THE LADY OF THE
AROOSTOOK

W. D. HOWELLS

1ˢᵗ WORLD
LIBRARY
Literary Society

The Lady of the Aroostook

W. D. Howells

© 1st World Library, 2007
PO Box 2211
Fairfield, IA 52556
www.1stworldlibrary.com
First Edition

LCCN: 2007927865

Softcover ISBN: 978-1-4218-4580-7
Hardcover ISBN: 978-1-4218-4496-1
eBook ISBN: 978-1-4218-4664-4

Purchase *"The Lady of the Aroostook"*
as a traditional bound book at:
www.1stWorldLibrary.com/purchase.asp?ISBN=978-1-4218-4580-7

1st World Library is a literary, educational organization
dedicated to:

- Creating a free internet library of downloadable ebooks

- Hosting writing competitions and offering book
publishing scholarships.

Interested in more 1st World Library books?
contact: literacy@1stworldlibrary.com
Check us out at: www.1stworldlibrary.com

1ˢᵗ World Library Literary Society

Giving Back to the World

"If you want to work on the core problem, it's early school literacy."

- James Barksdale, former CEO of Netscape

"No skill is more crucial to the future of a child, or to a democratic and prosperous society, than literacy."

- Los Angeles Times

"Literacy... means far more than learning how to read and write... The aim is to transmit... knowledge and promote social participation."

- UNESCO

"Literacy is not a luxury, it is a right and a responsibility. If our world is to meet the challenges of the twenty-first century we must harness the energy and creativity of all our citizens."

- President Bill Clinton

"Parents should be encouraged to read to their children, and teachers should be equipped with all available techniques for teaching literacy, so the varying needs and capacities of individual kids can be taken into account."

- Hugh Mackay

I

In the best room of a farm-house on the skirts of a village in the hills of Northern Massachusetts, there sat one morning in August three people who were not strangers to the house, but who had apparently assembled in the parlor as the place most in accord with an unaccustomed finery in their dress. One was an elderly woman with a plain, honest face, as kindly in expression as she could be perfectly sure she felt, and no more; she rocked herself softly in the haircloth arm-chair, and addressed as father the old man who sat at one end of the table between the windows, and drubbed noiselessly upon it with his stubbed fingers, while his lips, puckered to a whistle, emitted no sound. His face had that distinctly fresh-shaven effect which once a week is the advantage of shaving no oftener: here and there, in the deeper wrinkles, a frosty stubble had escaped the razor. He wore an old-fashioned, low black satin stock, over the top of which the linen of his unstarched collar contrived with difficulty to make itself seen; his high-crowned, lead-colored straw hat lay on the table before him. At the other end of the table sat a young girl, who leaned upon it with one arm, propping her averted face on her hand. The window was open beside her, and she was staring out upon the door-yard, where the hens were burrowing for coolness in the soft earth under the lilac bushes; from time to time she put her handkerchief to her eyes.

"I don't like this part of it, father," said the elderly woman, —"Lyddy's seeming to feel about it the way she does right at the last moment, as you may say." The old man made a noise in his throat as if he might speak; but he only unpuckered his mouth, and stayed his fingers, while the other continued: "I don't want her to go now, no more than ever I did. I ain't one to think that eatin' up everything on your plate keeps it from wastin', and I never was; and I say that even if you couldn't get the money back, it would cost no more to have her stay than to have her go."

"I don't suppose," said the old man, in a high, husky treble, "but what I could get some of it back from the captain; may be all. He didn't seem any ways graspin'. I don't want Lyddy should feel, any more than you do, Maria, that we're glad to have her go. But what I look at is this: as long as she has this idea—Well, it's like this—I d'know as I can express it, either." He relapsed into the comfort people find in giving up a difficult thing.

"Oh, I know!" returned the woman. "I understand it's an opportunity; you might call it a leadin', almost, that it would be flyin' in the face of Providence to refuse. I presume her gifts were given her for improvement, and it would be the same as buryin' them in the ground for her to stay up here. But I do say that I want Lyddy should feel just *so* about goin', or not go at all. It ain't like goin' among strangers, though, if it *is* in a strange land. They're her father's own kin, and if they're any ways like him they're warm-*hearted* enough, if that's all you want. I guess they'll do what's right by Lyddy when she gets there. And I try to look at it this way: that long before that maple by the gate is red she'll be with her father's own sister; and I for one don't mean to let it worry me." She made search for her handkerchief, and wiped away the tears that fell down her cheeks.

W. D. Howells

"Yes," returned the old man; "and before the leaves are on the ground we shall more'n have got our first letter from her. I declare for't," he added, after a tremulous pause, "I was goin' to say how Lyddy would enjoy readin' it to us! I don't seem to get it rightly into my head that she's goin' away."

"It ain't as if Lyddy was leavin' any life behind her that's over and above pleasant," resumed the woman. "She's a good girl, and I never want to see a more uncomplainin'; but I know it's duller and duller here all the while for her, with us two old folks, and no young company; and I d'know as it's been any better the two winters she's taught in the Mill Village. That's what reconciles me, on Lyddy's account, as much as anything. I ain't one to set much store on worldly ambition, and I never was; and I d'know as I care for Lyddy's advancement, as you may call it. I believe that as far forth as true happiness goes she'd be as well off here as there. But I don't say but what she would be more satisfied in the end, and as long as you can't have happiness, in this world, I say you'd better have satisfaction. Is that Josiah Whitman's hearse goin' past?" she asked, rising from her chair, and craning forward to bring her eyes on a level with the window, while she suspended the agitation of the palm-leaf fan which she had not ceased to ply during her talk; she remained a moment with the quiescent fan pressed against her bosom, and then she stepped out of the door, and down the walk to the gate. "Josiah!" she called, while the old man looked and listened at the window. "Who you be'n buryin'?"

The man halted his hearse, and answered briefly, "Mirandy Holcomb."

"Why, I thought the funeral wa'n't to be till tomorrow! Well, I declare," said the woman, as she reentered the room and sat down again in her rocking-chair, "I didn't ask him whether it was Mr. Goodlow or Mr. Baldwin preached the sermon. I was so put out hearin' it was Mirandy, you might say I forgot to ask him anything. Mirandy was always a well woman till they moved down to the Mill Village and began takin' the hands to board,— so many of 'em. When I think of Lyddy's teachin' there another winter,—well, I could almost rejoice that she was goin' away. She ain't a mite too strong as it is."

Here the woman paused, and the old man struck in with his quaint treble while she fanned herself in silence: "I do suppose the voyage is goin' to be everything for her health. She'll be from a month to six weeks gettin' to Try-East, and that'll be a complete change of air, Mr. Goodlow says. And she won't have a care on her mind the whole way out. It'll be a season of rest and quiet. I did wish, just for the joke of the thing, as you may say, that the ship had be'n goin' straight to Venus, and Lyddy could 'a' walked right in on 'em at breakfast, some morning. I should liked it to be'n a surprise. But there wa'n't any ship at Boston loadin' for Venus, and they didn't much believe I'd find one at New York. So I just took up with the captain of the Aroostook's offer. He says she can telegraph to her folks at Venus as soon as she gets to Try-East, and she's welcome to stay on the ship till they come for her. I didn't think of their havin' our mod'n improvements out there; but he says they have telegraphs and railroads every-wheres, the same as we do; and they're *real* kind and polite when you get used to 'em. The captain, he's as nice a man as I ever see. His wife's be'n two or three voyages with him in the Aroostook, and he'll know just how to have Lyddy's comfort looked after. He showed me the state-room she's goin' to have. Well, it ain't over and above large, but it's pretty as a pink: all clean white paint, with a solid mahogany edge to the berth, and a maho-gany-framed lookin'-glass on one side, and little winders at the top, and white lace curtains to the bed. He says he had it fixed up for his wife, and he lets Lyddy have it all for her own. She can set there and do her mendin' when she don't feel like comin' into the cabin. The cabin—well, I wish you could see that cabin, Maria! The first mate is a fine-appearing man, too. Some of the sailors looked pretty rough; but I guess it was as much their clothes as anything; and I d'know as Lyddy'd *have* a great deal to do with them, any way." The old man's treble ceased, and at the same moment the shrilling of a locust in one of the door-yard maples died away; both voices, arid, nasal, and high, lapsed as one into a common silence.

The woman stirred impatiently in her chair, as if both voices had been repeating something heard many times before. They seemed to renew her discontent. "Yes, I know; I know all that, father. But it ain't the mahogany I think of. It's the child's gettin' there safe and well."

"Well," said the old man, "I asked the captain about the seasickness, and he says she ain't nigh so likely to be sick as she would on the steamer; the motion's more regular, and she won't have the smell of the machinery. That's what he said. And he said the seasickness would do her good, any way. I'm sure I don't want her to be sick any more than you do, Maria." He added this like one who has been unjustly put upon his defense.

They now both remained silent, the woman rocking herself and fanning, and the old man holding his fingers suspended from their drubbing upon the table, and looking miserably from the woman in the rocking-chair to the girl at the window, as if a strict inquiry into the present situation might convict him of it in spite of his innocence. The girl still sat with her face turned from them, and still from time to time she put her handkerchief to her eyes and wiped away the tears. The locust in the maple began again, and shrilled inexorably. Suddenly the girl leaped to her feet.

"There's the stage!" she cried, with a tumult in her voice and manner, and a kind of choking sob. She showed, now that she stood upright, the slim and elegant shape which is the divine right of American girlhood, clothed with the stylishness that instinctive taste may evoke, even in a hill town, from study of paper patterns, Harper's Bazar, and the costume of summer boarders. Her dress was carried with spirit and effect.

"Lydia Blood!" cried the other woman, springing responsively to her feet, also, and starting toward the girl, "don't you go a step without you feel just like it! Take off your things this minute and stay, if you wouldn't jus' as lives go. It's hard enough to *have* you go, child, without seemin' to force you!"

"Oh, aunt Maria," answered the girl, piteously, "it almost kills me to go; but *I'm* doing it, not you. I know how you'd like to have me stay. But don't say it again, or I couldn't bear up; and I'm going now, if I have to be carried."

The old man had risen with the others; he was shorter than either, and as he looked at them he seemed half awed, half bewildered, by so much drama. Yet it was comparatively very little. The girl did not offer to cast herself upon her aunt's neck, and her aunt did not offer her an embrace, it was only their hearts that clung together as they simply shook hands and kissed each other. Lydia whirled away for her last look at herself in the glass over the table, and her aunt tremulously began to put to rights some slight disorder in the girl's hat.

"Father," she said sharply, "are Lyddy's things all ready there by the door, so's not to keep Ezra Perkins waitin'? You know he always grumbles so. And then he *gets* you to the cars so't you have to wait half an hour before they start." She continued to pin and pull at details of Lydia's dress, to which she descended from her hat. "It sets real nice on you, Lyddy. I guess you'll think of the time we had gettin' it made up, when you wear it out there." Miss Maria Latham laughed nervously.

With a harsh banging and rattling, a yellow Concord coach drew up at the gate where Miss Maria had stopped the hearse. The driver got down, and without a word put Lydia's boxes and bags into the boot, and left two or three light parcels for her to take into the coach with her.

Miss Maria went down to the gate with her father and niece. "Take the back seat, father!" she said, as the old man offered to take the middle place. "Let them that come later have what's left. You'll be home to-night, father; I'll set up for you. Good-by again, Lyddy." She did not kiss the girl again, or touch her hand. Their decent and sparing adieux had been made in the house. As Miss Maria returned to the door, the hens, cowering conscience-stricken under the lilacs, sprang up at sight of her with a screech of guilty alarm, and flew out over the fence.

"Well, I vow," soliloquized Miss Maria, "from where she set Lyddy must have seen them pests under the lilacs the whole time, and never said a word." She pushed the loosened soil into place with the side of her ample slipper, and then went into the house, where she kindled a fire in the kitchen stove, and made herself a cup of Japan tea: a variety of the herb which our country people prefer, apparently because it affords the same stimulus with none of the pleasure given by the Chinese leaf.

II

Lydia and her grandfather reached Boston at four o'clock, and the old man made a bargain, as he fancied, with an expressman to carry her baggage across the city to the wharf at which the Aroostook lay. The expressman civilly offered to take their small parcels without charge, and deliver them with the trunk and large bag; but as he could not check them all her grandfather judged it safest not to part with them, and he and Lydia crowded into the horse-car with their arms and hands full. The conductor obliged him to give up the largest of these burdens, and hung the old-fashioned oil-cloth sack on the handle of the brake behind, where Mr. Latham with keen anxiety, and Lydia with shame, watched it as it swayed back and forth with the motion of the car and threatened to break loose from its hand-straps and dash its bloated bulk to the ground. The old man called out to the conductor to be sure and stop in Scollay's Square, and the people, who had already stared uncomfortably at Lydia's bundles, all smiled. Her grandfather was going to repeat his direction as the conductor made no sign of having heard it, when his neighbor said kindly, "The car always stops in Scollay's Square."

"Then why couldn't he say so?" retorted the old man, in his high nasal key; and now the people laughed outright. He had the nervous restlessness of age when out of its

W. D. Howells

wonted place: he could not remain quiet in the car, for counting and securing his parcels; when they reached Scollay's Square, and were to change cars, he ran to the car they were to take, though there was abundant time, and sat down breathless from his effort. He was eager then that they should not be carried too far, and was constantly turning to look out of the window to ascertain their whereabouts. His vigilance ended in their getting aboard the East Boston ferry-boat in the car, and hardly getting ashore before the boat started. They now gathered up their burdens once more, and walked toward the wharf they were seeking, past those squalid streets which open upon the docks. At the corners they entangled themselves in knots of truck-teams and hucksters' wagons and horse-cars; once they brought the traffic of the neighborhood to a stand-still by the thoroughness of their inability and confusion. They wandered down the wrong wharf amidst the slime cast up by the fishing craft moored in the dock below, and made their way over heaps of chains and cordage, and through the hand-carts pushed hither and thither with their loads of fish, and so struggled back to the avenue which ran along the top of all the wharves. The water of the docks was of a livid turbidity, which teemed with the gelatinous globes of the sun-fish; and people were rowing about there in pleasure-boats, and sailors on floats were painting the hulls of the black ships. The faces of the men they met were red and sunburned mostly,—not with the sunburn of the fields, but of the sea; these men lurched in their gait with an uncouth heaviness, yet gave them way kindly enough; but certain dull-eyed, frowzy-headed women seemed to push purposely against her grandfather, and one of them swore at Lydia for taking up all the sidewalk with her bundles. There were such dull eyes and slattern heads at the open windows of the shabby houses; and there were gaunt, bold-faced young girls who strolled up and down the pavements, bonnetless and hatless, and chatted into the windows, and joked with other such girls whom they met. Suddenly a wild outcry rose from the swarming children up one of the intersecting streets, where a woman was beating a small boy over the head with a heavy stick: the boy fell howling and writhing to the ground, and the cruel blows still rained upon him, till another woman darted from an open door and caught the child up with one hand, and with the other wrenched the stick away and flung it into the street. No words passed, and there was nothing to show whose child the victim was; the first woman walked off, and while the boy rubbed his head and arms, and screamed with the pain, the other children, whose sports had been scarcely interrupted, were shouting and laughing all about him again.

"Grandfather," said Lydia faintly, "let us go down here, and rest a moment in the shade. I'm almost worn out." She pointed to the open and quiet space at the side of the lofty granite warehouse which they had reached.

"Well, I guess I'll set down a minute, too," said her grandfather. "Lyddy," he added, as they released their aching arms from their bags and bundles, and sank upon the broad threshold of a door which seemed to have been shut ever since the decay of the India trade, "I don't believe but what it would have be'n about as cheap in the end to come down in a hack. But I acted for what I thought was the best. I supposed we'd be'n there before now, and the idea of givin' a dollar for ridin' about ten minutes did seem sinful. I ain't noways afraid the ship will sail without you. Don't you fret any. I don't seem to know rightly just where I am, but after we've rested a spell I'll leave you here, and inquire round. It's a real quiet place, and I guess your things will be safe."

He took off his straw hat and fanned his face with it, while Lydia leaned her head against the door frame and

W. D. Howells

closed her eyes. Presently she heard the trampling of feet
going by, but she did not open her eyes till the feet paused
in a hesitating way, and a voice asked her grandfather, in
the firm, neat tone which she had heard summer boarders
from Boston use, "Is the young lady ill?" She now looked
up, and blushed like fire to see two handsome young men
regarding her with frank compassion.

"No," said her grandfather; "a little beat out, that's all.
We've been trying to find Lucas Wharf, and we don't
seem somehow just to hit on it."

"This is Lucas Wharf," said the young man. He made an
instinctive gesture of salutation toward his hat, with the
hand in which he held a cigar; he put the cigar into his
mouth as he turned from them, and the smoke drifted
fragrantly back to Lydia as he tramped steadily and
strongly on down the wharf, shoulder to shoulder with his
companion.

"Well, I declare for't, so it is," said her grandfather,
getting stiffly to his feet and retiring a few paces to gain a
view of the building at the base of which they had been
sitting. "Why, I might known it by this buildin'! But
where's the Aroostook, if this is Lucas Wharf?" He looked
wistfully in the direction the young men had taken, but
they were already too far to call after.

"Grandfather," said the girl, "do I look pale?"

"Well, you don't now," answered the old man, simply.
"You've got a good color now."

"What right had he," she demanded, "to speak to you
about me?"

"I d'know but what you did look rather pale, as you set

there with your head leaned back. I d'know as I noticed much."

"He took us for two beggars,—two tramps!" she exclaimed, "sitting here with our bundles scattered round us!"

The old man did not respond to this conjecture; it probably involved matters beyond his emotional reach, though he might have understood them when he was younger. He stood a moment with his mouth puckered to a whistle, but made no sound, and retired a step or two farther from the building and looked up at it again. Then he went toward the dock and looked down into its turbid waters, and returned again with a face of hopeless perplexity. "This is Lucas Wharf, and no mistake," he said. "I know the place first-rate, now. But what I can't make out is, What's got the Aroostook?"

A man turned the corner of the warehouse from the street above, and came briskly down towards them, with his hat off, and rubbing his head and face with a circular application of a red silk handkerchief. He was dressed in a suit of blue flannel, very neat and shapely, and across his ample waistcoat stretched a gold watch chain; in his left hand he carried a white Panama hat. He was short and stout; his round florid face was full of a sort of prompt kindness; his small blue eyes twinkled under shaggy brows whose sandy color had not yet taken the grizzled tone of his close-clipped hair and beard. From his clean wristbands his hands came out, plump and large; stiff, wiry hairs stood up on their backs, and under these various designs in tattooing showed their purple.

Lydia's grandfather stepped out to meet and halt this stranger, as he drew near, glancing quickly from the girl to the old man, and then at their bundles. "Can you tell me where a ship named the Aroostook is, that was layin' at

W. D. Howells

this wharf—Lucas Wharf—a fortnight ago, and better?"

"Well, I guess I can, Mr. Latham," answered the stranger, with a quizzical smile, offering one of his stout hands to Lydia's grandfather. "You don't seem to remember your friends very well, do you?"

The old man gave a kind of crow expressive of an otherwise unutterable relief and comfort. "Well, if it ain't Captain Jenness! I be'n so turned about, I declare for't, I don't believe I'd ever known you if you hadn't spoke up. Lyddy," he cried with a child-like joy, "this is Captain Jenness!"

Captain Jenness having put on his hat changed Mr. Latham's hand into his left, while he stretched his great right hand across it and took Lydia's long, slim fingers in its grasp, and looked keenly into her face. "Glad to see you, glad to see you, Miss Blood. (You see I've got your name down on my papers.) Hope you're well. Ever been a sea-voyage before? Little homesick, eh?" he asked, as she put her handkerchief to her eyes. He kept pressing Lydia's hand in the friendliest way. "Well, that's natural. And you're excited; that's natural, too. But we're not going to have any homesickness on the Aroostook, because we're going to make her home to you." At this speech all the girl's gathering forlornness broke in a sob. "That's right!" said Captain Jenness. "Bless you, I've got a girl just about your age up at Deer Isle, myself!" He dropped her hand, and put his arm across her shoulders. "Good land, I know what girls are, I hope! These your things?" He caught up the greater part of them into his capacious hands, and started off down the wharf, talking back at Lydia and her grandfather, as they followed him with the light parcels he had left them. "I hauled away from the wharf as soon as I'd stowed my cargo, and I'm at anchor out there in the stream now, waiting till I can finish up a few matters of business with the agents and get my passengers on board. When you get used to the strangeness," he said to Lydia, "you won't be a bit lonesome. Bless your heart! My wife's been with me many a voyage, and the last time I was out to Messina I had both my daughters."

At the end of the wharf, Captain Jenness stopped, and suddenly calling out, "Here!" began, as she thought, to hurl Lydia's things into the water. But when she reached the same point, she found they had all been caught, and deposited in a neat pile in a boat which lay below, where two sailors stood waiting the captain's further orders. He keenly measured the distance to the boat with his eye, and then he bade the men work round outside a schooner which lay near; and jumping on board this vessel, he helped Lydia and her grandfather down, and easily transferred them to the small boat. The men bent to their oars, and pulled swiftly out toward a ship that lay at anchor a little way off. A light breeze crept along the water, which was here blue and clear, and the grateful coolness and pleasant motion brought light into the girl's cheeks and eyes. Without knowing it she smiled. "That's right!" cried Captain Jenness, who had applauded her sob in the same terms. "*You'll* like it, first-rate. Look at that ship! *That's* the Aroostook. *Is* she a beauty, or ain't she?"

The stately vessel stood high from the water, for Captain Jenness's cargo was light, and he was going out chiefly for a return freight. Sharp jibs and staysails cut their white outlines keenly against the afternoon blue of the summer heaven; the topsails and courses dripped, half-furled, from the yards stretching across the yellow masts that sprang so far aloft; the hull glistened black with new paint. When Lydia mounted to the deck she found it as clean scrubbed as her aunt's kitchen floor. Her glance of admiration was not lost upon Captain Jenness. "Yes, Miss Blood," said he, "one difference between an American ship and any other sort is dirt. I wish I could take you aboard an English vessel, so you could appreciate the Aroostook. But I guess you don't need it," he added, with a proud satisfaction in his laugh. "The Aroostook ain't in order yet; wait till we've been a few days at sea." The captain swept the deck with a loving eye. It was spacious and handsome, with a stretch of some forty or fifty feet between the house at the stern and the forecastle, which rose considerably higher; a low bulwark was surmounted by a heavy rail supported upon turned posts painted white. Everything, in spite of the captain's boastful detraction, was in perfect trim, at least to landfolk's eyes. "Now come into the cabin," said the captain. He gave Lydia's traps, as he called them, in charge of a boy, while he led the way below, by a narrow stairway, warning Lydia and her grandfather to look out for their heads as they followed. "There!" he said, when they had safely arrived, inviting their inspection of the place with a general glance of his own.

"What did I tell you, Lyddy?" asked her grandfather, with simple joy in the splendors about them. "Solid mahogany trimmin's everywhere." There was also a great deal of milk-white paint, with some modest touches of gilding here and there. The cabin was pleasantly lit by the long low windows which its roof rose just high enough to lift above the deck, and the fresh air entered with the slanting sun. Made fast to the floor was a heavy table, over which hung from the ceiling a swinging shelf. Around the little saloon ran lockers cushioned with red plush. At either end were four or five narrow doors, which gave into as many tiny state-rooms. The boy came with Lydia's things, and set them inside one of these doors; and when he came out again the captain pushed it open, and called them in. "Here!" said he. "Here's where my girls made themselves at home the last voyage, and I expect you'll find it pretty comfortable. They say you don't feel the motion so much,—*I* don't know anything about the motion,—and in smooth weather you can have that window open sometimes, and change the air. It's light and it's large. Well, I had it fitted up for my wife; but she's got kind of on now, you know, and she don't feel much like going any more; and so I always give it to my nicest passenger." This was an unmistakable compliment, and Lydia blushed to the captain's entire content. "That's a rug she hooked," he continued, touching with his toe the carpet, rich in its artless domestic dyes as some Persian fabric, that lay before the berth. "These gimcracks belong to my girls; they left 'em." He pointed to various slight structures of card-board worked with crewel, which were tacked to the walls. "Pretty snug, eh?"

"Yes," said Lydia, "it's nicer than I thought it could be, even after what grandfather said."

"Well, that's right!" exclaimed the captain. "I like your way of speaking up. I wish you could know my girls. How old are you now?"

"I'm nineteen," said Lydia.

"Why, you're just between my girls!" cried the captain. "Sally is twenty-one, and Persis is eighteen. Well, now, Miss Blood," he said, as they returned to the cabin, "you can't begin to make yourself at home too soon for me. I used to sail to Cadiz and Malaga a good deal; and when I went to see any of them Spaniards he'd say, 'This house is yours.' Well, that's what I say: This ship is yours as long as you stay in her. And I *mean* it, and that's more than *they* did!" Captain Jenness laughed mightily, took some of Lydia's fingers in his left hand and squeezed them, and clapped her grandfather on the shoulder with his right. Then he slipped his hand down the old man's bony arm to the elbow, and held it, while he dropped his head towards

W. D. Howells

Lydia, and said, "We shall be glad to have him stay to supper, and as much longer as he likes, heh?"

"Oh, no!" said Lydia; "grandfather must go back on the six o'clock train. My aunt expects him." Her voice fell, and her face suddenly clouded.

"Good!" cried the captain. Then he pulled out his watch, and held it as far away as the chain would stretch, frowning at it with his head aslant. "Well!" he burst out. "He hasn't got any too much time on his hands." The old man gave a nervous start, and the girl trembled. "Hold on! Yes; there's time. It's only fifteen minutes after five."

"Oh, but we were more than half an hour getting down here," said Lydia, anxiously. "And grandfather doesn't know the way back. He'll be sure to get lost. I *wish* we'd come in a carriage."

"Couldn't 'a' kept the carriage waitin' on expense, Lyddy," retorted her grandfather, "But I tell you," he added, with something like resolution, "if I could find a carriage anywheres near that wharf, I'd take it, just as *sure*! I wouldn't miss that train for more'n half a dollar. It would cost more than that at a hotel to-night, let alone how your aunt Maria'd feel."

"Why, look here!" said Captain Jenness, naturally appealing to the girl. "Let *me* get your grandfather back. I've got to go up town again, any way, for some last things, with an express wagon, and we can ride right to the depot in that. Which depot is it?"

"Fitchburg," said the old man eagerly.

"That's right!" commented the captain. "Get you there in plenty of time, if we don't lose any now. And I'll tell you what, my little girl," he added, turning to Lydia: "if it'll be a comfort to you to ride up with us, and see your grandfather off, why come along! *My* girls went with me the last time on an express wagon."

"No," answered Lydia. "I want to. But it wouldn't be any comfort. I thought that out before I left home, and I'm going to say good-by to grandfather here."

"First-rate!" said Captain Jenness, bustling towards the gangway so as to leave them alone. A sharp cry from the old man arrested him.

"Lyddy! Where's your trunks?"

"Why!" said the girl, catching her breath in dismay, "where *can* they be? I forgot all about them."

"I got the checks fast enough," said the old man, "and I shan't give 'em up without I get the trunks. They'd ought to had 'em down here long ago; and now if I've got to pester round after 'em I'm sure to miss the train."

"What shall we do?" asked Lydia.

"Let's see your checks," said the captain, with an evident ease of mind that reassured her. When her grandfather had brought them with difficulty from the pocket visited last in the order of his search, and laid them in the captain's waiting palm, the latter endeavored to get them in focus. "What does it say on 'em?" he asked, handing them to Lydia. "My eyes never *did* amount to anything on shore." She read aloud the name of the express stamped on them. The captain gathered them back into his hand, and slipped them into his pocket, with a nod and wink full of comfort. "I'll see to it," he said. "At any rate, this ship ain't a-going to sail without them, if she waits a week. Now, then,

Mr. Latham!"

The old man, who waited, when not directly addressed or concerned, in a sort of blank patience, suddenly started out of his daze, and following the captain too alertly up the gangway stairs drove his hat against the hatch—with a force that sent him back into Lydia's arms.

"Oh, grandfather, are you hurt?" she piteously asked, trying to pull up the hat that was jammed down over his forehead.

"Not a bit! But I guess my hat's about done for,—without I can get it pressed over; and I d'know as this kind of straw *doos* press."

"First-rate!" called the captain from above. "Never mind the hat." But the girl continued fondly trying to reshape it, while the old man fidgeted anxiously, and protested that he would be sure to be left. It was like a half-shut accordion when she took it from his head; when she put it back it was like an accordion pulled out.

"All ready!" shouted Captain Jenness from the gap in the bulwark, where he stood waiting to descend into the small boat. The old man ran towards him in his senile haste, and stooped to get over the side into the boat below.

"Why, grandfather!" cried the girl in a breaking voice, full of keen, yet tender reproach.

"I declare for't," he said, scrambling back to the deck. "I 'most forgot. I be'n so put about." He took Lydia's hand loosely into his own, and bent forward to kiss her. She threw her arms round him, and while he remained looking over her shoulder, with a face of grotesque perplexity, and saying, "Don't cry, Lyddy, don't cry!" she pressed her face tighter into his withered neck, and tried to muffle her homesick sobs. The sympathies as well as the sensibilities often seem dulled by age. They have both perhaps been wrought upon too much in the course of the years, and can no longer respond to the appeal or distress which they can only dimly realize; even the heart grows old. "Don't you, don't you, Lyddy!" repeated the old man. "You mustn't. The captain's waitin'; and the cars—well, every minute I lose makes it riskier and riskier; and your aunt Maria, she's always so uneasy, you know!"

The girl was not hurt by his anxiety about himself; she was more anxious about him than about anything else. She quickly lifted her head, and drying her eyes, kissed him, forcing her lips into the smile that is more heart-breaking to see than weeping. She looked over the side, as her grandfather was handed carefully down to a seat by the two sailors in the boat, and the captain noted her resolute counterfeit of cheerfulness. "That's right!" he shouted up to her. "Just like my girls when their mother left 'em. But bless you, they soon got over it, and so'll you. Give way, men," he said, in a lower voice, and the boat shot from the ship's side toward the wharf. He turned and waved his handkerchief to Lydia, and, stimulated apparently by this, her grandfather felt in his pockets for his handkerchief; he ended after a vain search by taking off his hat and waving that.

When he put it on again, it relapsed into that likeness of a half-shut accordion from which Lydia had rescued it; but she only saw the face under it.

As the boat reached the wharf an express wagon drove down, and Lydia saw the sarcastic parley which she could not hear between the captain and the driver about the belated baggage which the latter put off. Then she saw the captain help her grandfather to the seat between himself and the driver, and the wagon rattled swiftly out of sight. One of the sailors lifted Lydia's baggage over the side of the wharf to the other in the boat, and they pulled off to the ship with it.

III

Lydia went back to the cabin, and presently the boy who had taken charge of her lighter luggage came dragging her trunk and bag down the gangway stairs. Neither was very large, and even a boy of fourteen who was small for his age might easily manage them.

"You can stow away what's in 'em in the drawers," said the boy. "I suppose you didn't notice the drawers," he added, at her look of inquiry. He went into her room, and pushing aside the valance of the lower berth showed four deep drawers below the bed; the charming snugness of the arrangement brought a light of housewifely joy to the girl's face.

"Why, it's as good as a bureau. They will hold everything."

"Yes," exulted the boy; "they're for two persons' things. The captain's daughters, they both had this room. Pretty good sized too; a good deal the captain's build. You won't find a better stateroom than this on a steamer. I've been on 'em." The boy climbed up on the edge of the upper drawer, and pulled open the window at the top of the wall. "Give you a little air, I guess. If you want I should, the captain said I was to bear a hand helping you to stow away what was in your trunks."

W. D. Howells

"No," said Lydia, quickly. "I'd just as soon do it alone."

"All right," said the boy. "If I was you, I'd do it now. I don't know just when the captain means to sail; but after we get outside, it might be rough, and it's better to have everything pretty snug by that time. I'll haul away the trunks when you've got 'em empty. If I shouldn't happen to be here, you can just call me at the top of the gangway, and I'll come. My name's Thomas," he said. He regarded Lydia inquiringly a moment before he added: "If you'd just as lives, I rather you'd call me Thomas, and not *steward*. They said you'd call me steward," he explained, in a blushing, deprecating confidence; "and as long as I've not got my growth, it kind of makes them laugh, you know,—especially the second officer."

"I will call you Thomas," said Lydia.

"Thank you." The boy glanced up at the round clock screwed to the cabin wall. "I guess you won't have to call me anything unless you hurry. I shall be down here, laying the table for supper, before you're done. The captain said I was to lay it for you and him, and if he didn't get back in time you was to go to eating, any way. Guess you won't think Captain Jenness is going to starve anybody."

"Have you been many voyages with Captain Jenness before this?" asked Lydia, as she set open her trunk, and began to lay her dresses out on the locker. Homesickness, like all grief, attacks in paroxysms. One gust of passionate regret had swept over the girl; before another came, she could occupy herself almost cheerfully with the details of unpacking.

"Only one before," said the boy. "The last one, when his daughters went out. I guess it was their coaxing got mother to let me go. *My* father was killed in the war."

"Was he?" asked Lydia, sympathetically.

"Yes. I didn't know much about it at the time; so little. Both your parents living?"

"No," said Lydia. "They're both dead. They died a long while ago. I've always lived with my aunt and grandfather."

"I thought there must be something the matter,—your coming with your grandfather," said the boy. "I don't see why you don't let me carry in some of those dresses for you. I'm used to helping about."

"Well, you may," answered Lydia, "if you want." A native tranquil kindness showed itself in her voice and manner, but something of the habitual authority of a school-mistress mingled with it. "You must be careful not to rumple them if I let you."

"I guess not. I've got older sisters at home. They hated to have me leave. But I looked at it this way: If I was ever going to sea—and I *was*—I couldn't get such another captain as Captain Jenness, nor such another crew; all the men from down our way; and I don't mind the second mate's jokes much. He doesn't mean anything by them; likes to plague, that's all. He's a first-rate sailor."

Lydia was kneeling before one of the trunks, and the boy was stooping over it, with a hand on either knee. She had drawn out her only black silk dress, and was finding it rather crumpled. "I shouldn't have thought it would have got so much jammed, coming fifty miles," she solilo-quized. "But they seemed to take a pleasure in seeing how much they could bang the trunks." She rose to her feet and shook out the dress, and drew the skirt several times over her left arm.

The boy's eyes glistened. "Goodness!" he said. "Just new, ain't it? Going to wear it any on board?"

"Sundays, perhaps," answered Lydia thoughtfully, still smoothing and shaping the dress, which she regarded at arm's-length, from time to time, with her head aslant.

"I suppose it's the latest style?" pursued the boy.

"Yes, it is," said Lydia. "We sent to Boston for the pattern. I hate to pack it into one of those drawers," she mused.

"You needn't," replied Thomas. "There's a whole row of hooks."

"I want to know!" cried Lydia. She followed Thomas into her state-room. "Well, well! They do seem to have thought of everything!"

"I should say so," exulted the boy. "Look here!" He showed her a little niche near the head of the berth strongly framed with glass, in which a lamp was made fast. "Light up, you know, when you want to read, or feel kind of lonesome." Lydia clasped her hands in pleasure and amaze. "Oh, I tell you Captain Jenness meant to have things about right. The other state-rooms don't begin to come up to this." He dashed out in his zeal, and opened their doors, that she might triumph in the superiority of her accommodations without delay. These rooms were cramped together on one side; Lydia's was in a comparatively ample corner by itself.

She went on unpacking her trunk, and the boy again took

his place near her, in the same attitude as before. "I tell you," he said, "I shall like to see you with that silk on. Have you got any other nice ones?"

"No; only this I'm wearing," answered Lydia, half amused and half honest in her sympathy with his ardor about her finery. "They said not to bring many clothes; they would be cheaper over there." She had now reached the bottom of her trunk. She knew by the clock that her grandfather could hardly have left the city on his journey home, but the interval of time since she had parted with him seemed vast. It was as if she had started to Boston in a former life; the history of the choosing and cutting and making of these clothes was like a dream of preexistence. She had never had so many things new at once, and it had been a great outlay, but her aunt Maria had made the money go as far as possible, and had spent it with that native taste, that genius for dress, which sometimes strikes the summer boarder in the sempstresses of the New England hills. Miss Latham's gift was quaintly unrelated to herself. In dress, as in person and manner, she was uncompromisingly plain and stiff. All the more lavishly, therefore, had it been devoted to the grace and beauty of her sister's child, who, ever since she came to find a home in her grandfather's house, had been more stylishly dressed than any other girl in the village. The summer boarders, whom the keen eye of Miss Latham studied with unerring sense of the best new effects in costume, wondered at Lydia's elegance, as she sat beside her aunt in the family pew, a triumph of that grim artist's skill. Lydia knew that she was well dressed, but she knew that after all she was only the expression of her aunt's inspirations. Her own gift was of another sort. Her father was a music-teacher, whose failing health had obliged him to give up his profession, and who had taken the traveling agency of a parlor organ manufactory for the sake of the out-door life. His business had brought him to South Bradfield, where he sold an organ to Deacon Latham's church, and fell in love with his younger daughter. He died a few years after his marriage, of an ancestral consumption, his sole heritage from the good New England stock of which he came. His skill as a pianist, which was considerable, had not descended to his daughter, but her mother had bequeathed her a peculiarly rich and flexible voice, with a joy in singing which was as yet a passion little affected by culture. It was this voice which, when Lydia rose to join in the terrible hymning of the congregation at South Bradfield, took the thoughts of people off her style and beauty; and it was this which enchanted her father's sister when, the summer before the date of which we write, that lady had come to America on a brief visit, and heard Lydia sing at her parlor organ in the old homestead.

Mrs. Erwin had lived many years abroad, chiefly in Italy, for the sake of the climate. She was of delicate health, and constantly threatened by the hereditary disease that had left her the last of her generation, and she had the fastidiousness of an invalid. She was full of generous impulses which she mistook for virtues; but the presence of some object at once charming and worthy was nece- ssary to rouse these impulses. She had been prosperously married when very young, and as a pretty American widow she had wedded in second marriage at Naples one of those Englishmen who have money enough to live at ease in Latin countries; he was very fond of her, and petted her. Having no children she might long before have thought definitely of poor Henry's little girl, as she called Lydia, but she had lived very comfortably indefinite in regard to her ever since the father's death. Now and then she had sent the child a handsome present or a sum of money. She had it on her conscience not to let her be wholly a burden to her grandfather; but often her conscience drowsed. When she came to South Bradfield, she won the hearts of the simple family, which had been

rather hardened against her, and she professed an enthusiasm for Lydia. She called her pretty names in Italian,
which she did not pronounce well; she babbled a great
deal about what ought to be done for her, and went away
without doing anything; so that when a letter finally came,
directing Lydia to be sent out to her in Venice, they were
all surprised, in the disappointment to which they had
resigned themselves.

Mrs. Erwin wrote an epistolary style exasperatingly
vacuous and diffuse, and, like many women of that sort,
she used pencil instead of ink, always apologizing for it as
due now to her weak eyes, and now to her weak wrist, and
again to her not being able to find the ink. Her hand was
full of foolish curves and dashes, and there were no
spaces between the words at times. Under these conditions it was no light labor to get at her meaning; but the
sum of her letter was that she wished Lydia to come out to
her at once, and she suggested that, as they could have
few opportunities or none to send her with people going
to Europe, they had better let her come the whole way by
sea. Mrs. Erwin remembered—in the space of a page and
a half—that nothing had ever done *her* so much good as a
long sea voyage, and it would be excellent for Lydia,
who, though she looked so strong, probably needed all the
bracing up she could get. She had made inquiries,—or,
what was the same thing, Mr. Erwin had, for her,—and
she found that vessels from American ports seldom came
to Venice; but they often came to Trieste, which was only
a few hours away; and if Mr. Latham would get Lydia a
ship for Trieste at Boston, she could come very safely and
comfortably in a few weeks. She gave the name of a
Boston house engaged in the Mediterranean trade to
which Mr. Latham could apply for passage; if they were
not sending any ship themselves, they could probably
recommend one to him.

This was what happened when Deacon Latham called at their office a few days after Mrs. Erwin's letter came. They directed him to the firm dispatching the Aroostook, and Captain Jenness was at their place when the deacon appeared there. The captain took cordial possession of the old man at once, and carried him down to the wharf to look at the ship and her accommodations. The matter was quickly settled between them. At that time Captain Jenness did not know but he might have other passengers out; at any rate he would look after the little girl (as Deacon Latham always said in speaking of Lydia) the same as if she were his own child.

Lydia knelt before her trunk, thinking of the remote events, the extinct associations of a few minutes and hours and days ago; she held some cuffs and collars in her hand, and something that her aunt Maria had said recurred to her. She looked up into the intensely interested face of the boy, and then laughed, bowing her forehead on the back of the hand that held these bits of linen.

The boy blushed. "What are you laughing at?" he asked, half piteously, half indignantly, like a boy used to being badgered.

"Oh, nothing," said Lydia. "My aunt told me if any of these things should happen to want doing up, I had better get the stewardess to help me." She looked at the boy in a dreadfully teasing way, softly biting her lip.

"Oh, if you're going to begin *that* way!" he cried in affliction.

"I'm not," she answered, promptly. "I like boys. I've taught school two winters, and I like boys first-rate."

Thomas was impersonally interested again. "Time! *You*

taught school?"

"Why not?"

"You look pretty young for a school-teacher!"

"Now you're making fun of me," said Lydia, astutely.

The boy thought he must have been, and was consoled. "Well, you began it," he said.

"I oughtn't to have done so," she replied with humility; "and I won't any more. There!" she said, "I'm not going to open my bag now. You can take away the trunk when you want, Thomas."

"Yes, ma'am," said the boy. The idea of a school-mistress was perhaps beginning to awe him a little. "Put your bag in your state-room first." He did this, and when he came back from carrying away her trunk he began to set the table. It was a pretty table, when set, and made the little cabin much cosier. When the boy brought the dishes from the cook's galley, it was a barbarously abundant table. There was cold boiled ham, ham and eggs, fried fish, baked potatoes, buttered toast, tea, cake, pickles, and watermelon; nothing was wanting. "I tell you," said Thomas, noticing Lydia's admiration, "the captain lives well lay-days."

"Lay-days?" echoed Lydia.

"The days we're in port," the boy explained.

"Well, I should think as much!" She ate with the hunger that tranquillity bestows upon youth after the swift succession of strange events, and the conflict of many emotions. The captain had not returned in time, and she

W. D. Howells

ate alone.

After a while she ventured to the top of the gangway stairs, and stood there, looking at the novel sights of the harbor, in the red sunset light, which rose slowly from the hulls and lower spars of the shipping, and kindled the tips of the high-shooting masts with a quickly fading splendor. A delicate flush responded in the east, and rose to meet the denser crimson of the west; a few clouds, incomparably light and diaphanous, bathed themselves in the glow. It was a summer sunset, portending for the land a morrow of great heat. But cool airs crept along the water, and the ferry-boats, thrust shuttlewise back and forth between either shore, made a refreshing sound as they crushed a broad course to foam with their paddles. People were pulling about in small boats; from some the gay cries and laughter of young girls struck sharply along the tide. The noise of the quiescent city came off in a sort of dull moan. The lamps began to twinkle in the windows and the streets on shore; the lanterns of the ships at anchor in the stream showed redder and redder as the twilight fell. The homesickness began to mount from Lydia's heart in a choking lump to her throat; for one must be very happy to endure the sights and sounds of the summer evening anywhere. She had to shield her eyes from the brilliancy of the kerosene when she went below into the cabin.

IV

Lydia did not know when the captain came on board. Once, talking in the cabin made itself felt through her dreams, but the dense sleep of weary youth closed over her again, and she did not fairly wake till morning. Then she thought she heard the crowing of a cock and the cackle of hens, and fancied herself in her room at home; the illusion passed with a pang. The ship was moving, with a tug at her side, the violent respirations of which were mingled with the sound of the swift rush of the vessels through the water, the noise of feet on the deck, and of orders hoarsely shouted.

The girl came out into the cabin, where Thomas was already busy with the breakfast table, and climbed to the deck. It was four o'clock of the summer's morning; the sun had not yet reddened the east, but the stars were extinct, or glimmered faint points immeasurably withdrawn in the vast gray of the sky. At that hour there is a hovering dimness over all, but the light on things near at hand is wonderfully keen and clear, and the air has an intense yet delicate freshness that seems to breathe from the remotest spaces of the universe,—a waft from distances beyond the sun. On the land the leaves and grass are soaked with dew; the densely interwoven songs of the birds are like a fabric that you might see and touch. But here, save for the immediate noises on the ship, which had already left her anchorage far behind, the shouting of the tug's escape-pipes, and the huge, swirling gushes from her powerful wheel, a sort of spectacular silence prevailed, and the sounds were like a part of this silence. Here and there a small fishing schooner came lagging slowly in, as if belated, with scarce wind enough to fill her sails; now and then they met a steamboat, towering white and high, a many-latticed bulk, with no one to be seen on board but the pilot at his wheel, and a few sleepy passengers on the forward promenade. The city, so beautiful and stately from the bay, was dropping, and sinking away behind. They passed green islands, some of which were fortified: the black guns looked out over the neatly shaven glacis; the sentinel paced the rampart.

"Well, well!" shouted Captain Jenness, catching sight of Lydia where she lingered at the cabin door. "You are an early bird. Glad to see you up! Hope you rested well! Saw your grandfather off all right, and kept him from taking the wrong train with my own hand. He's terribly excitable. Well, I suppose I shall be just so, at his age. Here!" The captain caught up a stool and set it near the bulwark for her. "There! You make yourself comfortable wherever you like. You're at home, you know." He was off again in a moment. Lydia cast her eye over at the tug. On the deck, near the pilot-house, stood the young man who had stopped the afternoon before, while she sat at the warehouse door, and asked her grandfather if she were not ill. At his feet was a substantial valise, and over his arm hung a shawl. He was smoking, and seated near him, on another valise, was his companion of the day before, also smoking. In the instant that Lydia caught sight of them, she perceived that they both recognized her and exchanged, as it were, a start of surprise. But they remained as before, except that he who was seated drew out a fresh cigarette, and without looking up reached to the other for a light. They were both men of good height, and they looked fresh and strong, with something very alert in their slight movements,—sudden turns of the head and brisk nods, which were not nervously quick. Lydia wondered at their presence there in an ignorance which could not even conjecture. She knew too little to know that they could not have any destination on the tug, and that they would not be making a pleasure-excursion at that hour in the morning. Their having their valises with them deepened the mystery, which was not solved till the tug's engines fell silent, and at an unnoticed order a space in the bulwark not far from Lydia was opened and steps were let down the side of the ship. Then the young men, who had remained, to all appearance, perfectly unconcerned, caught up their valises and climbed to the deck of the Aroostook. They did not give her more than a glance out of the corners of their eyes, but the surprise of their coming on board was so great a shock that she did not observe that the tug, casting loose from the ship, was describing a curt and foamy semicircle for her return to the city, and that the Aroostook, with a cloud of snowy canvas filling overhead, was moving over the level sea with the light ease of a bird that half swims, half flies, along the water. A sudden dismay, which was somehow not fear so much as an overpowering sense of isolation, fell upon the girl. She caught at Thomas, going forward with some dishes in his hand, with a pathetic appeal.

"Where are you going, Thomas?"

"I'm going to the cook's galley to help dish up the breakfast."

"What's the cook's galley?"

"Don't you know? The kitchen."

"Let me go with you. I should like to see the kitchen." She

trembled with eagerness. Arrived at the door of the narrow passage that ran across the deck aft of the fore-castle, she looked in and saw, amid a haze of frying and broiling, the short, stocky figure of a negro, bow-legged, and unnaturally erect from the waist up. At sight of Lydia, he made a respectful duck forward with his uncouth body. "Why, are you the cook?" she almost screamed in response to this obeisance.

"Yes, miss," said the man, humbly, with a turn of the pleading black eyes of the negro.

Lydia grew more peremptory: "Why—why—I thought the cook was a woman!"

"Very sorry, miss," began the negro, with a deprecatory smile, in a slow, mild voice.

Thomas burst into a boy's yelling laugh: "Well, if that ain't the best joke on Gabriel! He'll never hear the last of it when I tell it to the second officer!"

"Thomas!" cried Lydia, terribly, "you shall *not*!" She stamped her foot. "Do you hear me?"

The boy checked his laugh abruptly. "Yes, ma'am," he said submissively.

"Well, then!" returned Lydia. She stalked proudly back to the cabin gangway, and descending shut herself into her state-room.

V

A few hours later Deacon Latham came into the house with a milk-pan full of pease. He set this down on one end of the kitchen table, with his straw hat beside it, and then took a chair at the other end and fell into the attitude of the day before, when he sat in the parlor with Lydia and Miss Maria waiting for the stage; his mouth was puckered to a whistle, and his fingers were held above the board in act to drub it. Miss Maria turned the pease out on the table, and took the pan into her lap. She shelled at the pease in silence, till the sound of their pelting, as they were dropped on the tin, was lost in their multitude; then she said, with a sharp, querulous, pathetic impatience, "Well, father, I suppose you're thinkin' about Lyddy."

"Yes, Maria, I be," returned her father, with uncommon plumpness, as if here now were something he had made up his mind to stand to. "I been thinkin' that Lyddy's a woman grown, as you may say."

"Yes," admitted Miss Maria, "she's a woman, as far forth as that goes. What put it into your head?"

"Well, I d'know as I know. But it's just like this: I got to thinkin' whether she mightn't get to feelin' rather lonely on the voyage, without any other woman to talk to."

W. D. Howells

"I guess," said Miss Maria, tranquilly, "she's goin' to feel lonely enough at times, any way, poor thing! But I told her if she wanted advice or help about anything just to go to the stewardess. That Mrs. Bland that spent the summer at the Parkers' last year was always tellin' how they went to the stewardess for most everything, and she give her five dollars in gold when they got into Boston. I shouldn't want Lyddy should give so much as that, but I should want she should give something, as long's it's the custom."

"They don't have 'em on sailin' vessels, Captain Jenness said; they only have 'em on steamers," said Deacon Latham.

"Have what?" asked Miss Maria, sharply.

"Stewardesses. They've got a cabin-boy."

Miss Maria desisted a moment from her work; then she answered, with a gruff shortness peculiar to her, "Well, then, she can go to the cook, I suppose. It wouldn't matter which she went to, I presume."

Deacon Latham looked up with the air of confessing to sin before the whole congregation. "The cook's a man,—a black man," he said.

Miss Maria dropped a handful of pods into the pan, and sent a handful of peas rattling across the table on to the floor. "Well, who in Time"—the expression was strong, but she used it without hesitation, and was never known to repent it "*will* she go to, then?"

"I declare for't," said her father, "I don't know. I d'know as I ever thought it out fairly before; but just now when I was pickin' the pease for you, my mind got to dwellin' on

Lyddy, and then it come to me all at once: there she was, the only *one* among a whole shipful, and I—I didn't know but what she might think it rather of a strange position for her."

"*Oh!*" exclaimed Miss Maria, petulantly. "I guess Lyddy'd know how to conduct herself wherever she was; she's a born lady, if ever there was one. But what I think is—" Miss Maria paused, and did not say what she thought; but it was evidently not the social aspect of the matter which was uppermost in her mind. In fact, she had never been at all afraid of men, whom she regarded as a more inefficient and feebler-minded kind of women.

"The only thing't makes me feel easier is what the captain said about the young men," said Deacon Latham.

"What young men?" asked Miss Maria.

"Why, I told you about 'em!" retorted the old man, with some exasperation.

"You told me about two young men that stopped on the wharf and pitied Lyddy's worn-out looks."

"Didn't I tell you the rest? I declare for't, I don't believe I did; I be'n so put about. Well, as we was drivin' up to the depot, we met the same two young men, and the captain asked 'em, 'Are you goin' or not a-goin'?'—just that way; and they said, 'We're goin'.' And he said, 'When you comin' aboard?' and he told 'em he was goin' to haul out this mornin' at three o'clock. And they asked what tug, and he told 'em, and they fixed it up between 'em all then that they was to come aboard from the tug, when she'd got the ship outside; and that's what I suppose they did. The captain he said to me he hadn't mentioned it before, because he wa'n't sure't they'd go till that minute. He give

W. D. Howells

'em a first-rate of a character."

Miss Maria said nothing for a long while. The subject seemed one with which she did not feel herself able to grapple. She looked all about the kitchen for inspiration, and even cast a searching glance into the wood-shed. Suddenly she jumped from her chair, and ran to the open window: "Mr. Goodlow! Mr. Goodlow! I wish you'd come in here a minute."

She hurried to meet the minister at the front door, her father lagging after her with the infantile walk of an old man.

Mr. Goodlow took off his straw hat as he mounted the stone step to the threshold, and said good-morning; they did not shake hands. He wore a black alpaca coat, and waistcoat of farmer's satin; his hat was dark straw, like Deacon Latham's, but it was low-crowned, and a line of ornamental openwork ran round it near the top.

"Come into the settin'-room," said Miss Maria. "It's cooler, in there." She lost no time in laying the case before the minister. She ended by saying, "Father, he don't feel just right about it, and I d'know as I'm quite clear in my own mind."

The minister considered a while in silence before he said, "I think Lydia's influence upon those around her will be beneficial, whatever her situation in life may be."

"There, father!" cried Miss Maria, in reproachful relief.

"You're right, Maria, you're right!" assented the old man, and they both waited for the minister to continue.

"I rejoiced with you," he said, "when this opportunity for

Lydia's improvement offered, and I am not disposed to feel anxious as to the ways and means. Lydia is no fool. I have observed in her a dignity, a sort of authority, very remarkable in one of her years."

"I guess the boys at the school down to the Mill Village found out she had authority enough," said Miss Maria, promptly materializing the idea.

"Precisely," said Mr. Goodlow.

"That's what I told father, in the first place," said Miss Maria. "I guess Lyddy'd know how to conduct herself wherever she was,—just the words I used."

"I don't deny it, Maria, I don't deny it," shrilly piped the old man. "I ain't afraid of any harm comin' to Lyddy any more'n what you be. But what I said was, Wouldn't she feel kind of strange, sort of lost, as you may say, among so many, and she the only *one*?"

"She will know how to adapt herself to circumstances," said Mr. Goodlow. "I was conversing last summer with that Mrs. Bland who boarded at Mr. Parker's, and she told me that girls in Europe are brought up with no habits of self-reliance whatever, and that young ladies are never seen on the streets alone in France and Italy."

"Don't you think," asked Miss Maria, hesitating to accept this ridiculous statement, "that Mrs. Bland exaggerated some?"

"She *talked* a great deal," admitted Mr. Goodlow. "I should be sorry if Lydia ever lost anything of that native confidence of hers in her own judgment, and her ability to take care of herself under any circumstances, and I do not think she will. She never seemed conceited to me, but she *was* the most self-reliant girl I ever saw."

"You've hit it there, Mr. Goodlow. Such a spirit as she always had!" sighed Miss Maria. "It was just so from the first. It used to go to my heart to see that little thing lookin' after herself, every way, and not askin' anybody's help, but just as quiet and proud about it! She's her mother, all over. And yest'day, when she set here waitin' for the stage, and it did seem as if I should have to give up, hearin' her sob, sob, sob,—why, Mr. Goodlow, she hadn't any more idea of backin' out than—than—" Miss Maria relinquished the search for a comparison, and went into another room for a handkerchief. "I don't believe she cared over and above about goin', from the start," said Miss Maria, returning, "but when once she'd made up her mind to it, there she was. I d'know as she *took* much of a fancy to her aunt, but you couldn't told from anything that Lyddy said. Now, if I have anything on my mind, I have to blat it right out, as you may say; I can't seem to bear it a minute; but Lyddy's different. Well," concluded Miss Maria, "I guess there ain't goin' to any harm come to her. But it did give me a kind of start, first off, when father up and got to feelin' sort of bad about it. I d'know as I should thought much about it, if he hadn't seemed to. I d'know as I should ever thought about anything except her not havin' any one to advise with about her clothes. It's the only thing she ain't handy with: she won't know what to wear. I'm afraid she'll spoil her silk. I d'know but what father's *been* hasty in not lookin' into things carefuller first. He most always does repent afterwards."

"Couldn't repent beforehand!" retorted Deacon Latham. "And I tell you, Maria, I never saw a much finer man than Captain Jenness; and the cabin's everything I said it was, and more. Lyddy reg'larly went off over it; 'n' I guess, as Mr. Goodlow says, she'll influence 'em for good. Don't you fret about her clothes any. You fitted her out in apple-pie order, and she'll soon be there. 'T ain't but a little ways to Try-East, any way, to what it is some of them India voyages, Captain Jenness said. He had his own daughters out the last voyage; 'n' I guess he can tell Lyddy when it's weather to wear her silk. I d'know as I'd better said anything about what I was thinkin'. I don't want to be noways rash, and yet I thought I couldn't be too partic'lar."

For a silent moment Miss Maria looked sourly uncertain as to the usefulness of scruples that came so long after the fact. Then she said abruptly to Mr. Goodlow, "Was it you or Mr. Baldwin, preached Mirandy Holcomb's fune'l sermon?"

W. D. Howells

VI

One of the advantages of the negative part assigned to women in life is that they are seldom forced to commit themselves. They can, if they choose, remain perfectly passive while a great many things take place in regard to them; they need not account for what they do not do. From time to time a man must show his hand, but save for one supreme exigency a woman need never show hers. She moves in mystery as long as she likes; and mere reticence in her, if she is young and fair, interprets itself as good sense and good taste.

Lydia was, by convention as well as by instinct, mistress of the situation when she came out to breakfast, and confronted the young men again with collected nerves, and a reserve which was perhaps a little too proud. The captain was there to introduce them, and presented first Mr. Dunham, the gentleman who had spoken to her grandfather on the wharf, and then Mr. Staniford, his friend and senior by some four or five years. They were both of the fair New England complexion; but Dunham's eyes were blue, and Staniford's dark gray. Their mustaches were blonde, but Dunham's curled jauntily outward at the corners, and his light hair waved over either temple from the parting in the middle. Staniford's mustache was cut short; his hair was clipped tight to his shapely head, and not parted at all; he had a slightly aquiline nose, with sensitive nostrils, showing the cartilage; his face was darkly freckled. They were both handsome fellows, and fittingly dressed in rough blue, which they wore like men with the habit of good clothes; they made Lydia such bows as she had never seen before. Then the Captain introduced Mr. Watterson, the first officer, to all, and sat down, saying to Thomas, with a sort of guilty and embarrassed growl, "Ain't he out yet? Well, we won't wait," and with but little change of tone asked a blessing; for Captain Jenness in his way was a religious man.

There was a sixth plate laid, but the captain made no further mention of the person who was not out yet till shortly after the coffee was poured, when the absentee appeared, hastily closing his state-room door behind him, and then waiting on foot, with a half-impudent, half-intimidated air, while Captain Jenness, with a sort of elaborate repressiveness, presented him as Mr. Hicks. He was a short and slight young man, with a small sandy mustache curling tightly in over his lip, floating reddish-blue eyes, and a deep dimple in his weak, slightly retreating chin. He had an air at once amiable and baddish, with an expression, curiously blended, of monkey-like humor and spaniel-like apprehensiveness. He did not look well, and till he had swallowed two cups of coffee his hand shook. The captain watched him furtively from under his bushy eyebrows, and was evidently troubled and preoccupied, addressing a word now and then to Mr. Watterson, who, by virtue of what was apparently the ship's discipline, spoke only when he was spoken to, and then answered with prompt acquiescence. Dunham and Staniford exchanged not so much a glance as a consciousness in regard to him, which seemed to recognize and class him. They talked to each other, and sometimes to the captain. Once they spoke to Lydia. Mr. Dunham, for example, said, "Miss—ah—Blood, don't you think we are uncommonly fortunate in having such lovely weather for

W. D. Howells

a start-off?"

"I don't know," said Lydia.

Mr. Dunham arrested himself in the use of his fork. "I beg your pardon?" he smiled.

It seemed to be a question, and after a moment's doubt Lydia answered, "I didn't know it was strange to have fine weather at the start."

"Oh, but I can assure you it is," said Dunham, with a certain lady-like sweetness of manner which he had. "According to precedent, we ought to be all deathly seasick."

"Not at *this* time of year," said Captain Jenness.

"Not at this time of *year*," repeated Mr. Watterson, as if the remark were an order to the crew.

Dunham referred the matter with a look to his friend, who refused to take part in it, and then he let it drop. But presently Staniford himself attempted the civility of some conversation with Lydia. He asked her gravely, and somewhat severely, if she had suffered much from the heat of the day before.

"Yes," said Lydia, "it was very hot."

"I'm told it was the hottest day of the summer, so far," continued Staniford, with the same severity.

"I want to know!" cried Lydia.

The young man did not say anything more.

As Dunham lit his cigar at Staniford's on deck, the former said significantly, "What a very American thing!"

"What a bore!" answered the other.

Dunham had never been abroad, as one might imagine from his calling Lydia's presence a very American thing, but he had always consorted with people who had lived in Europe; he read the Revue des Deux Mondes habitually, and the London weekly newspapers, and this gave him the foreign stand-point from which he was fond of viewing his native world. "It's incredible," he added. "Who in the world can she be?"

"Oh, *I* don't know," returned Staniford, with a cold disgust. "I should object to the society of such a young person for a month or six weeks under the most favorable circumstances, and with frequent respites; but to be imprisoned on the same ship with her, and to have her on one's mind and in one's way the whole time, is more than I bargained for. Captain Jenness should have told us; though I suppose he thought that if *she* could stand it, *we* might. There's that point of view. But it takes all ease and comfort out of the prospect. Here comes that blackguard." Staniford turned his back towards Mr. Hicks, who was approaching, but Dunham could not quite do this, though he waited for the other to speak first.

"Will you—would you oblige me with a light?" Mr. Hicks asked, taking a cigar from his case.

"Certainly," said Dunham, with the comradery of the smoker.

Mr. Hicks seemed to gather courage from his cigar. "You didn't expect to find a lady passenger on board, did you?" His poor disagreeable little face was lit up with unpleasant enjoyment of the anomaly. Dunham hesitated for an answer.

"One never can know what one's fellow passengers are going to be," said Staniford, turning about, and looking not at Mr. Hicks's face, but his feet, with an effect of being, upon the whole, disappointed not to find them cloven. He added, to put the man down rather than from an exact belief in his own suggestion, "She's probably some relation of the captain's."

"Why, that's the joke of it," said Hicks, fluttered with his superior knowledge. "I've been pumping the cabin-boy, and he says the captain never saw her till yesterday. She's an up-country school-marm, and she came down here with her grandfather yesterday. She's going out to meet friends of hers in Venice." The little man pulled at his cigar, and coughed and chuckled, and waited confidently for the impression.

"Dunham," said Staniford, "did I hand you that sketch-block of mine to put in your bag, when we were packing last night?"

"Yes, I've got it."

"I'm glad of that. Did you see Murray yesterday?"

"No; he was at Cambridge."

"I thought he was to have met you at Parker's." The conversation no longer included Mr. Hicks or the subject he had introduced; after a moment's hesitation, he walked away to another part of the ship. As soon as he was beyond ear-shot, Staniford again spoke: "Dunham, this girl is plainly one of those cases of supernatural innocence, on the part of herself and her friends, which, as you suggested, wouldn't occur among any other people in the world but ours."

"You're a good fellow, Staniford!" cried Dunham.

"Not at all. I call myself simply a human being, with the elemental instincts of a gentleman, as far as concerns this matter. The girl has been placed in a position which could be made very painful to her. It seems to me it's our part to prevent it from being so. I doubt if she finds it at all anomalous, and if we choose she need never do so till after we've parted with her. I fancy we can preserve her unconsciousness intact."

"Staniford, this is like you," said his friend, with glistening eyes. "I had some wild notion of the kind myself, but I'm so glad you spoke of it first."

"Well, never mind," responded Staniford. "We must make her feel that there is nothing irregular or uncommon in her being here as she is. I don't know how the matter's to be managed, exactly; it must be a negative benevolence for the most part; but it can be done. The first thing is to cow that nuisance yonder. Pumping the cabin-boy! The little sot! Look here, Dunham; it's such a satisfaction to me to think of putting that fellow under foot that I'll leave you all the credit of saving the young lady's feelings. I should like to begin stamping on him at once."

"I think you have made a beginning already. I confess I wish you hadn't such heavy nails in your boots!"

"Oh, they'll do him good, confound him!" said Staniford.

"I should have liked it better if her name hadn't been Blood," remarked Dunham, presently.

W. D. Howells

"It doesn't matter what a girl's surname is. Besides, Blood is very frequent in some parts of the State."

"She's very pretty, isn't she?" Dunham suggested.

"Oh, pretty enough, yes," replied Staniford. "Nothing is so common as the pretty girl of our nation. Her beauty is part of the general tiresomeness of the whole situation."

"Don't you think," ventured his friend, further, "that she has rather a lady-like air?"

"She wanted to know," said Staniford, with a laugh.

Dunham was silent a while before he asked, "What do you suppose her first name is?"

"Jerusha, probably."

"Oh, impossible!"

"Well, then,—Lurella. You have no idea of the grotesqueness of these people's minds. I used to see a great deal of their intimate life when I went on my tramps, and chanced it among them, for bed and board, wherever I happened to be. We cultivated Yankees and the raw material seem hardly of the same race. Where the Puritanism has gone out of the people in spots, there's the rankest growth of all sorts of crazy heresies, and the old scriptural nomenclature has given place to something compounded of the fancifulness of story-paper romance and the gibberish of spiritualism. They make up their names, sometimes, and call a child by what sounds pretty to them. I wonder how the captain picked up that scoundrel."

The turn of Staniford's thought to Hicks was suggested by

the appearance of Captain Jenness, who now issued from the cabin gangway, and came toward them with the shadow of unwonted trouble in his face. The captain, too, was smoking.

"Well, gentlemen," he began, with the obvious indirectness of a man not used to diplomacy, "how do you like your accommodations?"

Staniford silently acquiesced in Dunham's reply that they found them excellent. "But you don't mean to say," Dunham added, "that you're going to give us beefsteak and all the vegetables of the season the whole way over?"

"No," said the captain; "we shall put you on sea-fare soon enough. But you'll like it. You don't want the same things at sea that you do on shore; your appetite chops round into a different quarter altogether, and you want salt beef; but you'll get it good. Your room's pretty snug," he suggested.

"Oh, it's big enough," said Staniford, to whom he had turned as perhaps more in authority than Dunham. "While we're well we only sleep in it, and if we're seasick it doesn't matter where we are."

The captain knocked the ash from his cigar with the tip of his fat little finger, and looked down. "I was in hopes I could have let you had a room apiece, but I had another passenger jumped on me at the last minute. I suppose you see what's the matter with Mr. Hicks?" He looked up from one to another, and they replied with a glance of perfect intelligence. "I don't generally talk my passengers over with one another, but I thought I'd better speak to you about him. I found him yesterday evening at my agents', with his father. He's just been on a spree, a regular two weeks' tear, and the old gentleman didn't know what to do

W. D. Howells

with him, on shore, any longer. He thought he'd send him to sea a voyage, and see what would come of it, and he plead hard with me to take him. I didn't want to take him, but he worked away at me till I couldn't say no. I argued in my own mind that he couldn't get anything to drink on my ship, and that he'd behave himself well enough as long as he was sober." The captain added ruefully, "He looks worse this morning than he did last night. He looks bad. I told the old gentleman that if he got into any trouble at Try-East, or any of the ports where we touched, he shouldn't set foot on my ship again. But I guess he'll keep pretty straight. He hasn't got any money, for one thing."

Staniford laughed. "He stops drinking for obvious reasons, if for no others, like Artemus Ward's destitute inebriate. Did you think only of us in deciding whether you should take him?"

The captain looked up quickly at the young men, as if touched in a sore place. "Well, there again I didn't seem to get my bearings just right. I suppose you mean the young lady?" Staniford motionlessly and silently assented. "Well, she's more of a young lady than I thought she was, when her grandfather first come down here and talked of sending her over with me. He was always speaking about his little girl, you know, and I got the idea that she was about thirteen, or eleven, may be. I thought the child might be some bother on the voyage, but thinks I, I'm used to children, and I guess I can manage. Bless your soul! when I first see her on the wharf yesterday, it most knocked me down! I never believed she was half so tall, nor half so good-looking." Staniford smiled at this expression of the captain's despair, but the captain did not smile. "Why, she was as pretty as a bird. Well, there I was. It was no time then to back out. The old man wouldn't understood. Besides, there was the young lady herself, and she seemed so forlorn and helpless that I kind of pitied her. I thought, What if it was one of my own girls? And I made up my mind that she shouldn't know from anything I said or did that she wasn't just as much at home and just as much in place on my ship as she would be in my house. I suppose what made me feel easier about it, and took the queerness off some, was my having my own girls along last voyage. To be sure, it ain't quite the same thing," said the captain, interrogatively.

"Not quite," assented Staniford.

"If there was two of them," said the captain, "I don't suppose I should feel so bad about it. But thinks I, A lady's a lady the world over, and a gentleman's a gentleman." The captain looked significantly at the young men. "As for that other fellow," added Captain Jenness, "if I can't take care of him, I think I'd better stop going to sea altogether, and go into the coasting trade."

He resumed his cigar with defiance, and was about turning away when Staniford spoke. "Captain Jenness, my friend and I had been talking this little matter over just before you came up. Will you let me say that I'm rather proud of having reasoned in much the same direction as yourself?"

This was spoken with that air which gave Staniford a peculiar distinction, and made him the despair and adoration of his friend: it endowed the subject with seriousness, and conveyed a sentiment of grave and noble sincerity. The captain held out a hand to each of the young men, crossing his wrists in what seemed a favorite fashion with him. "Good!" he cried, heartily. "I *thought* I knew you."

VII

Staniford and Dunham drew stools to the rail, and sat down with their cigars after the captain left them. The second mate passed by, and cast a friendly glance at them; he had whimsical brown eyes that twinkled under his cap-peak, while a lurking smile played under his heavy mustache; but he did not speak. Staniford said, there was a pleasant fellow, and he should like to sketch him. He was only an amateur artist, and he had been only an amateur in life otherwise, so far; but he did not pretend to have been anything else.

"Then you're not sorry you came, Staniford?" asked Dunham, putting his hand on his friend's knee. "He characteristically assumed the responsibility, although the voyage by sailing-vessel rather than steamer was their common whim, and it had been Staniford's preference that decided them for Trieste rather than any nearer port.

"No, I'm not sorry,—if you call it come, already. I think a bit of Europe will be a very good thing for the present, or as long as I'm in this irresolute mood. If I understand it, Europe is the place for American irresolution. When I've made up my mind, I'll come home again. I still think Colorado is the thing, though I haven't abandoned California altogether; it's a question of cattle-range and sheep-ranch."

"You'll decide against both," said Dunham.

"How would you like West Virginia? They cattle-range in West Virginia, too. They may sheep-ranch, too, for all I know,—no, that's in Old Virginia. The trouble is that the Virginias, otherwise irreproachable, are not paying fields for such enterprises. They say that one is a sure thing in California, and the other is a sure thing in Colorado. They give you the figures." Staniford lit another cigar.

"But why shouldn't you stay where you are, Staniford? You've money enough left, after all."

"Yes, money enough for one. But there's something ignoble in living on a small stated income, unless you have some object in view besides living, and I haven't, you know. It's a duty I owe to the general frame of things to make more money."

"If you turned your mind to any one thing, I'm sure you'd succeed where you are," Dunham urged.

"That's just the trouble," retorted his friend. "I can't turn my mind to any one thing,—I'm too universally gifted. I paint a little, I model a little, I play a very little indeed; I can write a book notice. The ladies praise my art, and the editors keep my literature a long time before they print it. This doesn't seem the highest aim of being. I have the noble earth-hunger; I must get upon the land. That's why I've got upon the water." Staniford laughed again, and pulled comfortably at his cigar. "Now, you," he added, after a pause, in which Dunham did not reply, "you have not had losses; you still have everything comfortable about you. *Du hast Alles was Menschen begehr*, even to the *schonsten Augen* of the divine Miss Hibbard."

"Yes, Staniford, that's it. I hate your going out there all

alone. Now, if you were taking some nice girl with you!" Dunham said, with a lover's fond desire that his friend should be in love, too.

"To those wilds? To a redwood shanty in California, or a turf hovel in Colorado? What nice girl would go? 'I will take some savage woman, she shall rear my dusky race.'"

"I don't like to have you take any risks of degenerating," began Dunham.

"With what you know to be my natural tendencies? Your prophetic eye prefigures my pantaloons in the tops of my boots. Well, there is time yet to turn back from the brutality of a patriarchal life. You must allow that I've taken the longest way round in going West. In Italy there are many chances; and besides, you know, I like to talk."

It seemed to be an old subject between them, and they discussed it languidly, like some abstract topic rather than a reality.

"If you only had some tie to bind you to the East, I should feel pretty safe about you," said Dunham, presently.

"I have you," answered his friend, demurely.

"Oh, I'm nothing," said Dunham, with sincerity.

"Well, I may form some tie in Italy. Art may fall in love with me, there. How would you like to have me settle in Florence, and set up a studio instead of a ranch,—choose between sculpture and painting, instead of cattle and sheep? After all, it does grind me to have lost that money! If I had only been swindled out of it, I shouldn't have cared; but when you go and make a bad thing of it yourself, with your eyes open, there's a reluctance to place the responsibility where it belongs that doesn't occur in the other case. Dunham, do you think it altogether ridiculous that I should feel there was something sacred in the money? When I remember how hard my poor old father worked to get it together, it seems wicked that I should have stupidly wasted it on the venture I did. I want to get it back; I want to make money. And so I'm going out to Italy with you, to waste more. I don't respect myself as I should if I were on a Pullman palace car, speeding westward. I'll own I like this better."

"Oh, it's all right, Staniford," said his friend. "The voyage will do you good, and you'll have time to think everything over, and start fairer when you get back."

"That girl," observed Staniford, with characteristic abruptness, "is a type that is commoner than we imagine in New England. We fair people fancy we are the only genuine Yankees. I guess that's a mistake. There must have been a good many dark Puritans. In fact, we always think of Puritans as dark, don't we?"

"I believe we do," assented Dunham. "Perhaps on account of their black clothes."

"Perhaps," said Staniford. "At any rate, I'm so tired of the blonde type in fiction that I rather like the other thing in life. Every novelist runs a blonde heroine; I wonder why. This girl has the clear Southern pallor; she's of the olive hue; and her eyes are black as sloes,—not that I know what sloes are. Did she remind you of anything in particular?"

"Yes; a little of Faed's Evangeline, as she sat in the doorway of the warehouse yesterday."

"Exactly. I wish the picture were more of a picture; but I

W. D. Howells

don't know that it matters. *She's* more of a picture."

"'Pretty as a bird,' the captain said."

"Bird isn't bad. But the bird is in her manner. There's something tranquilly alert in her manner that's like a bird; like a bird that lingers on its perch, looking at you over its shoulder, if you come up behind. That trick of the heavily lifted, half lifted eyelids,—I wonder if it's a trick. The long lashes can't be; she can't make them curl up at the edges. Blood,—Lurella Blood. And she wants to know." Staniford's voice fell thoughtful.

"She's more slender than Faed's Evangeline. Faed painted rather too fat a sufferer on that tombstone. Lurella Blood has a very pretty figure. Lurella. Why Lurella?"

"Oh, come, Staniford!" cried Dunham. "It isn't fair to call the girl by that jingle without some ground for it."

"I'm sure her name's Lurella, for she wanted to know. Besides, there's as much sense in it as there is in any name. It sounds very well. Lurella. It is mere prejudice that condemns the novel collocation of syllables."

"I wonder what she's thinking of now,—what's passing in her mind," mused Dunham aloud.

"*You* want to know, too, do you?" mocked his friend. "I'll tell you what: processions of young men so long that they are an hour getting by a given point. That's what's passing in every girl's mind—when she's thinking. It's perfectly right. Processsions of young girls are similarly passing in our stately and spacious intellects. It's the chief business of the youth of one sex to think of the youth of the other sex."

"Oh, yes, I know," assented Dunham; "and I believe in it, too—"

"Of course you do, you wicked wretch, you abandoned Lovelace, you bruiser of ladies' hearts! You hope the procession is composed entirely of yourself. What would the divine Hibbard say to your goings-on?"

"Oh, don't, Staniford! It isn't fair," pleaded Dunham, with the flattered laugh which the best of men give when falsely attainted of gallantry. "I was wondering whether she was feeling homesick, or strange, or—"

"I will go below and ask her," said Staniford. "I know she will tell me the exact truth. They always do. Or if you will take a guess of mine instead of her word for it, I will hazard the surmise that she is not at all homesick. What has a pretty young girl to regret in such a life as she has left? It's the most arid and joyless existence under the sun. She has never known anything like society. In the country with us, the social side must always have been somewhat paralyzed, but there are monumental evidences of pleasures in other days that are quite extinct now. You see big dusty ball-rooms in the old taverns: ball-rooms that have had no dancing in them for half a century, and where they give you a bed sometimes. There used to be academies, too, in the hill towns, where they furnished a rude but serviceable article of real learning, and where the local octogenarian remembers seeing something famous in the way of theatricals on examination-day; but neither his children nor his grandchildren have seen the like. There's a decay of the religious sentiment, and the church is no longer a social centre, with merry meetings among the tombstones between the morning and the afternoon service. Superficial humanitarianism of one kind or another has killed the good old orthodoxy, as the railroads have killed the turnpikes and the country taverns; and the common schools have killed the academies. Why, I don't suppose this girl ever saw anything livelier than a township cattle show, or a Sunday-school picnic, in her life. They don't pay visits in the country except at rare intervals, and their evening parties, when they have any, are something to strike you dead with pity. They used to clear away the corn-husks and pumpkins on the barn floor, and dance by the light of tin lanterns. At least, that's the traditional thing. The actual thing is sitting around four sides of the room, giggling, whispering, looking at photograph albums, and coaxing somebody to play on the piano. The banquet is passed in the form of apples and water. I have assisted at *some* rural festivals where the apples were omitted. Upon the whole, I wonder our country people don't all go mad. They do go mad, a great many of them, and manage to get a little glimpse of society in the insane asylums." Staniford ended his tirade with a laugh, in which he vented his humorous sense and his fundamental pity of the conditions he had caricatured.

"But how," demanded Dunham, breaking rebelliously from the silence in which he had listened, "do you account for her good manner?"

"She probably was born with a genius for it. Some people are born with a genius for one thing, and some with a genius for another. I, for example, am an artistic genius, forced to be an amateur by the delusive possession of early wealth, and now burning with a creative instinct in the direction of the sheep or cattle business; you have the gift of universal optimism; Lurella Blood has the genius of good society. Give that girl a winter among nice people in Boston, and you would never know that she was not born on Beacon Hill."

"Oh, I doubt that," said Dunham.

"You doubt it? Pessimist!"

"But you implied just now that she had no sensibility," pursued Dunham.

"So I did!" cried Staniford, cheerfully. "Social genius and sensibility are two very different things; the cynic might contend they were incompatible, but I won't insist so far. I dare say she may regret the natal spot; most of us have a dumb, brutish attachment to the *cari luoghi*; but if she knows anything, she hates its surroundings, and must be glad to get out into the world. I should like mightily to know how the world strikes her, as far as she's gone. But I doubt if she's one to betray her own counsel in any way. She looks deep, Lurella does." Staniford laughed again at the pain which his insistence upon the name brought into Dunham's face.

VIII

After dinner, nature avenged herself in the young men for their vigils of the night before, when they had stayed up so late, parting with friends, that they had found themselves early risers without having been abed. They both slept so long that Dunham, leaving Staniford to a still unfinished nap, came on deck between five and six o'clock.

Lydia was there, wrapped against the freshening breeze in a red knit shawl, and seated on a stool in the waist of the ship, in the Evangeline attitude, and with the wistful, Evangeline look in her face, as she gazed out over the far-weltering sea-line, from which all trace of the shore had vanished. She seemed to the young man very interesting, and he approached her with that kindness for all other women in his heart which the lover feels in absence from his beloved, and with a formless sense that some retribution was due her from him for the roughness with which Staniford had surmised her natural history. Women had always been dear and sacred to him; he liked, beyond most young men, to be with them; he was forever calling upon them, getting introduced to them, waiting upon them, inventing little services for them, corresponding with them, and wearing himself out in their interest. It is said that women do not value men of this sort so much as men of some other sorts. It was long, at any rate, before

Dunham—whom people always called Charley Dunham —found the woman who thought him more lovely than every other woman pronounced him; and naturally Miss Hibbard was the most exacting of her sex. She required all those offices which Dunham delighted to render, and many besides: being an invalid, she needed devotion. She had refused Dunham before going out to Europe with her mother, and she had written to take him back after she got there. He was now on his way to join her in Dresden, where he hoped that he might marry her, and be perfectly sacrificed to her ailments. She only lacked poverty in order to be thoroughly displeasing to most men; but Dunham had no misgiving save in regard to her money; he wished she had no money.

"A good deal more motion, isn't there?" he said to Lydia, smiling sunnily as he spoke, and holding his hat with one hand. "Do you find it unpleasant?"

"No," she answered, "not at all. I like it."

"Oh, there isn't enough swell to make it uncomfortable, yet," asserted Dunham, looking about to see if there were not something he could do for her. "And you may turn out a good sailor. Were you ever at sea before?"

"No; this is the first time I was ever on a ship."

"Is it possible!" cried Dunham; he was now fairly at sea for the first time himself, though by virtue of his European associations he seemed to have made many voyages. It appeared to him that if there was nothing else he could do for Lydia, it was his duty to talk to her. He found another stool, and drew it up within easier conversational distance. "Then you've never been out of sight of land before?"

W. D. Howells

"No," said Lydia.

"That's very curious—I beg your pardon; I mean you must find it a great novelty."

"Yes, it's very strange," said the girl, seriously. "It looks like the Flood. It seems as if all the rest of the world was drowned."

Dunham glanced round the vast horizon. "It *is* like the Flood. And it has that quality, which I've often noticed in sublime things, of seeming to be for this occasion only."

"Yes?" said Lydia.

"Why, don't you know? It seems as if it must be like a fine sunset, and would pass in a few minutes. Perhaps we feel that we can't endure sublimity long, and want it to pass."

"I could look at it forever," replied Lydia.

Dunham turned to see if this were young-ladyish rapture, but perceived that she was affecting nothing. He liked seriousness, for he was, with a great deal of affectation for social purposes, a very sincere person. His heart warmed more and more to the lonely girl; to be talking to her seemed, after all, to be doing very little for her, and he longed to be of service. "Have you explored our little wooden world, yet?" he asked, after a pause.

Lydia paused too. "The ship?" she asked presently. "No; I've only been in the cabin, and here; and this morning," she added, conscientiously, "Thomas showed me the cook's galley,—the kitchen."

"You've seen more than I have," said Dunham. "Wouldn't

you like to go forward, to the bow, and see how it looks there?"

"Yes, thank you," answered Lydia, "I would."

She tottered a little in gaining her feet, and the wind drifted her slightness a step or two aside. "Won't you take my arm, perhaps?" suggested Dunham.

"Thank you," said Lydia, "I think I can get along." But after a few paces, a lurch of the ship flung her against Dunham's side; he caught her hand, and passed it through his arm without protest from her.

"Isn't it grand?" he asked triumphantly, as they stood at the prow, and rose and sank with the vessel's careering plunges. It was no gale, but only a fair wind; the water foamed along the ship's sides, and, as her bows descended, shot forward in hissing jets of spray; away on every hand flocked the white caps. "You had better keep my arm, here." Lydia did so, resting her disengaged hand on the bulwarks, as she bent over a little on that side to watch the rush of the sea. "It really seems as if there were more of a view here."

"It does, somehow," admitted Lydia."

"Look back at the ship's sails," said Dunham. The swell and press of the white canvas seemed like the clouds of heaven swooping down upon them from all the airy heights. The sweet wind beat in their faces, and they laughed in sympathy, as they fronted it. "Perhaps the motion is a little too strong for you here?" he asked.

"Oh, not at all!" cried the girl.

He had done something for her by bringing her here, and

he hoped to do something more by taking her away. He was discomfited, for he was at a loss what other attention to offer. Just at that moment a sound made itself heard above the whistling of the cordage and the wash of the sea, which caused Lydia to start and look round.

"Didn't you think," she asked, "that you heard hens?"

"Why, yes," said Dunham. "What could it have been? Let us investigate."

He led the way back past the forecastle and the cook's galley, and there, in dangerous proximity to the pots and frying pans, they found a coop with some dozen querulous and meditative fowl in it.

"I heard them this morning," said Lydia. "They seemed to wake me with their crowing, and I thought—I was at home!"

"I'm very sorry," said Dunham, sympathetically. He wished Staniford were there to take shame to himself for denying sensibility to this girl.

The cook, smoking a pipe at the door of his galley, said, "Dey won't trouble you much, miss. Dey don't gen'ly last us long, and I'll kill de roosters first."

"Oh, come, now!" protested Dunham. "I wouldn't say that!" The cook and Lydia stared at him in equal surprise.

"Well," answered the cook, "I'll kill the hens first, den. It don't make any difference to me which I kill. I dunno but de hens is tenderer." He smoked in a bland indifference.

"Oh, hold on!" exclaimed Dunham, in repetition of his helpless protest.

Lydia stooped down to make closer acquaintance with the devoted birds. They huddled themselves away from her in one corner of their prison, and talked together in low tones of grave mistrust. "Poor things!" she said. As a country girl, used to the practical ends of poultry, she knew as well as the cook that it was the fit and simple destiny of chickens to be eaten, sooner or later; and it must have been less in commiseration of their fate than in self-pity and regret for the scenes they recalled that she sighed. The hens that burrowed yesterday under the lilacs in the door-yard; the cock that her aunt so often drove, insulted and exclamatory, at the head of his harem, out of forbidden garden bounds; the social groups that scratched and descanted lazily about the wide, sunny barn doors; the anxious companies seeking their favorite perches, with alarming outcries, in the dusk of summer evenings; the sentinels answering each other from farm to farm before winter dawns, when all the hills were drowned in snow, were of kindred with these hapless prisoners.

Dunham was touched at Lydia's compassion. "Would you like—would you like to feed them?" he asked by a happy inspiration. He turned to the cook, with his gentle politeness: "There's no objection to our feeding them, I suppose?"

"Laws, no!" said the cook. "Fats 'em up." He went inside, and reappeared with a pan full of scraps of meat and crusts of bread.

"Oh, I say!" cried Dunham. "Haven't you got some grain, you know, of some sort; some seeds, don't you know?"

"They will like this," said Lydia, while the cook stared in perplexity. She took the pan, and opening the little door of the coop flung the provision inside. But the fowls were either too depressed in spirit to eat anything, or they were not hungry; they remained in their corner, and merely fell silent, as if a new suspicion had been roused in their unhappy breasts.

"Dey'll come, to it," observed the cook.

Dunham felt far from content, and regarded the poultry with silent disappointment. "Are you fond of pets?" he asked, after a while.

"Yes, I used to have pet chickens when I was a little thing."

"You ought to adopt one of these," suggested Dunham. "That white one is a pretty creature."

"Yes," said Lydia. "He looks as if he were Leghorn. Leghorn breed," she added, in reply to Dunham's look of inquiry. "He's a beauty."

"Let me get him out for you a moment!" cried the young man, in his amiable zeal. Before Lydia could protest, or the cook interfere, he had opened the coop-door and plunged his arm into the tumult which his manoeuvre created within. He secured the cockerel, and drawing it forth was about to offer it to Lydia, when in its struggles to escape it drove one of its spurs into his hand. Dunham suddenly released it; and then ensued a wild chase for its recapture, up and down the ship, in which it had every advantage of the young man. At last it sprang upon the rail; he put out his hand to seize it, when it rose with a desperate screech, and flew far out over the sea. They watched the suicide till it sank exhausted into a distant white-cap.

"Dat's gone," said the cook, philosophically. Dunham looked round. Half the ship's company, alarmed by his steeple-chase over the deck, were there, silently agrin.

Lydia did not laugh. When he asked, still with his habitual sweetness, but entirely at random, "Shall we—ah—go below?" she did not answer definitely, and did not go. At the same time she ceased to be so timidly intangible and aloof in manner. She began to talk to Dunham, instead of letting him talk to her; she asked him questions, and listened with deference to what he said on such matters as the probable length of the voyage and the sort of weather they were likely to have. She did not take note of his keeping his handkerchief wound round his hand, nor of his attempts to recur to the subject of his mortifying adventure. When they were again quite alone, the cook's respect having been won back through his ethnic susceptibility to silver, she remembered that she must go to her room.

"In other words," said Staniford, after Dunham had reported the whole case to him, "she treated your hurt vanity as if you had been her pet schoolboy. She lured you away from yourself, and got you to talking and thinking of other things. Lurella is deep, I tell you. What consummate tacticians the least of women are! It's a pity that they have to work so often in such dull material as men; they ought always to have women to operate on. The youngest of them has more wisdom in human nature than the sages of our sex. I must say, Lurella is magnanimous, too. She might have taken her revenge on you for pitying her yesterday when she sat in that warehouse door on the wharf. It was rather fine in Lurella not to do it. What did she say, Dunham? What did she talk about? Did she want to know?"

"No!" shouted Dunham. "She talked very well, like any young lady."

"Oh, all young ladies talk well, of course. But what did this one say? What did she do, except suffer a visible pang of homesickness at the sight of unattainable poultry? Come, you have represented the interview with Miss Blood as one of great brilliancy."

"I haven't," said Dunham. "I have done nothing of the kind. Her talk was like any pleasant talk; it was refined and simple, and— unobtrusive."

"That is, it was in no way remarkable," observed Staniford, with a laugh. "I expected something better of Lurella; I expected something salient. Well, never mind. She's behaved well by you, seeing what a goose you had made of yourself. She behaved like a lady, and I've noticed that she eats with her fork. It often happens in the country that you find the women practicing some of the arts of civilization, while their men folk are still sunk in barbaric uses. Lurella, I see, is a social creature; she was born for society, as you were, and I suppose you will be thrown a good deal together. We're all likely to be associated rather familiarly, under the circumstances. But I wish you would note down in your mind some points of her conversation. I'm really curious to know what a girl of her traditions thinks about the world when she first sees it. Her mind must be in most respects an unbroken wilderness. She's had schooling, of course, and she knows her grammar and algebra; but she can't have had any cultivation. If she were of an earlier generation, one would expect to find something biblical in her; but you can't count upon a Puritanic culture now among our country folks."

"If you are so curious," said Dunham, "why don't you study her mind, yourself?"

"No, no, that wouldn't do," Staniford answered. "The light

of your innocence upon hers is invaluable. I can understand her better through you. You must go on. I will undertake to make your peace with Miss Hibbard."

The young men talked as they walked the deck and smoked in the starlight. They were wakeful after their long nap in the afternoon, and they walked and talked late, with the silences that old friends can permit themselves. Staniford recurred to his loss of money and his Western projects, which took more definite form now that he had placed so much distance between himself and their fulfillment. With half a year in Italy before him, he decided upon a cattle-range in Colorado. Then, "I should like to know," he said, after one of the pauses, "how two young men of our form strike that girl's fancy. I haven't any personal curiosity about her impressions, but I should like to know, as an observer of the human race. If my conjectures are right, she's never met people of our sort before."

"What sort of men has she been associated with?" asked Dunham.

"Well, I'm not quite prepared to say. I take it that it isn't exactly the hobbledehoy sort. She has probably looked high,—as far up as the clerk in the store. He has taken her to drive in a buggy Saturday afternoons, when he put on his ready-made suit,—and looked very well in it, too; and they've been at picnics together. Or may be, as she's in the school-teaching line, she's taken some high-browed, hollow-cheeked high-school principal for her ideal. Or it is possible that she has never had attention from any one. That is apt to happen to self-respectful girls in rural communities, and their beauty doesn't save them. Fellows, as they call themselves, like girls that have what they call go, that make up to them. Lurella doesn't seem of that kind; and I should not be surprised if you were the first gentleman who had ever offered her his arm. I wonder what she thought of you. She's acquainted by sight with the ordinary summer boarder of North America; they penetrate everywhere, now; but I doubt if she's talked with them much, if at all. She must be ignorant of our world beyond anything we can imagine."

"But how do you account for her being so well dressed?"

"Oh, that's instinct. You find it everywhere. In every little village there is some girl who knows how to out-preen all the others. I wonder," added Staniford, in a more deeply musing tone, "if she kept from laughing at you out of good feeling, or if she was merely overawed by your splendor."

"She didn't laugh," Dunham answered, "because she saw that it would have added to my annoyance. My splendor had nothing to do with it."

"Oh, don't underrate your splendor, my dear fellow!" cried Staniford, with a caressing ridicule that he often used with Dunham. "Of course, *I* know what a simple and humble fellow you are, but you've no idea how that exterior of yours might impose upon the agricultural imagination; it has its effect upon me, in my pastoral moods." Dunham made a gesture of protest, and Staniford went on: "Country people have queer ideas of us, sometimes. Possibly Lurella was afraid of you. Think of that, Dunham,—having a woman afraid of you, for once in your life! Well, hurry up your acquaintance with her, Dunham, or I shall wear myself out in mere speculative analysis. I haven't the *aplomb* for studying the sensibilities of a young lady, and catching chickens for her, so as to produce a novel play of emotions. I thought this voyage was going to be a season of mental quiet, but having a young lady on board seems to forbid that kind of repose. I shouldn't mind a half dozen, but *one* is altogether too many. Poor little thing! I say, Dunham! There's something rather pretty about having her with us, after all, isn't there? It gives a certain distinction to our voyage. We shall not degenerate. We shall shave every day, wind and weather permitting, and wear our best things." They talked of other matters, and again Staniford recurred to Lydia: "If she has any regrets for her mountain home,—though I don't see why she should have,—I hope they haven't kept her awake. My far-away cot on the plains is not going to interfere with my slumbers."

Staniford stepped to the ship's side, and flung the end of his cigarette overboard; it struck, a red spark amidst the lurid phosphorescence of the bubbles that swept backward from the vessel's prow.

IX

The weather held fine. The sun shone, and the friendly winds blew out of a cloudless heaven; by night the moon ruled a firmament powdered with stars of multitudinous splendor. The conditions inspired Dunham with a restless fertility of invention in Lydia's behalf. He had heard of the game of shuffle-board, that blind and dumb croquet, with which the jaded passengers on the steamers appease their terrible leisure, and with the help of the ship's carpenter he organized this pastime, and played it with her hour after hour, while Staniford looked on and smoked in grave observance, and Hicks lurked at a distance, till Dunham felt it on his kind heart and tender conscience to invite him to a share in the diversion. As his nerves recovered their tone, Hicks showed himself a man of some qualities that Staniford would have liked in another man: he was amiable, and he was droll, though apt to turn sulky if Staniford addressed him, which did not often happen. He knew more than Dunham of shuffle-board, as well as of tossing rings of rope over a peg set up a certain space off in the deck,—a game which they eagerly took up in the afternoon, after pushing about the flat wooden disks all the morning. Most of the talk at the table was of the varying fortunes of the players; and the yarn of the story-teller in the forecastle remained half-spun, while the sailors off watch gathered to look on, and to bet upon Lydia's skill. It puzzled Staniford to make out whether she felt any strangeness in the situation, which she accepted with so much apparent serenity. Sometimes, in his frequently recurring talks with Dunham, he questioned whether their delicate precautions for saving her feelings were not perhaps thrown away upon a young person who played shuffle-board and ring-toss on the deck of the Aroostook with as much self-possession as she would have played croquet on her native turf at South Bradfield.

"Their ideal of propriety up country is very different from ours," he said, beginning one of his long comments. "I don't say that it concerns the conscience more than ours does; but they think evil of different things. We're getting Europeanized,—I don't mean you, Dunham; in spite of your endeavors you will always remain one of the most hopelessly American of our species,—and we have our little borrowed anxieties about the free association of young people. They have none whatever; though they are apt to look suspiciously upon married people's friendships with other people's wives and husbands. It's quite likely that Lurella, with the traditions of her queer world, has not imagined anything anomalous in her position. She may realize certain inconveniences. But she must see great advantages in it. Poor girl! How she must be rioting on the united devotion of cabin and forecastle, after the scanty gallantries of a hill town peopled by elderly unmarried women! I'm glad of it, for her sake. I wonder which she really prizes most: your ornate attentions, or the uncouth homage of those sailors, who are always running to fetch her rings and blocks when she makes a wild shot. I believe I don't care and shouldn't disapprove of her preference, whichever it was." Staniford frowned before he added: "But I object to Hicks and his drolleries. It's impossible for that little wretch to think reverently of a young girl; it's shocking to see her treating him as if he were a gentleman." Hicks's behavior really gave no grounds for reproach; and it was only his moral

mechanism, as Staniford called the character he cons-
tructed for him, which he could blame; nevertheless, the
thought of him gave an oblique cast to Staniford's reflec-
tions, which he cut short by saying, "This sort of worship
is every woman's due in girlhood; but I suppose a
fortnight of it will make her a pert and silly coquette.
What does she say to your literature, Dunham?"

Dunham had already begun to lend Lydia books,—his
own and Staniford's,—in which he read aloud to her, and
chose passages for her admiration; but he was obliged to
report that she had rather a passive taste in literature. She
seemed to like what he said was good, but not to like it
very much, or to care greatly for reading; or else she had
never had the habit of talking books. He suggested this to
Staniford, who at once philosophized it.

"Why, I rather like that, you know. We all read in such a
literary way, now; we don't read simply for the joy or
profit of it; we expect to talk about it, and say how it is
this and that; and I've no doubt that we're sub-consciously
harassed, all the time, with an automatic process of
criticism. Now Lurella, I fancy, reads with the sense of
the days when people read in private, and not in public, as
we do. She believes that your serious books are all true;
and she knows that my novels are all lies—that's what
some excellent Christians would call the fiction even of
George Eliot or of Hawthorne; she would be ashamed to
discuss the lives and loves of heroes and heroines who
never existed. I think that's first-rate. She must wonder at
your distempered interest in them. If one could get at it, I
suppose the fresh wholesomeness of Lurella's mind would
be something delicious, —a quality like spring water."

He was one of those men who cannot rest in regard to
people they meet till they have made some effort to
formulate them. He liked to ticket them off; but when he

could not classify them, he remained content with his mere study of them. His habit was one that does not promote sympathy with one's fellow creatures. He confessed even that it disposed him to wish for their less acquaintance when once he had got them generalized; they became then collected specimens. Yet, for the time being, his curiosity in them gave him a specious air of sociability. He lamented the insincerity which this involved, but he could not help it. The next novelty in character was as irresistible as the last; he sat down before it till it yielded its meaning, or suggested to him some analogy by which he could interpret it.

With this passion for the arrangement and distribution of his neighbors, it was not long before he had placed most of the people on board in what he called the psychology of the ship. He did not care that they should fit exactly in their order. He rather preferred that they should have idiosyncrasies which differentiated them from their species, and he enjoyed Lydia's being a little indifferent about books for this and for other reasons. "If she were literary, she would be like those vulgar little persons of genius in the magazine stories. She would have read all sorts of impossible things up in her village. She would have been discovered by some aesthetic summer boarder, who had happened to identify her with the gifted Daisy Dawn, and she would be going out on the aesthetic's money for the further expansion of her spirit in Europe. Somebody would be obliged to fall in love with her, and she would sacrifice her career for a man who was her inferior, as we should be subtly given to understand at the close. I think it's going to be as distinguished by and by not to like books as it is not to write them. Lurella is a prophetic soul; and if there's anything comforting about her, it's her being so merely and stupidly pretty."

"She is not merely and stupidly pretty!" retorted Dunham.

"She never does herself justice when you are by. She can talk very well, and on some subjects she thinks strongly."

"Oh, I'm sorry for that!" said Staniford. "But call me some time when she's doing herself justice."

"I don't mean that she's like the women we know. She doesn't say witty things, and she hasn't their responsive quickness; but her ideas are her own, no matter how old they are; and what she says she seems to be saying for the first time, and as if it had never been thought out before."

"That is what I have been contending for," said Staniford; "that is what I meant by spring water. It is that thrilling freshness which charms me in Lurella." He laughed. "Have you converted her to your spectacular faith, yet?" Dunham blushed. "You have tried," continued Staniford. "Tell me about it!"

"I will not talk with you on such matters," said Dunham, "till you know how to treat serious things seriously."

"I shall know how when I realize that they are serious with you. Well, I don't object to a woman's thinking strongly on religious subjects: it's the only safe ground for her strong thinking, and even there she had better feel strongly. Did you succeed in convincing her that Archbishop Laud was a *saint incompris*, and the good King Charles a blessed martyr."

Dunham did not answer till he had choked down some natural resentment. He had, several years earlier, forsaken the pale Unitarian worship of his family, because, Staniford always said, he had such a feeling for color, and had adopted an extreme tint of ritualism. It was rumored at one time, before his engagement to Miss Hibbard, that he was going to unite with a celibate brotherhood; he went regularly into retreat at certain seasons, to the vast entertainment of his friend; and, within the bounds of good taste, he was a zealous propagandist of his faith, of which he had the practical virtues in high degree. "I hope," he said presently, "that I know how to respect convictions, even of those adhering to the Church in Error."

Staniford laughed again. "I see you have not converted Lurella. Well, I like that in her, too. I wish I could have the arguments, *pro* and *con*. It would have been amusing. I suppose," he pondered aloud, "that she is a Calvinist of the deepest dye, and would regard me as a lost spirit for being outside of her church. She would look down upon me from one height, as I look down upon her from another. And really, as far as personal satisfaction in superiority goes, she might have the advantage of me. That's very curious, very interesting."

As the first week wore away, the wonted incidents of a sea voyage lent their variety to the life on board. One day the ship ran into a school of whales, which remained heavily thumping and lolling about in her course, and blowing jets of water into the air, like so many breaks in garden hose, Staniford suggested. At another time some flying-fish came on board. The sailors caught a dolphin, and they promised a shark, by and by. All these things were turned to account for the young girl's amusement, as if they had happened for her. The dolphin died that she might wonder and pity his beautiful death; the cook fried her some of the flying-fish; some one was on the lookout to detect even porpoises for her. A sail in the offing won the discoverer envy when he pointed it out to her; a steamer, celebrity. The captain ran a point out of his course to speak to a vessel, that she might be able to tell what speaking a ship at sea was like.

At table the stores which the young men had laid in for private use became common luxuries, and she fared sumptuously every day upon dainties which she supposed were supplied by the ship,—delicate jellies and canned meats and syruped fruits; and, if she wondered at anything, she must have wondered at the scrupulous abstinence with which Captain Jenness, seconded by Mr. Watterson, refused the luxuries which his bounty provided them, and at the constancy with which Staniford declined some of these dishes, and Hicks declined others. Shortly after the latter began more distinctly to be tolerated, he appeared one day on deck with a steamer-chair in his hand, and offered it to Lydia's use, where she sat on a stool by the bulwark. After that, as she reclined in this chair, wrapped in her red shawl, and provided with a book or some sort of becoming handiwork, she was even more picturesquely than before the centre about which the ship's pride and chivalrous sentiment revolved. They were Americans, and they knew how to worship a woman.

Staniford did not seek occasions to please and amuse her, as the others did. When they met, as they must, three times a day, at table, he took his part in the talk, and now and then addressed her a perfunctory civility. He imagined that she disliked him, and he interested himself in imagining the ignorant grounds of her dislike. "A woman," he said, "must always dislike some one in company; it's usually another woman; as there's none on board, I accept her enmity with meekness." Dunham wished to persuade him that he was mistaken. "Don't try to comfort me, Dunham," he replied. "I find a pleasure in being detested which is inconceivable to your amiable bosom."

Dunham turned to go below, from where they stood at the head of the cabin stairs. Staniford looked round, and saw Lydia, whom they had kept from coming up; she must have heard him. He took his cigar from his mouth, and caught up a stool, which he placed near the ship's side, where Lydia usually sat, and without waiting for her concurrence got a stool for himself, and sat down with her.

"Well, Miss Blood," he said, "it's Saturday afternoon at last, and we're at the end of our first week. Has it seemed very long to you?"

Lydia's color was bright with consciousness, but the glance she gave Staniford showed him looking tranquilly and honestly at her. "Yes," she said, "it *has* seemed long."

"That's merely the strangeness of everything. There's nothing like local familiarity to make the time pass,— except monotony; and one gets both at sea. Next week will go faster than this, and we shall all be at Trieste before we know it. Of course we shall have a storm or two, and that will retard us in fact as well as fancy. But you wouldn't feel that you'd been at sea if you hadn't had a storm."

He knew that his tone was patronizing, but he had theorized the girl so much with a certain slight in his mind that he was not able at once to get the tone which he usually took towards women. This might not, indeed, have pleased some women any better than patronage: it mocked while it caressed all their little pretenses and artificialities; he addressed them as if they must be in the joke of themselves, and did not expect to be taken seriously. At the same time he liked them greatly, and would not on any account have had the silliest of them different from what she was. He did not seek them as Dunham did; their society was not a matter of life or death with him; but he had an elder-brotherly kindness for the whole sex.

W. D. Howells

Lydia waited awhile for him to say something more, but he added nothing, and she observed, with a furtive look: "I presume you've seen some very severe storms at sea."

"No," Staniford answered, "I haven't. I've been over several times, but I've never seen anything alarming. I've experienced the ordinary seasickening tempestuousness."

"Have you—have you ever been in Italy?" asked Lydia, after another pause.

"Yes," he said, "twice; I'm very fond of Italy." He spoke of it in a familiar tone that might well have been discouraging to one of her total unacquaintance with it. Presently he added of his own motion, looking at her with his interest in her as a curious study, "You're going to Venice, I think Mr. Dunham told me."

"Yes," said Lydia.

"Well, I think it's rather a pity that you shouldn't arrive there directly, without the interposition of Trieste." He scanned her yet more closely, but with a sort of absence in his look, as if he addressed some ideal of her.

"Why?" asked Lydia, apparently pushed to some self-assertion by this way of being looked and talked at.

"It's the strangest place in the world," said Staniford; and then he mused again. "But I suppose—" He did not go on, and the word fell again to Lydia.

"I'm going to visit my aunt, who is staying there. She was where I live, last summer, and she told us about it. But I couldn't seem to understand it."

"No one can understand it, without seeing it."

"I've read some descriptions of it," Lydia ventured.

"They're of no use,—the books."

"Is Trieste a strange place, too?"

"It's strange, as a hundred other places are,—and it's picturesque; but there's only one Venice."

"I'm afraid sometimes," she faltered, as if his manner in regard to this peculiar place had been hopelessly exclusive, "that it will be almost too strange."

"Oh, that's another matter," said Staniford. "I confess I should be rather curious to know whether you liked Venice. I like it, but I can imagine myself sympathizing with people who detested it,—if they said so. Let me see what will give you some idea of it. Do you know Boston well?"

"No; I've only been there twice," Lydia acknowledged.

"Then you've never seen the Back Bay by night, from the Long Bridge. Well, let me see—"

"I'm afraid," interposed Lydia, "that I've not been about enough for you to give me an idea from other places. We always go to Greenfield to do our trading; and I've been to Keene and Springfield a good many times."

"I'm sorry to say I haven't," said Staniford. "But I'll tell you: Venice looks like an inundated town. If you could imagine those sunset clouds yonder turned marble, you would have Venice as she is at sunset. You must first think of the sea when you try to realize the place. If you don't find the sea too strange, you won't find Venice so."

"I wish it would ever seem half as home-like!" cried the girl.

"Then you find the ship—I'm glad you find the ship—home-like," said Staniford, tentatively.

"Oh, yes; everything is so convenient and pleasant. It seems sometimes as if I had always lived here."

"Well, that's very nice," assented Staniford, rather blankly. "Some people feel a little queer at sea—in the beginning. And you haven't —at all?" He could not help this leading question, yet he knew its meanness, and felt remorse for it.

"Oh, *I* did, at first," responded the girl, but went no farther; and Staniford was glad of it. After all, why should he care to know what was in her mind?

"Captain Jenness," he merely said, "understands making people at home."

"Oh, yes, indeed," assented Lydia. "And Mr. Watterson is very agreeable, and Mr. Mason. I didn't suppose sailors were so. What soft, mild voices they have!"

"That's the speech of most of the Down East coast people."

"Is it? I like it better than our voices. Our voices are so sharp and high, at home."

"It's hard to believe that," said Staniford, with a smile.

Lydia looked at him. "Oh, I wasn't born in South Bradfield. I was ten years old when I went there to live."

"Where *were* you born, Miss Blood?" he asked.

"In California. My father had gone out for his health, but he died there."

"Oh!" said Staniford. He had a book in his hand, and he began to scribble a little sketch of Lydia's pose, on a fly-leaf. She looked round and saw it. "You've detected me," he said; "I haven't any right to keep your likeness, now. I must make you a present of this work of art, Miss Blood." He finished the sketch with some ironical flourishes, and made as if to tear out the leaf.

"Oh!" cried Lydia, simply, "you will spoil the book!"

"Then the book shall go with the picture, if you'll let it," said Staniford.

"Do you mean to give it to me?" she asked, with surprise.

"That was my munificent intention. I want to write your name in it. What's the initial of your first name, Miss Blood?"

"L, thank you," said Lydia.

Staniford gave a start. "No!" he exclaimed. It seemed a fatality.

"My name is Lydia," persisted the girl. "What letter should it begin with?"

"Oh—oh, I knew Lydia began with an L," stammered Staniford, "but I—I—I thought your first name was—"

"What?" asked Lydia sharply.

"I don't know. Lily," he answered guiltily.

"Lily *Blood*!" cried the girl. "Lydia is bad enough; but *Lily* Blood! They couldn't have been such fools!"

"I beg your pardon. Of course not. I don't know how I could have got the idea. It was one of those impressions—hallucinations—" Staniford found himself in an attitude of lying excuse towards the simple girl, over whom he had been lording it in satirical fancy ever since he had seen her, and meekly anxious that she should not be vexed with him. He began to laugh at his predicament, and she smiled at his mistake. "What is the date?" he asked.

"The 15th," she said; and he wrote under the sketch, *Lydia Blood. Ship Aroostook, August* 15, 1874, and handed it to her, with a bow surcharged with gravity.

She took it, and regarded the picture without comment.

"Ah!" said Staniford, "I see that you know how bad my sketch is. You sketch."

"No, I don't know how to draw," replied Lydia.

"You criticise."

"No."

"So glad," said Staniford. He began to like this. A young man must find pleasure in sitting alone near a pretty young girl, and talking with her about herself and himself, no matter how plain and dull her speech is; and Staniford, though he found Lydia as blankly unresponsive as might be to the flattering irony of his habit, amused himself in realizing that here suddenly he was almost upon the terms of window-seat flirtation with a girl whom lately he had treated with perfect indifference, and just now with fatherly patronage. The situation had something more even than the usual window-seat advantages; it had qualities as of a common shipwreck, of their being cast away on a desolate island together. He felt more than ever that he must protect this helpless loveliness, since it had begun to please his imagination. "You don't criticise," he said. "Is that because you are so amiable? I'm sure you could, if you would."

"No," returned Lydia; "I don't really know. But I've often wished I did know."

"Then you didn't teach drawing, in your school?"

"How did you know I had a school?" asked Lydia quickly.

He disliked to confess his authority, because he disliked the authority, but he said, "Mr. Hicks told us."

"Mr. Hicks!" Lydia gave a little frown as of instinctive displeasure, which gratified Staniford.

"Yes; the cabin-boy told him. You see, we are dreadful gossips on the Aroostook,—though there are so few ladies—" It had slipped from him, but it seemed to have no personal slant for Lydia.

"Oh, yes; I told Thomas," she said. "No; it's only a country school. Once I thought I should go down to the State Normal School, and study drawing there; but I never did. Are you—are you a painter, Mr. Staniford?"

He could not recollect that she had pronounced his name before; he thought it came very winningly from her lips. "No, I'm not a painter. I'm not anything." He hesitated; then he added recklessly, "I'm a farmer."

"A farmer?" Lydia looked incredulous, but grave.

"Yes; I'm a horny-handed son of the soil. I'm a cattle-farmer; I'm a sheep-farmer; I don't know which. One day I'm the one, and the next day I'm the other." Lydia looked mystified, and Staniford continued: "I mean that I have no profession, and that sometimes I think of going into farming, out West."

"Yes?" said Lydia.

"How should I like it? Give me an opinion, Miss Blood."

"Oh, I don't know," answered the girl.

"You would never have dreamt that I was a farmer, would you?"

"No, I shouldn't," said Lydia, honestly. "It's very hard work."

"And I don't look fond of hard work?"

"I didn't say that."

"And I've no right to press you for your meaning."

"What I meant was—I mean—Perhaps if you had never tried it you didn't know what very hard work it was. Some of the summer boarders used to think our farmers had easy times."

"I never was a summer boarder of that description. I know that farming is hard work, and I'm going into it because I dislike it. What do you think of that as a form of self-sacrifice?"

"I don't see why any one should sacrifice himself uselessly."

"You don't? You have very little conception of martyrdom. Do you like teaching school?"

"No," said Lydia promptly.

"Why do you teach, then?" Staniford had blundered. He knew why she taught, and he felt instantly that he had hurt her pride, more sensitive than that of a more sophisticated person, who would have had no scruple in saying that she did it because she was poor. He tried to retrieve himself. "Of course, I understand that school-teaching is useful self-sacrifice." He trembled lest she should invent some pretext for leaving him; he could not afford to be left at a disadvantage. "But do you know, I would no more have taken you for a teacher than you me for a farmer."

"Yes?" said Lydia.

He could not tell whether she was appeased or not, and he rather feared not. "You don't ask why. And I asked you why at once."

Lydia laughed. "Well, why?"

"Oh, that's a secret. I'll tell you one of these days." He had really no reason; he said this to gain time. He was always honest in his talk with men, but not always with women.

"I suppose I look very young," said Lydia. "I used to be afraid of the big boys."

"If the boys were big enough," interposed Staniford, "they must have been afraid of you."

Lydia said, as if she had not understood, "I had hard work to get my certificate. But I was older than I looked."

"That is much better," remarked Staniford, "than being younger than you look. I am twenty-eight, and people take me for thirty-four. I'm a prematurely middle-aged man. I wish you would tell me, Miss Blood, a little about South Bradfield. I've been trying to make out whether I was ever there. I tramped nearly everywhere when I was a student. What sort of people are they there?"

"Oh, they are very nice people," said Lydia.

"Do you like them?"

"I never thought whether I did. They are nearly all old. Their children have gone away; they don't seem to live; they are just staying. When I first came there I was a little girl. One day I went into the grave-yard and counted the stones; there were three times as many as there were living persons in the village."

"I think I know the kind of place," said Staniford. "I suppose you're not very homesick?"

"Not for the place," answered Lydia, evasively.

"Of course," Staniford hastened to add, "you miss your own family circle." To this she made no reply. It is the habit of people bred like her to remain silent for want of some sort of formulated comment upon remarks to which they assent.

Staniford fell into a musing mood, which was without visible embarrassment to the young girl, who must have been inured to much severer silences in the society of South Bradfield. He remained staring at her throughout his reverie, which in fact related to her. He was thinking what sort of an old maid she would have become if she had remained in that village. He fancied elements of hardness and sharpness in her which would have asserted themselves as the joyless years went on, like the bony structure of her face as the softness of youth left it. She was saved from that, whatever was to be her destiny in Italy. From South Bradfield to Venice,—what a prodigious transition! It seemed as if it must transfigure her. "Miss Blood," he exclaimed, "I wish I could be with you when you first see Venice!"

"Yes?" said Lydia.

Even the interrogative comment, with the rising inflection, could not chill his enthusiasm. "It is really the greatest sight in the world."

Lydia had apparently no comment to make on this fact. She waited tranquilly a while before she said, "My father used to talk about Italy to me when I was little. He wanted to go. My mother said afterwards—after she had come home with me to South Bradfield—that she always believed he would have lived if he had gone there. He had consumption."

"Oh!" said Staniford softly. Then he added, with the tact of his sex, "Miss Blood, you mustn't take cold, sitting here with me. This wind is chilly. Shall I go below and get you some more wraps?"

"No, thank you," said Lydia; "I believe I will go down, now."

She went below to her room, and then came out into the cabin with some sewing at which she sat and stitched by the lamp. The captain was writing in his log-book;

W. D. Howells

Dunham and Hicks were playing checkers together. Staniford, from a corner of a locker, looked musingly upon this curious family circle. It was not the first time that its occupations had struck him oddly. Sometimes when they were all there together, Dunham read aloud. Hicks knew tricks of legerdemain which he played cleverly. The captain told some very good stories, and led off in the laugh. Lydia always sewed and listened. She did not seem to find herself strangely placed, and her presence characterized all that was said and done with a charming innocence. As a bit of life, it was as pretty as it was quaint.

"Really," Staniford said to Dunham, as they turned in, that night, "she has domesticated us."

"Yes," assented Dunham with enthusiasm; "isn't she a nice girl?"

"She's intolerably passive. Or not passive, either. She says what she thinks, but she doesn't seem to have thought of many things. Did she ever tell you about her father?"

"No," said Dunham.

"I mean about his dying of consumption?"

"No, she never spoke of him to me. Was he—"

"Um. It appears that we have been upon terms of confidence, then." Staniford paused, with one boot in his hand. "I should never have thought it."

"What was her father?" asked Dunham.

"Upon my word, I don't know. I didn't seem to get beyond elemental statements of intimate fact with her. He died in

California, where she was born; and he always had a longing to go to Italy. That was rather pretty."

"It's very touching, I think."

"Yes, of course. We might fancy this about Lurella: that she has a sort of piety in visiting the scenes that her father wished to visit, and that—Well, anything is predicable of a girl who says so little and looks so much. She's certainly very handsome; and I'm bound to say that her room could not have been better than her company, so far."

W. D. Howells

X

The dress that Lydia habitually wore was one which her aunt Maria studied from the costume of a summer boarder, who had spent a preceding summer at the seashore, and who found her yachting-dress perfectly adapted to tramping over the South Bradfield hills. Thus reverting to its original use on shipboard, the costume looked far prettier on Lydia than it had on the summer boarder from whose unconscious person it had been plagiarized. It was of the darkest blue flannel, and was fitly set off with those bright ribbons at the throat which women know how to dispose there according to their complexions. One day the bow was scarlet, and another crimson; Staniford did not know which was better, and disputed the point in vain with Dunham. They all grew to have a taste in such matters. Captain Jenness praised her dress outright, and said that he should tell his girls about it. Lydia, who had always supposed it was a walking costume, remained discreetly silent when the young men recognized its nautical character. She enjoyed its success; she made some little changes in the hat she wore with it, which met the approval of the cabin family; and she tranquilly kept her black silk in reserve for Sunday. She came out to breakfast in it, and it swept the narrow spaces, as she emerged from her state-room, with so rich and deep a murmur that every one looked up. She sustained their united glance with something tenderly deprecatory and appealingly conscious in her manner, much as a very sensitive girl in some new finery meets the eyes of her brothers when she does not know whether to cry or laugh at what they will say. Thomas almost dropped a plate. "Goodness!" he said, helplessly expressing the public sentiment in regard to a garment of which he alone had been in the secret. No doubt it passed his fondest dreams of its splendor; it fitted her as the sheath of the flower fits the flower.

Captain Jenness looked hard at her, but waited a decent season after saying grace before offering his compliment, which he did in drawing the carving-knife slowly across the steel. "Well, Miss Blood, that's right!" Lydia blushed richly, and the young men made their obeisances across the table.

The flushes and pallors chased each other over her face, and the sight of her pleasure in being beautiful charmed Staniford. "If she were used to worship she would have taken our adoration more arrogantly," he said to his friend when they went on deck after breakfast. "I can place her; but one's circumstance doesn't always account for one in America, and I can't make out yet whether she's ever been praised for being pretty. Some of our hill-country people would have felt like hushing up her beauty, as almost sinful, and some would have gone down before it like Greeks. I can't tell whether she knows it all or not; but if you suppose her unconscious till now, it's pathetic. And black silks must be too rare in her life not to be celebrated by a high tumult of inner satisfaction. I'm glad we bowed down to the new dress."

"Yes," assented Dunham, with an uneasy absence; "but— Staniford, I should like to propose to Captain Jenness our having service this morning. It is the eleventh Sunday after—"

"Ah, yes!" said Staniford. "It is Sunday, isn't it? I *thought* we had breakfast rather later than usual. All over the Christian world, on land and sea, there is this abstruse relation between a late breakfast and religious observances."

Dunham looked troubled. "I wish you wouldn't talk that way, Staniford, and I hope you won't say anything—"

"To interfere with your proposition? My dear fellow, I am at least a gentleman."

"I beg your pardon," said Dunham, gratefully.

Staniford even went himself to the captain with Dunham's wish; it is true the latter assumed the more disagreeable part of proposing the matter to Hicks, who gave a humorous assent, as one might to a joke of doubtful feasibility.

Dunham gratified both his love for social management and his zeal for his church in this organization of worship; and when all hands were called aft, and stood round in decorous silence, he read the lesson for the day, and conducted the service with a gravity astonishing to the sailors, who had taken him for a mere dandy. Staniford bore his part in the responses from the same prayer-book with Captain Jenness, who kept up a devout, inarticulate under-growl, and came out strong on particular words when he got his bearings through his spectacles. Hicks and the first officer silently shared another prayer-book, and Lydia offered half hers to Mr. Mason.

When the hymn was given out, she waited while an experimental search for the tune took place among the rest. They were about to abandon the attempt, when she lifted her voice and began to sing. She sang as she did in the meeting-house at South Bradfield, and her voice seemed to fill all the hollow height and distance; it rang far off like a mermaid's singing, on high like an angel's; it called with the same deep appeal to sense and soul alike. The sailors stood rapt; Dunham kept up a show of singing for the church's sake. The others made no pretense of looking at the words; they looked at her, and she began to falter, hearing herself alone. Then Staniford struck in again wildly, and the sea-voices lent their powerful discord, while the girl's contralto thrilled through all.

"Well, Miss Blood," said the captain, when the service had ended in that subordination of the spiritual to the artistic interest which marks the process and the close of so much public worship in our day, "you've given us a surprise. I guess we shall keep you pretty busy with our calls for music, after this."

"She is a genius!" observed Staniford at his first opportunity with Dunham. "I knew there must be something the matter. Of course she's going out to school her voice; and she hasn't strained it in idle babble about her own affairs! I must say that Lu—Miss Blood's power of holding her tongue commands my homage. Was it her little *coup* to wait till we got into that hopeless hobble before she struck in?"

"Coup? For shame, Staniford! Coup at such a time!"

"Well, well! I don't say so. But for the theatre one can't begin practicing these effects too soon. Really, that voice puts a new complexion on Miss Blood. I have a theory to reconstruct. I have been philosophizing her as a simple country girl. I must begin on an operatic novice. I liked the other better. It gave value to the black silk; as a singer she'll wear silk as habitually as a cocoon. She will have to take some stage name; translate Blood into Italian. We

W. D. Howells

shall know her hereafter as La Sanguinelli; and when she comes to Boston we shall make our modest brags about going out to Europe with her. I don't know; I think I preferred the idyllic flavor I was beginning to find in the presence of the ordinary, futureless young girl, voyaging under the chaperonage of her own innocence,—the Little Sister of the Whole Ship. But this crepusculant prima donna—no, I don't like it. Though it explains some things. These splendid creatures are never sent half equipped into the world. I fancy that where there's an operatic voice, there's an operatic soul to go with it. Well, La Sanguinelli will wear me out, yet! Suggest some new topic, Dunham; talk of something else, for heaven's sake!"

"Do you suppose," asked Dunham, "that she would like to help get up some *musicales*, to pass away the time?"

"Oh, do you call that talking of something else? What an insatiate organizer you are! You organize shuffleboard; you organize public worship; you want to organize musicales. She would have to do all your music for you."

"I think she would like to go in for it," said Dunham. "It must be a pleasure to exercise such a gift as that, and now that it's come out in the way it has, it would be rather awkward for us not to recognize it."

Staniford refused point-blank to be a party to the new enterprise, and left Dunham to his own devices at dinner, where he proposed the matter.

"If you had my Persis here, now," observed Captain Jenness, "with her parlor organ, you could get along."

"I wish Miss Jenness was here," said Dunham, politely. "But we must try to get on as it is. With Miss Blood's voice to start with, nothing ought to discourage us."

Dunham had a thin and gentle pipe of his own, and a fairish style in singing, but with his natural modesty he would not offer himself as a performer except in default of all others. "Don't you sing, Mr. Hicks?"

"Anything to oblige a friend," returned Hicks. "But I don't sing —before Miss Blood."

"Miss Blood," said Staniford, listening in ironic safety, "you overawe us all. I never did sing, but I think I should want to make an effort if you were not by."

"But don't you—don't you play something, anything?" persisted Dunham, in desperate appeal to Hicks.

"Well, yes," the latter admitted, "I play the flute a little."

"Flutes on water!" said Staniford. Hicks looked at him in sulky dislike, but as if resolved not to be put down by him.

"And have you got your flute with you?" demanded Dunham, joyously.

"Yes, I have," replied Hicks.

"Then we are all right. I think I can carry a part, and if you will play to Miss Blood's singing—"

"Try it this evening, if you like," said the other.

"Well, ah—I don't know. Perhaps—we hadn't better begin this evening."

Staniford laughed at Dunham's embarrassment. "You might have a sacred concert, and Mr. Hicks could represent the shawms and cymbals with his flute."

Dunham looked sorry for Staniford's saying this. Captain Jenness stared at him, as if his taking the names of these scriptural instruments in vain were a kind of blasphemy, and Lydia seemed puzzled and a little troubled.

"I didn't think of its being Sunday," said Hicks, with what Staniford felt to be a cunning assumption of manly frankness, "or any more Sunday than usual; seems as if we had had a month of Sundays already since we sailed. I'm not much on religion myself, but I shouldn't like to interfere with other people's principles."

Staniford was vexed with himself for his scornful pleasantry, and vexed with the others for taking it so seriously and heavily, and putting him so unnecessarily in the wrong. He was angry with Dunham, and he said to Hicks, "Very just sentiments."

"I am glad you like them," replied Hicks, with sullen apprehension of the offensive tone.

Staniford turned to Lydia. "I suppose that in South Bradfield your Sabbath is over at sundown on Sunday evening."

"That used to be the custom," answered the girl. "I've heard my grandfather tell of it."

"Oh, yes," interposed Captain Jenness. "They used to keep Saturday night down our way, too. I can remember when I was a boy. It came pretty hard to begin so soon, but it seemed to kind of break it, after all, having a night in."

The captain did not know what Staniford began to laugh at. "Our Puritan ancestors knew just how much human nature could stand, after all. We did not have an uninterrupted Sabbath till the Sabbath had become much milder. Is that it?"

The captain had probably no very clear notion of what this meant, but simply felt it to be a critical edge of some sort. "I don't know as you can have too much religion," he remarked. "I've seen some pretty rough customers in the church, but I always thought, What would they be out of it!"

"Very true!" said Staniford, smiling. He wanted to laugh again, but he liked the captain too well to do that; and then he began to rage in his heart at the general stupidity which had placed him in the attitude of mocking at religion, a thing he would have loathed to do. It seemed to him that Dunham was answerable for his false position. "But we shall not see the right sort of Sabbath till Mr. Dunham gets his Catholic church fully going," he added.

They all started, and looked at Dunham as good Protestants must when some one whom they would never have suspected of Catholicism turns out to be a Catholic. Dunham cast a reproachful glance at his friend, but said simply, "I am a Catholic,—that is true; but I do not admit the pretensions of the Bishop of Rome."

The rest of the company apparently could not follow him in making this distinction; perhaps some of them did not quite know who the Bishop of Rome was. Lydia continued to look at him in fascination; Hicks seemed disposed to whistle, if such a thing were allowable; Mr. Watterson devoutly waited for the captain. "Well," observed the captain at last, with the air of giving the devil his due, "I've seen some very good people among the Catholics."

"That's so, Captain Jenness," said the first officer.

W. D. Howells

"I don't see," said Lydia, without relaxing her gaze, "why, if you are a Catholic, you read the service of a Protestant church."

"It is not a Protestant church," answered Dunham, gently, "as I have tried to explain to you."

"The Episcopalian?" demanded Captain Jenness.

"The Episcopalian," sweetly reiterated Dunham.

"I should like to know what kind of a church it is, then," said Captain Jenness, triumphantly.

"An Apostolic church."

Captain Jenness rubbed his nose, as if this were a new kind of church to him.

"Founded by Saint Henry VIII. himself," interjected Staniford.

"No, Staniford," said Dunham, with a soft repressiveness. And now a threatening light of zeal began to burn in his kindly eyes. These souls had plainly been given into his hands for ecclesiastical enlightenment. "If our friends will allow me, I will explain—"

Staniford's shaft had recoiled upon his own head. "O Lord!" he cried, getting up from the table, "I can't stand *that*!" The others regarded him, as he felt, even to that weasel of a Hicks, as a sheep of uncommon blackness. He went on deck, and smoked a cigar without relief. He still heard the girl's voice in singing; and he still felt in his nerves the quality of latent passion in it which had thrilled him when she sang. His thought ran formlessly upon her future, and upon what sort of being was already fated to waken her to those possibilities of intense suffering and joy which he imagined in her. A wound at his heart, received long before, hurt vaguely; and he felt old.

W. D. Howells

XI

No one said anything more of the musicales, and the afternoon and evening wore away without general talk. Each seemed willing to keep apart from the rest. Dunham suffered Lydia to come on deck alone after tea, and Staniford found her there, in her usual place, when he went up some time later. He approached her at once, and said, smiling down into her face, to which the moonlight gave a pale mystery, "Miss Blood, did you think I was very wicked to-day at dinner?"

Lydia looked away, and waited a moment before she spoke. "I don't know," she said. Then, impulsively, "Did you?" she asked.

"No, honestly, I don't think I was," answered Staniford. "But I seemed to leave that impression on the company. I felt a little nasty, that was all; and I tried to hurt Mr. Dunham's feelings. But I shall make it right with him before I sleep; he knows that. He's used to having me repent at leisure. Do you ever walk Sunday night?"

"Yes, sometimes," said Lydia interrogatively.

"I'm glad of that. Then I shall not offend against your scruples if I ask you to join me in a little ramble, and you will refuse from purely personal considerations. Will you walk with me?"

"Yes." Lydia rose.

"And will you take my arm?" asked Staniford, a little surprised at her readiness.

"Thank you."

She put her hand upon his arm, confidently enough, and they began to walk up and down the stretch of open deck together.

"Well," said Staniford, "did Mr. Dunham convince you all?"

"I think he talks beautifully about it," replied Lydia, with quaint stiffness.

"I am glad you see what a very good fellow he is. I have a real affection for Dunham."

"Oh, yes, he's good. At first it surprised me. I mean—"

"No, no," Staniford quickly interrupted, "why did it surprise you to find Dunham good?"

"I don't know. You don't expect a person to be serious who is so—so—"

"Handsome?"

"No,—so—I don't know just how to say it: fashionable."

Staniford laughed. "Why, Miss Blood, you're fashionably dressed yourself, not to go any farther, and you're serious."

"It's different with a man," the girl explained.

"Well, then, how about me?" asked Staniford. "Am I too well dressed to be expected to be serious?"

"Mr. Dunham always seems in earnest," Lydia answered, evasively.

"And you think one can't be in earnest without being serious?" Lydia suffered one of those silences to ensue in which Staniford had already found himself helpless. He knew that he should be forced to break it: and he said, with a little spiteful mocking, "I suppose the young men of South Bradfield are both serious and earnest."

"How?" asked Lydia.

"The young men of South Bradfield."

"I told you that there were none. They all go away."

"Well, then, the young men of Springfield, of Keene, of Greenfield."

"I can't tell. I am not acquainted there."

Staniford had begun to have a disagreeable suspicion that her ready consent to walk up and down with a young man in the moonlight might have come from a habit of the kind. But it appeared that her fearlessness was like that of wild birds in those desert islands where man has never come. The discovery gave him pleasure out of proportion to its importance, and he paced back and forth in a silence that no longer chafed. Lydia walked very well, and kept his step with rhythmic unison, as if they were walking to music together. "That's the time in her pulses," he thought, and then he said, "Then you don't have a great deal of social excitement, I suppose,—dancing, and that kind of thing? Though perhaps you don't approve of dancing?"

"Oh, yes, I like it. Sometimes the summer boarders get up little dances at the hotel."

"Oh, the summer boarders!" Staniford had overlooked them. "The young men get them up, and invite the ladies?" he pursued.

"There are no young men, generally, among the summer boarders. The ladies dance together. Most of the gentlemen are old, or else invalids."

"Oh!" said Staniford.

"At the Mill Village, where I've taught two winters, they have dances sometimes,—the mill hands do."

"And do you go?"

"No. They are nearly all French Canadians and Irish people."

"Then you like dancing because there are no gentlemen to dance with?"

"There are gentlemen at the picnics."

"The picnics?"

"The teachers' picnics. They have them every summer, in a grove by the pond."

There was, then, a high-browed, dyspeptic high-school principal, and the desert-island theory was probably all wrong. It vexed Staniford, when he had so nearly got the compass of her social life, to find this unexplored corner in it.

"And I suppose you are leaving very agreeable friends among the teachers?"

"Some of them are pleasant. But I don't know them very well. I've only been to one of the picnics."

Staniford drew a long, silent breath. After all, he knew everything. He mechanically dropped a little the arm on which her hand rested, that it might slip farther within. Her timid remoteness had its charm, and he fell to thinking, with amusement, how she who was so subordinate to him was, in the dimly known sphere in which he had been groping to find her, probably a person of authority and consequence. It satisfied a certain domineering quality in him to have reduced her to this humble attitude, while it increased the protecting tenderness he was beginning to have for her. His mind went off further upon this matter of one's different attitudes toward different persons; he thought of men, and women too, before whom he should instantly feel like a boy, if he could be confronted with them, even in his present lordliness of mood. In a fashion of his when he convicted himself of anything, he laughed aloud. Lydia shrank a little from him, in question. "I beg your pardon," he said. "I was laughing at something I happened to think of. Do you ever find yourself struggling very hard to be what you think people think you are?"

"Oh, yes," replied Lydia. "But I thought no one else did."

"Everybody does the thing that we think no one else does," said Staniford, sententiously.

"I don't know whether I quite like it," said Lydia. "It seems like hypocrisy. It used to worry me. Sometimes I wondered if I had any real self. I seemed to be just what people made me, and a different person to each."

"I'm glad to hear it, Miss Blood. We are companions in hypocrisy. As we are such nonentities we shall not affect each other at all." Lydia laughed. "Don't you think so? What are you laughing at? I told you what I was laughing at!"

"But I didn't ask you."

"You wished to know."

"Yes, I did."

"Then you ought to tell me what I wish to know."

"It's nothing," said Lydia. "I thought you were mistaken in what you said."

"Oh! Then you believe that there's enough of you to affect me?"

"No."

"The other way, then?"

She did not answer.

"I'm delighted!" exclaimed Staniford. "I hope I don't exert an uncomfortable influence. I should be very unhappy to think so." Lydia stooped side-wise, away from him, to get a fresh hold of her skirt, which she was carrying in her right hand, and she hung a little more heavily upon his arm. "I hope I make you think better of yourself,—very self-satisfied, very conceited even."

"No," said Lydia.

"You pique my curiosity beyond endurance. Tell me how I make you feel."

She looked quickly round at him, as if to see whether he was in earnest. "Why, it's nothing," she said. "You made me feel as if you were laughing at everybody."

It flatters a man to be accused of sarcasm by the other sex, and Staniford was not superior to the soft pleasure of the reproach. "Do you think I make other people feel so, too?"

"Mr. Dunham said—"

"Oh! Mr. Dunham has been talking me over with you, has he? What did he tell you of me? There is nobody like a true friend for dealing an underhand blow at one's repu- tation. Wait till you hear my account of Dunham! What did he say?"

"He said that was only your way of laughing at yourself."

"The traitor! What did you say?"

"I don't know that I said anything."

"You were reserving your opinion for my own hearing?"

"No."

"Why don't you tell me what you thought? It might be of great use to me. I'm in earnest, now; I'm serious. Will you tell me?"

"Yes, some time," said Lydia, who was both amused and mystified at this persistence.

"When? To-morrow?"

"Oh, that's too soon. When I get to Venice!"

"Ah! That's a subterfuge. You know we shall part in Trieste."

"I thought," said Lydia, "you were coming to Venice, too."

"Oh, yes, but I shouldn't be able to see you there."

"Why not?"

"Why not? Why, because—" He was near telling the young girl who hung upon his arm, and walked up and down with him in the moonlight, that in the wicked Old World towards which they were sailing young people could not meet save in the sight and hearing of their elders, and that a confidential analysis of character would be impossible between them there. The wonder of her being where she was, as she was, returned upon him with a freshness that it had been losing in the custom of the week past. "Because you will be so much taken up with your friends," he said, lamely. He added quickly, "There's one thing I should like to know, Miss Blood: did you hear what Mr. Dunham and I were saying, last night, when we stood in the gangway and kept you from coming up?"

Lydia waited a moment. Then she said, "Yes. I couldn't help hearing it."

"That's all right. I don't care for your hearing what I said. But—I hope it wasn't true?"

"I couldn't understand what you meant by it," she answered, evasively, but rather faintly.

"Thanks," said Staniford. "I didn't mean anything. It was merely the guilty consciousness of a generally disagreeable person." They walked up and down many turns without saying anything. She could not have made any direct protest, and it pleased him that she could not frame any flourishing generalities. "Yes," Staniford resumed, "I will try to see you as I pass through Venice. And I will come to hear you sing when you come out at Milan."

"Come out? At Milan?"

"Why, yes! You are going to study at the conservatory in Milan?"

"How did you know that?" demanded Lydia.

"From hearing you to-day. May I tell you how much I liked your singing?"

"My aunt thought I ought to cultivate my voice. But I would never go upon the stage. I would rather sing in a church. I should like that better than teaching."

"I think you're quite right," said Staniford, gravely. "It's certainly much better to sing in a church than to sing in a theatre. Though I believe the theatre pays best."

"Oh, I don't care for that. All I should want would be to make a living."

The reference to her poverty touched him. It was a confidence, coming from one so reticent, that was of value. He waited a moment and said, "It's surprising how well we keep our footing here, isn't it? There's hardly any swell, but the ship pitches. I think we walk better together than alone."

"Yes," answered Lydia, "I think we do."

"You mustn't let me tire you. I'm indefatigable."

"Oh, I'm not tired. I like it,—walking."

"Do you walk much at home?"

"Not much. It's a pretty good walk to the school-house."

"Oh! Then you like walking at sea better than you do on shore?"

"It isn't the custom, much. If there were any one else, I should have liked it there. But it's rather dull, going by yourself."

"Yes, I understand how that is," said Staniford, dropping his teasing tone. "It's stupid. And I suppose it's pretty lonesome at South Bradfield every way."

"It is,—winters," admitted Lydia. "In the summer you see people, at any rate, but in winter there are days and days when hardly any one passes. The snow is banked up everywhere."

He felt her give an involuntary shiver; and he began to talk to her about the climate to which she was going. It was all stranger to her than he could have realized, and less intelligible. She remembered California very dimly, and she had no experience by which she could compare and adjust his facts. He made her walk up and down more and more swiftly, as he lost himself in the comfort of his own talking and of her listening, and he failed to note the little falterings with which she expressed her weariness.

All at once he halted, and said, "Why, you're out of breath! I beg your pardon. You should have stopped me. Let us sit down." He wished to walk across the deck to where the seats were, but she just perceptibly withstood his motion, and he forbore.

"I think I won't sit down," she said. "I will go downstairs." She began withdrawing her hand from his arm. He put his right hand upon hers, and when it came out of his arm it remained in his hand.

"I'm afraid you won't walk with me again," said Staniford. "I've tired you shamefully."

"Oh, not at all!"

"And you will?"

"Yes."

"Thanks. You're very amiable." He still held her hand. He pressed it. The pressure was not returned, but her hand seemed to quiver and throb in his like a bird held there. For the time neither of them spoke, and it seemed a long time. Staniford found himself carrying her hand towards his lips; and she was helplessly, trustingly, letting him.

He dropped her hand, and said, abruptly, "Good-night."

"Good-night," she answered, and ceased from his side like a ghost.

XII

Staniford sat in the moonlight, and tried to think what the steps were that had brought him to this point; but there were no steps of which he was sensible. He remembered thinking the night before that the conditions were those of flirtation; to-night this had not occurred to him. The talk had been of the dullest commonplaces; yet he had pressed her hand and kept it in his, and had been about to kiss it. He bitterly considered the disparity between his present attitude and the stand he had taken when he declared to Dunham that it rested with them to guard her peculiar isolation from anything that she could remember with pain or humiliation when she grew wiser in the world. He recalled his rage with Hicks, and the insulting condemnation of his bearing towards him ever since; and could Hicks have done worse? He had done better: he had kept away from her; he had let her alone.

That night Staniford slept badly, and woke with a restless longing to see the girl, and to read in her face whatever her thought of him had been. But Lydia did not come out to breakfast. Thomas reported that she had a headache, and that he had already carried her the tea and toast she wanted. "Well, it seems kind of lonesome without her," said the captain. "It don't seem as if we could get along."

It seemed desolate to Staniford, who let the talk flag and

W. D. Howells

fail round him without an effort to rescue it. All the morning he lurked about, keeping out of Dunham's way, and fighting hard through a dozen pages of a book, to which he struggled to nail his wandering mind. A headache was a little matter, but it might be even less than a headache. He belated himself purposely at dinner, and entered the cabin just as Lydia issued from her stateroom door.

She was pale and looked heavy-eyed. As she lifted her glance to him, she blushed; and he felt the answering red stain his face. When she sat down, the captain patted her on the shoulder with his burly right hand, and said he could not navigate the ship if she got sick. He pressed her to eat of this and that; and when she would not, he said, well, there was no use trying to force an appetite, and that she would be better all the sooner for dieting. Hicks went to his state-room, and came out with a box of guava jelly, from his private stores, and won a triumph enviable in all eyes when Lydia consented to like it with the chicken. Dunham plundered his own and Staniford's common stock of dainties for her dessert; the first officer agreed and applauded right and left; Staniford alone sat taciturn and inoperative, watching her face furtively. Once her eyes wandered to the side of the table where he and Dunham sat; then she colored and dropped her glance.

He took his book again after dinner, and with his finger between the leaves, at the last-read, unintelligible page, he went out to the bow, and crouched down there to renew the conflict of the morning. It was not long before Dunham followed. He stooped over to lay a hand on either of Staniford's shoulders.

"What makes you avoid me, old man?" he demanded, looking into Staniford's face with his frank, kind eyes.

"And I avoid you?" asked Staniford.

"Yes; why?"

"Because I feel rather shabby, I suppose. I knew I felt shabby, but I didn't know I was avoiding you."

"Well, no matter. If you feel shabby, it's all right; but I hate to have you feel shabby." He got his left hand down into Staniford's right, and a tacit reconciliation was transacted between them. Dunham looked about for a seat, and found a stool, which he planted in front of Staniford. "Wasn't it pleasant to have our little lady back at table, again?"

"Very," said Staniford.

"I couldn't help thinking how droll it was that a person whom we all considered a sort of incumbrance and superfluity at first should really turn out an object of prime importance to us all. Isn't it amusing?"

"Very droll."

"Why, we were quite lost without her, at breakfast. I couldn't have imagined her taking such a hold upon us all, in so short a time. But she's a pretty creature, and as good as she's pretty."

"I remember agreeing with you on those points before." Staniford feigned to suppress fatigue.

Dunham observed him. "I know you don't take so much interest in her as—as the rest of us do, and I wish you did. You don't know what a lovely nature she is."

"No?"

"No; and I'm sure you'd like her."

"Is it important that I should like her? Don't let your enthusiasm for the sex carry you beyond bounds, Dunham."

"No, no. Not important, but very pleasant. And I think acquaintance with such a girl would give you some new ideas of women."

"Oh, my old ones are good enough. Look here, Dunham," said Staniford, sharply, "what are you after?"

"What makes you think I'm after anything?"

"Because you're not a humbug, and because I am. My depraved spirit instantly recognized the dawning duplicity of yours. But you'd better be honest. You can't make the other thing work. What do you want?"

"I want your advice. I want your help, Staniford."

"I thought so! Coming and forgiving me in that— apostolic manner."

"Don't!"

"Well. What do you want my help for? What have you been doing?" Staniford paused, and suddenly added: "Have you been making love to Lurella?" He said this in his ironical manner, but his smile was rather ghastly.

"For shame, Staniford!" cried Dunham. But he reddened violently.

"Then it isn't with Miss Hibbard that you want my help. I'm glad of that. It would have been awkward. I'm a little afraid of Miss Hibbard. It isn't every one has your courage, my dear fellow."

"I haven't been making love to her," said Dunham, "but—I—"

"But you what?" demanded Staniford sharply again. There had been less tension of voice in his joking about Miss Hibbard.

"Staniford," said his friend, "I don't know whether you noticed her, at dinner, when she looked across to our own side?"

"What did she do?"

"Did you notice that she—well, that she blushed a little?"

Staniford waited a while before he answered, after a gulp, "Yes, I noticed that."

"Well, I don't know how to put it exactly, but I'm afraid that I have unwittingly wronged this young girl."

"Wronged her? What the devil *do* you mean, Dunham?" cried Staniford, with bitter impatience.

"I'm afraid—I'm afraid—Why, it's simply this: that in trying to amuse her, and make the time pass agreeably, and relieve her mind, and all that, don't you know, I've given her the impression that I'm—well—interested in her, and that she may have allowed herself—insensibly, you know—to look upon me in that light, and that she may have begun to think—that she may have become—"

"Interested in you?" interrupted Staniford rudely.

W. D. Howells

"Well—ah—well, that is—ah—well—yes!" cried Dunham, bracing himself to sustain a shout of ridicule. But Staniford did not laugh, and Dunham had courage to go on. "Of course, it sounds rather conceited to say so, but the circumstances are so peculiar that I think we ought to recognize even any possibilities of that sort."

"Oh, yes," said Staniford, gravely. "Most women, I believe, are so innocent as to think a man in love when he behaves like a lover. And this one," he added ruefully, "seems more than commonly ignorant of our ways,—of our infernal shilly-shallying, purposeless no-mindedness. She couldn't imagine a man—a gentleman—devoting himself to her by the hour, and trying by every art to show his interest and pleasure in her society, without imagining that he wished her to like him,—love him; there's no half-way about it. She couldn't suppose him the shallow, dawdling, soulless, senseless ape he really was." Staniford was quite in a heat by this time, and Dunham listened in open astonishment.

"You are hard upon me," he said. "Of course, I have been to blame; I know that, I acknowledge it. But my motive, as you know well enough, was never to amuse myself with her, but to contribute in any way I could to her enjoyment and happiness. I—"

"*You!*" cried Staniford. "What are you talking about?"

"What are *you* talking about?" demanded Dunham, in his turn.

Staniford recollected himself. "I was speaking of abstract flirtation. I was firing into the air."

"In my case, I don't choose to call it flirtation," returned Dunham. "My purpose, I am bound to say, was thoroughly unselfish and kindly."

"My dear fellow," said Staniford, with a bitter smile, "there can be no unselfishness and no kindliness between us and young girls, unless we mean business,—love-making. You may be sure that they feel it so, if they don't understand it so."

"I don't agree with you. I don't believe it. My own experience is that the sweetest and most generous friendships may exist between us, without a thought of anything else. And as to making love, I must beg you to remember that my love has been made once for all. I never dreamt of showing Miss Blood anything but polite attention."

"Then what are you troubled about?"

"I am troubled—" Dunham stopped helplessly, and Staniford laughed in a challenging, disagreeable way, so that the former perforce resumed:

"I'm troubled about—about her possible misinter-pretation."

"Oh! Then in this case of sweet and generous friendship the party of the second part may have construed the sentiment quite differently! Well, what do you want me to do? Do you want me to take the contract off your hands?"

"You put it grossly," said Dunham.

"And *you* put it offensively!" cried the other. "My regard for the young lady is as reverent as yours. You have no right to miscolor my words."

"Staniford, you are too bad," said Dunham, hurt even more than angered. "If I've come to you in the wrong moment—if you are vexed at anything, I'll go away, and beg your pardon for boring you."

Staniford was touched; he looked cordially into his friend's face. "I *was* vexed at something, but you never can come to me at the wrong moment, old fellow. I beg *your* pardon. *I* see your difficulty plainly enough, and I think you're quite right in proposing to hold up,—for that's what you mean, I take it?"

"Yes," said Dunham, "it is. And I don't know how she will like it. She will be puzzled and grieved by it. I hadn't thought seriously about the matter till this morning, when she didn't come to breakfast. You know I've been in the habit of asking her to walk with me every night after tea; but Saturday evening you were with her, and last night I felt sore about the affairs of the day, and rather dull, and I didn't ask her. I think she noticed it. I think she was hurt."

"You think so?" said Staniford, peculiarly.

"I might not have thought so," continued Dunham, "merely because she did not come to breakfast; but her blushing when she looked across at dinner really made me uneasy."

"Very possibly you're right." Staniford mused a while before he spoke again. "Well, what do you wish me to do?"

"I must hold up, as you say, and of course she will feel the difference. I wish—I wish at least you wouldn't avoid her, Staniford. That's all. Any little attention from you—I know it bores you—would not only break the loneliness, but it would explain that—that my—attentions didn't— ah—hadn't meant anything."

"Oh!"

"Yes; that it's common to offer them. And she's a girl of so much force of character that when she sees the affair in its true light—I suppose I'm to blame! Yes, I ought to have told her at the beginning that I was engaged. But you can't force a fact of that sort upon a new acquaintance: it looks silly." Dunham hung his head in self-reproach.

"Well?" asked Staniford.

"Well, that's all! No, it *isn't* all, either. There's something else troubles me. Our poor little friend is a blackguard, I suppose?"

"Hicks?"

"Yes."

"You have invited him to be the leader of your orchestra, haven't you?"

"Oh, don't, Staniford!" cried Dunham in his helplessness. "I should hate to see her dependent in any degree upon that little cad for society." Cad was the last English word which Dunham had got himself used to. "That was why I hoped that you wouldn't altogether neglect her. She's here, and she's no choice but to remain. We can't leave her to herself without the danger of leaving her to Hicks. You see?"

"Well," said Staniford gloomily, "I'm not sure that you couldn't leave her to a worse cad than Hicks." Dunham looked up in question. "To me, for example."

"Oh, hallo!" cried Dunham.

W. D. Howells

"I don't see how I'm to be of any use," continued the other. "I'm not a squire of dames; I should merely make a mess of it."

"You're mistaken, Staniford,—I'm sure you are,—in supposing that she dislikes you," urged his friend.

"Oh, very likely."

"I know that she's simply afraid of you."

"Don't flatter, Dunham. Why should I care whether she fears me or affects me? No, my dear fellow. This is irretrievably your own affair. I should be glad to help you out if I knew how. But I don't. In the mean time your duty is plain, whatever happens. You can't overdo the sweet and the generous in this wicked world without paying the penalty."

Staniford smiled at the distress in which Dunham went his way. He understood very well that it was not vanity, but the liveliness of a sensitive conscience, that had made Dunham search his conduct for the offense against the young girl's peace of heart which he believed he had committed, and it was the more amusing because he was so guiltless of harm. Staniford knew who was to blame for the headache and the blush. He knew that Dunham had never gone so far; that his chivalrous pleasure in her society might continue for years free from flirtation. But in spite of this conviction a little poignant doubt made itself felt, and suddenly became his whole consciousness. "Confound him!" he mused. "I wonder if she really could care anything for him!" He shut his book, and rose to his feet with such a burning in his heart that he could not have believed himself capable of the greater rage he felt at what he just then saw. It was Lydia and Hicks seated together in the place where he had sat with her. She leaned with one arm upon the rail, in an attitude that brought all her slim young grace into evidence. She seemed on very good terms with him, and he was talking and making her laugh as Staniford had never heard her laugh before—so freely, so heartily.

W. D. Howells

XIII

The atoms that had been tending in Staniford's being toward a certain form suddenly arrested and shaped themselves anew at the vibration imparted by this laughter. He no longer felt himself Hicks's possible inferior, but vastly better in every way, and out of the turmoil of his feelings in regard to Lydia was evolved the distinct sense of having been trifled with. Somehow, an advantage had been taken of his sympathies and purposes, and his forbearance had been treated with contempt.

The conviction was neither increased nor diminished by the events of the evening, when Lydia brought out some music from her state-room, and Hicks appeared, flute in hand, from his, and they began practicing one of the pieces together. It was a pretty enough sight. Hicks had been gradually growing a better-looking fellow; he had an undeniable picturesqueness, as he bowed his head over the music towards hers; and she, as she held the sheet with one hand for him to see, while she noiselessly accompanied herself on the table with the fingers of the other, and tentatively sang now this passage and now that, was divine. The picture seemed pleasing to neither Staniford nor Dunham; they went on deck together, and sat down to their cigarettes in their wonted place. They did not talk of Lydia, or of any of the things that had formed the basis of their conversation hitherto, but

Staniford returned to his Colorado scheme, and explained at length the nature of his purposes and expectations. He had discussed these matters before, but he had never gone into them so fully, nor with such cheerful earnestness. He said he should never marry,—he had made up his mind to that; but he hoped to make money enough to take care of his sister's boy Jim handsomely, as the little chap had been named for him. He had been thinking the matter over, and he believed that he should get back by rail and steamer as soon as he could after they reached Trieste. He was not sorry he had come; but he could not afford to throw away too much time on Italy, just then.

Dunham, on his part, talked a great deal of Miss Hibbard, and of some curious psychological characteristics of her dyspepsia. He asked Staniford whether he had ever shown him the photograph of Miss Hibbard taken by Sarony when she was on to New York the last time: it was a three-quarters view, and Dunham thought it the best she had had done. He spoke of her generous qualities, and of the interest she had always had in the Diet Kitchen, to which, as an invalid, her attention had been particularly directed: and he said that in her last letter she had mentioned a project for establishing diet kitchens in Europe, on the Boston plan. When their talk grew more impersonal and took a wider range, they gathered suggestion from the situation, and remarked upon the immense solitude of the sea. They agreed that there was something weird in the long continuance of fine weather, and that the moon had a strange look. They spoke of the uncertainty of life. Dunham regretted, as he had often regretted before, that his friend had no fixed religious belief; and Staniford gently accepted his solicitude, and said that he had at least a conviction if not a creed. He then begged Dunham's pardon in set terms for trying to wound his feelings the day before; and in the silent hand-clasp that followed they renewed all the cordiality of their friendship. From time to time, as they talked, the music from below came up fitfully, and once they had to pause as Lydia sang through the song that she and Hicks were practicing.

As the days passed their common interest in the art brought Hicks and the young girl almost constantly together, and the sound of their concerting often filled the ship. The musicales, less formal than Dunham had intended, and perhaps for that reason a source of rapidly diminishing interest with him, superseded both ring-toss and shuffle-board, and seemed even more acceptable to the ship's company as an entertainment. One evening, when the performers had been giving a piece of rather more than usual excellence and difficulty, one of the sailors, deputed by his mates, came aft, with many clumsy shows of deference, and asked them to give Marching through Georgia. Hicks found this out of his repertory, but Lydia sang it. Then the group at the forecastle shouted with one voice for Tramp, Tramp, Tramp, the Boys are Marching, and so beguiled her through the whole list of war-songs. She ended with one unknown to her listeners, but better than all the rest in its pathetic words and music, and when she had sung The Flag's come back to Tennessee, the spokesman of the sailors came aft again, to thank her for his mates, and to say they would not spoil that last song by asking for anything else. It was a charming little triumph for her, as she sat surrounded by her usual court: the captain was there to countenance the freedom the sailors had taken, and Dunham and Staniford stood near, but Hicks, at her right hand, held the place of honor.

The next night Staniford found her alone in the waist of the ship, and drew up a stool beside the rail where she sat.

"We all enjoyed your singing so much, last night, Miss

Blood. I think Mr. Hicks plays charmingly, but I believe I prefer to hear your voice alone."

"Thank you," said Lydia, looking down, demurely.

"It must be a great satisfaction to feel that you can give so much pleasure."

"I don't know," she said, passing the palm of one hand over the back of the other.

"When you are a *prima donna* you mustn't forget your old friends of the Aroostook. We shall all take vast pride in you."

It was not a question, and Lydia answered nothing. Staniford, who had rather obliged himself to this advance, with some dim purpose of showing that nothing had occurred to alienate them since the evening, of their promenade, without having proved to himself that it was necessary to do this, felt that he was growing angry. It irritated him to have her sit as unmoved after his words as if he had not spoken.

"Miss Blood," he said, "I envy you your gift of snubbing people."

Lydia looked at him. "Snubbing people?" she echoed.

"Yes; your power of remaining silent when you wish to put down some one who has been wittingly or unwittingly impertinent."

"I don't know what you mean," she said, in a sort of breathless way.

"And you didn't intend to mark your displeasure at my

planning your future?"

"No! We had talked of that. I—"

"And you were not vexed with me for anything? I have
been afraid that I—that you—" Staniford found that he
was himself getting short of breath. He had begun with
the intention of mystifying her, but matters had suddenly
taken another course, and he was really anxious to know
whether any disagreeable associations with that night
lingered in her mind. With this longing came a natural
inability to find the right word. "I was afraid—" he
repeated, and then he stopped again. Clearly, he could not
tell her that he was afraid he had gone too far; but this
was what he meant. "You don't walk with me, any more,
Miss Blood," he concluded, with an air of burlesque
reproach.

"You haven't asked me—since," she said.

He felt a singular value and significance in this word,
since. It showed that her thoughts had been running
parallel with his own; it permitted, if it did not signify,
that he should resume the mood of that time, where their
parting had interrupted it. He enjoyed the fact to the
utmost, but he was not sure that he wished to do what he
was permitted. "Then I didn't tire you?" he merely asked.
He was not sure, now he came to think of it, that he liked
her willingness to recur to that time. He liked it, but not
quite in the way he would have liked to like it.

"No," she said.

"The fact is," he went on aimlessly, "that I thought I had
rather abused your kindness. Besides," he added, veering
off, "I was afraid I should be an interruption to the
musical exercises."

"Oh, no," said Lydia. "Mr. Dunham hasn't arranged anything yet." Staniford thought this uncandid. It was fighting shy of Hicks, who was the person in his own mind; and it reawakened a suspicion which was lurking there. "Mr. Dunham seems to have lost his interest."

This struck Staniford as an expression of pique; it reawakened quite another suspicion. It was evident that she was hurt at the cessation of Dunham's attentions. He was greatly minded to say that Dunham was a fool, but he ended by saying, with sarcasm, "I suppose he saw that he was superseded."

"Mr. Hicks plays well," said Lydia, judicially, "but he doesn't really know so much of music as Mr. Dunham."

"No?" responded Staniford, with irony. "I will tell Dunham. No doubt he's been suffering the pangs of professional jealousy. That must be the reason why he keeps away."

"Keeps away?" asked Lydia.

"*Now* I've made an ass of myself!" thought Staniford. "You said that he seemed to have lost his interest," he answered her.

"Oh! Yes!" assented Lydia. And then she remained rather distraught, pulling at the ruffling of her dress.

"Dunham is a very accomplished man," said Staniford, finding the usual satisfaction in pressing his breast against the thorn. "He's a great favorite in society. He's up to no end of things." Staniford uttered these praises in a curiously bitter tone. "He's a capital talker. Don't you think he talks well?"

"I don't know; I suppose I haven't seen enough people to be a good judge."

"Well, you've seen enough people to know that he's very good looking?"

"Yes?"

"You don't mean to say you don't think him good looking?"

"No,—oh, no, I mean—that is—I don't know anything about his looks. But he resembles a lady who used to come from Boston, summers. I thought he must be her brother."

"Oh, then you think he looks effeminate!" cried Staniford, with inner joy. "I assure you," he added with solemnity, "Dunham is one of the manliest fellows in the world!"

"Yes?" said Lydia.

Staniford rose. He was smiling gayly as he looked over the broad stretch of empty deck, and down into Lydia's eyes. "Wouldn't you like to take a turn, now?"

"Yes," she said promptly, rising and arranging her wrap across her shoulders, so as to leave her hands free. She laid one hand in his arm and gathered her skirt with the other, and they swept round together for the start and confronted Hicks.

"Oh!" cried Lydia, with what seemed dismay, "I promised Mr. Hicks to practice a song with him." She did not try to release her hand from Staniford's arm, but was letting it linger there irresolutely.

Staniford dropped his arm, and let her hand fall. He bowed with icy stiffness, and said, with a courtesy so fierce that Mr. Hicks, on whom he glared as he spoke, quailed before it, "I yield to your prior engagement."

W. D. Howells

XIV

It was nothing to Staniford that she should have promised Hicks to practice a song with him, and no process of reasoning could have made it otherwise. The imaginary opponent with whom he scornfully argued the matter had not a word for himself. Neither could the young girl answer anything to the cutting speeches which he mentally made her as he sat alone chewing the end of his cigar; and he was not moved by the imploring looks which his fancy painted in her face, when he made believe that she had meekly returned to offer him some sort of reparation. Why should she excuse herself? he asked. It was he who ought to excuse himself for having been in the way. The dialogue went on at length, with every advantage to the inventor.

He was finally aware of some one standing near and looking down at him. It was the second mate, who supported himself in a conversational posture by the hand which he stretched to the shrouds above their heads. "Are you a good sailor, Mr. Staniford?" he inquired. He and Staniford were friends in their way, and had talked together before this.

"Do you mean seasickness? Why?" Staniford looked up at the mate's face.

"Well, we're going to get it, I guess, before long. We shall soon be off the Spanish coast. We've had a great run so far."

"If it comes we must stand it. But I make it a rule never to be seasick beforehand."

"Well, I ain't one to borrow trouble, either. It don't run in the family. Most of us like to chance things, I chanced it for the whole war, and I come out all right. Sometimes it don't work so well."

"Ah?" said Staniford, who knew that this was a leading remark, but forbore, as he knew Mason wished, to follow it up directly.

"One of us chanced it once too often, and of course it was a woman."

"The risk?"

"Not the risk. My oldest sister tried tamin' a tiger. Ninety-nine times out of a hundred, a tiger won't tame worth a cent. But her pet was such a lamb most the while that she guessed she'd chance it. It didn't work. She's at home with mother now,—three children, of course,—and he's in hell, I s'pose. He was killed 'long-side o' me at Gettysburg. Ike was a good fellow when he was sober. But my souls, the life he led that poor girl! Yes, when a man's got that tiger in him, there ought to be some quiet little war round for puttin' him out of his misery." Staniford listened silently, waiting for the mate to make the application of his grim allegory. "I s'pose I'm prejudiced; but I do *hate* a drunkard; and when I see one of 'em makin' up to a girl, I want to go to her, and tell her she'd better take a real tiger out the show, at once."

W. D. Howells

The idea which these words suggested sent a thrill to Staniford's heart, but he continued silent, and the mate went on, with the queer smile, which could be inferred rather than seen, working under his mustache and the humorous twinkle of his eyes evanescently evident under his cap peak.

"I don't go round criticisn' my superior officers, and *I* don't say anything about the responsibility the old man took. The old man's all right, accordin' to his lights; he ain't had a tiger in the family. But if that chap was to fall overboard,—well, I don't know *how* long it would take to lower a boat, if I was to listen to my *conscience*. There ain't really any help for him. He's begun too young ever to get over it. He won't be ashore at Try-East an hour before he's drunk. If our men had any spirits amongst 'em that could be begged, bought, or borrowed, he'd be drunk now, right along. Well, I'm off watch," said the mate, at the tap of bells. "Guess we'll get our little gale pretty soon."

"Good-night," said Staniford, who remained pondering. He presently rose, and walked up and down the deck. He could hear Lydia and Hicks trying that song: now the voice, and now the flute; then both together; and presently a burst of laughter. He began to be angry with her ignorance and inexperience. It became intolerable to him that a woman should be going about with no more knowledge of the world than a child, and entangling herself in relations with all sorts of people. It was shocking to think of that little sot, who had now made his infirmity known for all the ship's company, admitted to association with her which looked to common eyes like courtship. From the mate's insinuation that she ought to be warned, it was evident that they thought her interested in Hicks; and the mate had come, like Dunham, to leave the responsibility with Staniford. It only wanted now that Captain Jenness should appear with his appeal, direct or indirect.

While Staniford walked up and down, and scorned and raged at the idea that he had anything to do with the matter, the singing and fluting came to a pause in the cabin; and at the end of the next tune, which brought him to the head of the gangway stairs, he met Lydia emerging. He stopped and spoke to her, having instantly resolved, at sight of her, not to do so.

"Have you come up for breath, like a mermaid?" he asked. "Not that I'm sure mermaids do."

"Oh, no," said Lydia. "I think I dropped my handkerchief where we were sitting."

Staniford suspected, with a sudden return to a theory of her which he had already entertained, that she had not done so. But she went lightly by him, where he stood stolid, and picked it up; and now he suspected that she had dropped it there on purpose.

"You have come back to walk with me?"

"No!" said the girl indignantly. "I have not come back to walk with you!" She waited a moment; then she burst out with, "How dare you say such a thing to me? What right have you to speak to me so? What have I done to make you think that I would come back to—"

The fierce vibration in her voice made him know that her eyes were burning upon him and her lips trembling. He shrank before her passion as a man must before the justly provoked wrath of a woman, or even of a small girl.

"I stated a hope, not a fact," he said in meek uncandor. "Don't you think you ought to have done so?"

"I don't—I don't understand you," panted Lydia, confusedly arresting her bolts in mid-course.

Staniford pursued his guilty advantage; it was his only chance. "I gave way to Mr. Hicks when you had an engagement with me. I thought— you would come back to keep your engagement." He was still very meek.

"Excuse me," she said with self-reproach that would have melted the heart of any one but a man who was in the wrong, and was trying to get out of it at all hazards. "I didn't know what you meant—I—"

"If I had meant what you thought," interrupted Staniford nobly, for he could now afford to be generous, "I should have deserved much more than you said. But I hope you won't punish my awkwardness by refusing to walk with me."

He knew that she regarded him earnestly before she said, "I must get my shawl and hat."

"Let me go!" he entreated.

"You couldn't find them," she answered, as she vanished past him. She returned, and promptly laid her hand in his proffered arm; it was as if she were eager to make him amends for her harshness.

Staniford took her hand out, and held it while he bowed low toward her. "I declare myself satisfied."

"I don't understand," said Lydia, in alarm and mortification.

"When a subject has been personally aggrieved by his sovereign, his honor is restored if they merely cross swords."

The girl laughed her delight in the extravagance. She must have been more or less than woman not to have found his flattery delicious. "But we are republicans!" she said in evasion.

"To be sure, we are republicans. Well, then, Miss Blood, answer your free and equal one thing: is it a case of conscience?"

"How?" she asked, and Staniford did not recoil at the rusticity. This how for what, and the interrogative yes, still remained. Since their first walk, she had not wanted to know, in however great surprise she found herself.

"Are you going to walk with me because you had promised?"

"Why, of course," faltered Lydia.

"That isn't enough."

"Not enough?"

"Not enough. You must walk with me because you like to do so."

Lydia was silent.

"Do you like to do so?"

"I can't answer you," she said, releasing her hand from him.

"It was not fair to ask you. What I wish to do is to restore the original status. You have kept your engagement to

W. D. Howells

walk with me, and your conscience is clear. Now, Miss Blood, may I have your company for a little stroll over the deck of the Aroostook?" He made her another very low bow.

"What must I say?" asked Lydia, joyously.

"That depends upon whether you consent. If you consent, you must say, 'I shall be very glad.'"

"And if I don't?"

"Oh, I can't put any such decision into words."

Lydia mused a moment. "I shall be very glad," she said, and put her hand again into the arm he offered.

As happens after such a passage they were at first silent, while they walked up and down.

"If this fine weather holds," said Staniford, "and you continue as obliging as you are to-night, you can say, when people ask you how you went to Europe, that you walked the greater part of the way. Shall you continue so obliging? Will you walk with me every fine night?" pursued Staniford.

"Do you think I'd better say so?" she asked, with the joy still in her voice.

"Oh, I can't decide for you. I merely formulate your decisions after you reach them,—if they're favorable."

"Well, then, what is this one?"

"Is it favorable?"

"You said you would formulate it." She laughed again, and Staniford started as one does when a nebulous association crystallizes into a distinctly remembered fact.

"What a curious laugh you have!" he said. "It's like a nun's laugh. Once in France I lodged near the garden of a convent where the nuns kept a girls' school, and I used to hear them laugh. You never happened to be a nun, Miss Blood?"

"No, indeed!" cried Lydia, as if scandalized.

"Oh, I merely meant in some previous existence. Of course, I didn't suppose there was a convent in South Bradfield." He felt that the girl did not quite like the little slight his irony cast upon South Bradfield, or rather upon her for never having been anywhere else. He hastened to say, "I'm sure that in the life before this you were of the South somewhere."

"Yes?" said Lydia, interested and pleased again as one must be in romantic talk about one's self. "Why do you think so?"

He bent a little over toward her, so as to look into the face she instinctively averted, while she could not help glancing at him from the corner of her eye. "You have the color and the light of the South," he said. "When you get to Italy, you will live in a perpetual mystification. You will go about in a dream of some self of yours that was native there in other days. You will find yourself retrospectively related to the olive faces and the dark eyes you meet; you will recognize sisters and cousins in the patrician ladies when you see their portraits in the palaces where you used to live in such state."

Staniford spiced his flatteries with open burlesque; the

girl entered into his fantastic humor. "But if I was a nun?" she asked, gayly.

"Oh, I forgot. You were a nun. There was a nun in Venice once, about two hundred years ago, when you lived there, and a young English lord who was passing through the town was taken to the convent to hear her sing; for she was not only of 'an admirable beauty,' as he says, but sang 'extremely well.' She sang to him through the grating of the convent, and when she stopped he said, 'Die when-soever you will, you need to change neither voice nor face to be an angel!' Do you think—do you dimly recollect anything that makes you think—it might—Consider care-fully: the singing extremely well, and—" He leant over again, and looked up into her face, which again she could not wholly withdraw.

"No, no!" she said, still in his mood.

"Well, you must allow it was a pretty speech."

"Perhaps," said Lydia, with sudden gravity, in which there seemed to Staniford a tender insinuation of reproach, "he was laughing at her."

"If he was, he was properly punished. He went on to Rome, and when he came back to Venice the beautiful nun was dead. He thought that his words 'seemed fatal.' Do you suppose it would kill you *now* to be jested with?"

"I don't think people like it generally."

"Why, Miss Blood, you are intense!"

"I don't know what you mean by that," said Lydia.

"You like to take things seriously. You can't bear to think that people are not the least in earnest, even when they least seem so."

"Yes," said the girl, thoughtfully, "perhaps that's true. Should you like to be made fun of, yourself?"

"I shouldn't mind it, I fancy, though it would depend a great deal upon who made fun of me. I suppose that women always laugh at men,—at their clumsiness, their want of tact, the fit of their clothes."

"I don't know. I should not do that with any one I—"

"You liked? Oh, none of them do!" cried Staniford.

"I was not going to say that," faltered the girl.

"What were you going to say?"

She waited a moment. "Yes, I was going to say that," she assented with a sigh of helpless veracity. "What makes you laugh?" she asked, in distress.

"Something I like. I'm different from you: I laugh at what I like; I like your truthfulness,—it's charming."

"I didn't know that truth need be charming."

"It had better be, in women, if it's to keep even with the other thing." Lydia seemed shocked; she made a faint, involuntary motion to withdraw her hand, but he closed his arm upon it. "Don't condemn me for thinking that fibbing is charming. I shouldn't like it at all in you. Should you in me?"

"I shouldn't in any one," said Lydia.

"Then what is it you dislike in me?" he suddenly demanded.

"I didn't say that I disliked anything in you."

"But you have made fun of something in me?"

"No, no!"

"Then it wasn't the stirring of a guilty conscience when you asked me whether I should like to be made fun of? I took it for granted you'd been doing it."

"You are very suspicious."

"Yes; and what else?"

"Oh, you like to know just what every one thinks and feels."

"Go on!" cried Staniford. "Analyze me, formulate me!"

"That's all."

"All I come to?"

"All I have to say."

"That's very little. Now, I'll begin on you. You don't care what people think or feel."

"Oh, yes, I do. I care too much."

"Do you care what I think?"

"Yes."

"Then I think you're too unsuspicious."

"Ought I to suspect somebody?" she asked, lightly.

"Oh, that's the way with all your sex. One asks you to be suspicious, and you ask whom you shall suspect. You can do nothing in the abstract. I should like to be suspicious for you. Will you let me?"

"Oh, yes, if you like to be."

"Thanks. I shall be terribly vigilant,—a perfect dragon. And you really invest me with authority?"

"Yes."

"That's charming." Staniford drew a long breath. After a space of musing, he said, "I thought I should be able to begin by attacking some one else, but I must commence at home, and denounce myself as quite unworthy of walking to and fro, and talking nonsense to you. You must beware of me, Miss Blood."

"Why?" asked the girl.

"I am very narrow-minded and prejudiced, and I have violent antipathies. I shouldn't be able to do justice to any one I disliked."

"I think that's the trouble with all of us," said Lydia.

"Oh, but only in degree. I should not allow, if I could help it, a man whom I thought shabby, and coarse at heart, the privilege of speaking to any one I valued,—to my sister, for instance. It would shock me to find her have any taste in common with such a man, or amused by him. Don't you understand?"

W. D. Howells

"Yes," said Lydia. It seemed to him as if by some infinitely subtle and unconscious affinition she relaxed toward him as they walked. This was incomparably sweet and charming to Staniford,—too sweet as recognition of his protecting friendship to be questioned as anything else. He felt sure that she had taken his meaning, and he rested content from further trouble in regard to what it would have been impossible to express. Her tacit confidence touched a kindred spring in him, and he began to talk to her of himself: not of his character or opinions,— they had already gone over them,—but of his past life, and his future. Their strangeness to her gave certain well-worn topics novelty, and the familiar project of a pastoral career in the far West invested itself with a color of romance which it had not worn before. She tried to remember, at his urgence, something about her childhood in California; and she told him a great deal more about South Bradfield. She described its characters and customs, and, from no vantage-ground or stand-point but her native feeling of their oddity, and what seemed her sympathy with him, made him see them as one might whose life had not been passed among them. Then they began to compare their own traits, and amused themselves to find how many they had in common. Staniford related a singular experience of his on a former voyage to Europe, when he dreamed of a collision, and woke to hear a great trampling and uproar on deck, which afterwards turned out to have been caused by their bare escape from running into an iceberg. She said that she had had strange dreams, too, but mostly when she was a little girl; once she had had a presentiment that troubled her, but it did not come true. They both said they did not believe in such things, and agreed that it was only people's love of mystery that kept them noticed. He permitted himself to help her, with his disengaged hand, to draw her shawl closer about the shoulder that was away from him. He gave the action a philosophical and impersonal character by saying immediately afterwards: "The sea is really the only mystery left us, and that will never be explored. They circumnavigate the whole globe,—" here he put the gathered shawl into the fingers which she stretched through his arm to take it, and she said, "Oh, thank you!"—"but they don't describe the sea. War and plague and famine submit to the ameliorations of science,"—the closely drawn shawl pressed her against his shoulder; his mind wandered; he hardly knew what he was saying,— "but the one utterly inexorable calamity—the same now as when the first sail was spread—is a shipwreck."

"Yes," she said, with a deep inspiration. And now they walked back and forth in silence broken only by a casual word or desultory phrase. Once Staniford had thought the conditions of these promenades perilously suggestive of love-making; another time he had blamed himself for not thinking of this; now he neither thought nor blamed himself for not thinking. The fact justified itself, as if it had been the one perfectly right and wise thing in a world where all else might be questioned.

"Isn't it pretty late?" she asked, at last.

"If you're tired, we'll sit down," he said.

"What time is it?" she persisted.

"Must I look?" he pleaded. They went to a lantern, and he took out his watch and sprang the case open. "Look!" he said. "I sacrifice myself on the altar of truth." They bent their heads low together over the watch; it was not easy to make out the time. "It's nine o'clock," said Staniford.

"It can't be; it was half past when I came up," answered Lydia.

"One hand's at twelve and the other at nine," he said, conclusively.

"Oh, then it's a quarter to twelve." She caught away her hand from his arm, and fled to the gangway. "I didn't dream it was so late."

The pleasure which her confession brought to his face faded at sight of Hicks, who was turning the last pages of a novel by the cabin lamp, as he followed Lydia in. It was the book that Staniford had given her.

"Hullo!" said Hicks, with companionable ease, looking up at her. "Been having quite a tramp."

She did not seem troubled by the familiarity of an address that incensed Staniford almost to the point of taking Hicks from his seat, and tossing him to the other end of the cabin. "Oh, you've finished my book," she said. "You must tell me how you like it, to-morrow."

"I doubt it," said Hicks. "I'm going to be seasick to-morrow. The captain's been shaking his head over the barometer and powwowing with the first officer. Something's up, and I guess it's a gale. Good-by; I shan't see you again for a week or so."

He nodded jocosely to Lydia, and dropped his eyes again to his book, ignoring Staniford's presence. The latter stood a moment breathing quick; then he controlled himself and went into his room. His coming roused Dunham, who looked up from his pillow. "What time is it?" he asked, stupidly.

"Twelve," said Staniford.

"Had a pleasant walk?"

"If you still think," said Staniford, savagely, "that she's painfully interested in you, you can make your mind easy. She doesn't care for either of us."

"*Either* of us?" echoed Dunham. He roused himself.

"Oh, go to sleep; *go* to sleep!" cried Staniford.

XV

The foreboded storm did not come so soon as had been feared, but the beautiful weather which had lasted so long was lost in a thickened sky and a sullen sea. The weather had changed with Staniford, too. The morning after the events last celebrated, he did not respond to the glance which Lydia gave him when they met, and he hardened his heart to her surprise, and shunned being alone with her. He would not admit to himself any reason for his attitude, and he could not have explained to her the mystery that at first visibly grieved her, and then seemed merely to benumb her. But the moment came when he ceased to take a certain cruel pleasure in it, and he approached her one morning on deck, where she stood holding fast to the railing where she usually sat, and said, as if there had been no interval of estrangement between them, but still coldly, "We have had our last walk for the present, Miss Blood. I hope you will grieve a little for my loss."

She turned on him a look that cut him to the heart, with what he fancied its reproach and its wonder. She did not reply at once, and then she did not reply to his hinted question.

"Mr. Staniford," she began. It was the second time he had heard her pronounce his name; he distinctly remembered the first.

"Well?" he said.

"I want to speak to you about lending that book to Mr. Hicks. I ought to have asked you first."

"Oh, no," said Staniford. "It was yours."

"You gave it to me," she returned.

"Well, then, it was yours,—to keep, to lend, to throw away."

"And you didn't mind my lending it to him?" she pursued. "I—"

She stopped, and Staniford hesitated, too. Then he said, "I didn't dislike your lending it; I disliked his having it. I will acknowledge that."

She looked up at him as if she were going to speak, but checked herself, and glanced away. The ship was plunging heavily, and the livid waves were racing before the wind. The horizon was lit with a yellow brightness in the quarter to which she turned, and a pallid gleam defined her profile. Captain Jenness was walking fretfully to and fro; he glanced now at the yellow glare, and now cast his eye aloft at the shortened sail. While Staniford stood questioning whether she meant to say anything more, or whether, having discharged her conscience of an imagined offense, she had now reached one of her final, precipitous silences, Captain Jenness suddenly approached them, and said to him, "I guess you'd better go below with Miss Blood."

The storm that followed had its hazards, but Staniford's

consciousness was confined to its discomforts. The day came, and then the dark came, and both in due course went, and came again. Where he lay in his berth, and whirled and swung, and rose and sank, as lonely as a planetary fragment tossing in space, he heard the noises of the life without. Amidst the straining of the ship, which was like the sharp sweep of a thunder-shower on the deck overhead, there plunged at irregular intervals the wild trample of heavily-booted feet, and now and then the voices of the crew answering the shouted orders made themselves hollowly audible. In the cabin there was talking, and sometimes even laughing. Sometimes he heard the click of knives and forks, the sardonic rattle of crockery. After the first insane feeling that somehow he must get ashore and escape from his torment, he hardened himself to it through an immense contempt, equally insane, for the stupidity of the sea, its insensate uproar, its blind and ridiculous and cruel mischievousness. Except for this delirious scorn he was a surface of perfect passivity.

Dunham, after a day of prostration, had risen, and had perhaps shortened his anguish by his resolution. He had since taken up his quarters on a locker in the cabin; he looked in now and then upon Staniford, with a cup of tea, or a suggestion of something light to eat; once he even dared to boast of the sublimity of the ocean. Staniford stared at him with eyes of lack-lustre indifference, and waited for him to be gone. But he lingered to say, "You would laugh to see what a sea-bird our lady is! She hasn't been sick a minute. And Hicks, you'll be glad to know, is behaving himself very well. Really, I don't think we've done the fellow justice. I think you've overshadowed him, and that he's needed your absence to show himself to advantage."

Staniford disdained any comment on this except a fierce

"Humph!" and dismissed Dunham by turning his face to the wall. He refused to think of what he had said. He lay still and suffered indefinitely, and no longer waited for the end of the storm. There had been times when he thought with acquiescence of going to the bottom, as a probable conclusion; now he did not expect anything. At last, one night, he felt by inexpressibly minute degrees something that seemed surcease of his misery. It might have been the end of all things, for all he cared; but as the lull deepened, he slept without knowing what it was, and when he woke in the morning he found the Aroostook at anchor in smooth water.

She was lying in the roads at Gibraltar, and before her towered the embattled rock. He crawled on deck after a while. The captain was going ashore, and had asked such of his passengers as liked, to go with him and see the place. When Staniford appeared, Dunham was loyally refusing to leave his friend till he was fairly on foot. At sight of him they suspended their question long enough to welcome him back to animation, with the patronage with which well people hail a convalescent. Lydia looked across the estrangement of the past days with a sort of inquiry, and Hicks chose to come forward and accept a cold touch of the hand from him. Staniford saw, with languid observance, that Lydia was very fresh and bright; she was already equipped for the expedition, and could never have had any doubt in her mind as to going. She had on a pretty walking dress which he had not seen before, and a hat with the rim struck sharply upward behind, and her masses of dense, dull black hair pulled up and fastened somewhere on the top of her head. Her eyes shyly sparkled under the abrupt descent of the hat-brim over her forehead.

His contemptuous rejection of the character of invalid prevailed with Dunham; and Staniford walked to another

W. D. Howells

part of the ship, to cut short the talk about himself, and saw them row away.

"Well, you've had a pretty tough time, they say," said the second mate, lounging near him. "I don't see any fun in seasickness *myself.*"

"It's a ridiculous sort of misery," said Staniford.

"I hope we shan't have anything worse on board when that chap gets back. The old man thinks he can keep an eye on him." The mate was looking after the boat.

"The captain says he hasn't any money," Staniford remarked carelessly. The mate went away without saying anything more, and Staniford returned to the cabin, where he beheld without abhorrence the preparations for his breakfast. But he had not a great appetite, in spite of his long fast. He found himself rather light-headed, and came on deck again after a while, and stretched himself in Hicks's steamer chair, where Lydia usually sat in it. He fell into a dull, despairing reverie, in which he blamed himself for not having been more explicit with her. He had merely expressed his dislike of Hicks; but expressed without reasons it was a groundless dislike, which she had evidently not understood, or had not cared to heed; and since that night, now so far away, when he had spoken to her, he had done everything he could to harden her against himself. He had treated her with a stupid cruelty, which a girl like her would resent to the last; he had forced her to take refuge in the politeness of a man from whom he was trying to keep her.

His heart paused when he saw the boat returning in the afternoon without Hicks. The others reported that they had separated before dinner, and that they had not seen him since, though Captain Jenness had spent an hour trying to look him up before starting back to the ship. The captain wore a look of guilty responsibility, mingled with intense exasperation, the two combining in as much haggardness as his cheerful visage could express. "If he's here by six o'clock," he said, grimly, "all well and good. If not, the Aroostook sails, any way."

Lydia crept timidly below. Staniford complexly raged to see that the anxiety about Hicks had blighted the joy of the day for her.

"How the deuce could he get about without any money?" he demanded of Dunham, as soon as they were alone.

Dunham vainly struggled to look him in the eye. "Staniford," he faltered, with much more culpability than some criminals would confess a murder, "I lent him five dollars!"

"You lent him five dollars!" gasped Staniford.

"Yes," replied Dunham, miserably; "he got me aside, and asked me for it. What could I do? What would you have done yourself?"

Staniford made no answer. He walked some paces away, and then returned to where Dunham stood helpless. "He's lying about there dead-drunk, somewhere, I suppose. By Heaven, I could almost wish he was. He couldn't come back, then, at any rate."

The time lagged along toward the moment appointed by the captain, and the preparations for the ship's departure were well advanced, when a boat was seen putting out from shore with two rowers, and rapidly approaching the Aroostook. In the stern, as it drew nearer, the familiar figure of Hicks discovered itself in the act of waving a handkerchief He scrambled up the side of the ship in excellent spirits, and gave Dunham a detailed account of his adventures since they had parted. As always happens with such scapegraces, he seemed to have had a good time, however he had spoiled the pleasure of the others. At tea, when Lydia had gone away, he clapped down a sovereign near Dunham's plate.

"Your five dollars," he said.

"Why, how—" Dunham began.

"How did I get on without it? My dear boy, I sold my watch! A ship's time is worth no more than a setting hen's,—eh, captain?—and why take note of it? Besides, I always like to pay my debts promptly: there's nothing mean about me. I'm not going ashore again without my pocket-book, I can tell you." He winked shamelessly at Captain Jenness. "If you hadn't been along, Dunham, I couldn't have made a raise, I suppose. *You* wouldn't have lent me five dollars, Captain Jenness."

"No, I wouldn't," said the captain, bluntly.

"And I believe you'd have sailed without me, if I hadn't got back on time."

"I would," said the captain, as before.

Hicks threw back his head, and laughed. Probably no human being had ever before made so free with Captain Jenness at his own table; but the captain must have felt that this contumacy was part of the general risk which he had taken in taking Hicks, and he contented himself with maintaining a silence that would have appalled a less audacious spirit. Hicks's gayety, however, was not to be quelled in that way.

"Gibraltar wouldn't be a bad place to put up at for a while," he said. "Lots of good fellows among the officers, they say, and fun going all the while. First-class gunning in the Cork Woods at St. Roque. If it hadn't been for the *res angusta domi*,—you know what I mean, captain,—I should have let you get along with your old dug-out, as the gentleman in the water said to Noah." His hilarity had something alarmingly knowing in it; there was a wildness in the pleasure with which he bearded the captain, like that of a man in his first cups; yet he had not been drinking. He played round the captain's knowledge of the sanative destitution in which he was making the voyage with mocking recurrence; but he took himself off to bed early, and the captain came through his trials with unimpaired temper. Dunham disappeared not long afterwards; and Staniford's vague hope that Lydia might be going on deck to watch the lights of the town die out behind the ship as they sailed away was disappointed. The second mate made a point of lounging near him where he sat alone in their wonted place.

"Well," he said, "he did come back sober."

"Yes," said Staniford.

"Next to not comin' back at all," the mate continued, "I suppose it was the best thing he could do." He lounged away. Neither his voice nor his manner had that quality of disappointment which characterizes those who have mistakenly prophesied evil. Staniford had a mind to call him back, and ask him what he meant; but he refrained, and he went to bed at last resolved to unburden himself of the whole Hicks business once for all. He felt that he had had quite enough of it, both in the abstract and in its relation to Lydia.

XVI

Hicks did not join the others at breakfast. They talked of what Lydia had seen at Gibraltar, where Staniford had been on a former voyage. Dunham had made it a matter of conscience to know all about it beforehand from his guide-books, and had risen early that morning to correct his science by his experience in a long entry in the diary which he was keeping for Miss Hibbard. The captain had the true sea-farer's ignorance, and was amused at the things reported by his passengers of a place where he had been ashore so often; Hicks's absence doubtless relieved him, but he did not comment on the cabin-boy's announcement that he was still asleep, except to order him let alone.

They were seated at their one o'clock dinner before the recluse made any sign. Then he gave note of his continued existence by bumping and thumping sounds within his state-room, as if some one were dressing there in a heavy sea.

"Mr. Hicks seems to be taking his rough weather retrospectively," said Staniford, with rather tremulous humor.

The door was flung open, and Hicks reeled out, staying himself by the door-knob. Even before he appeared, a reek of strong waters had preceded him. He must have been drinking all night. His face was flushed, and his eyes were bloodshot. He had no collar on; but he wove a cravat and otherwise he was accurately and even fastidiously dressed. He balanced himself by the door-knob, and measured the distance he had to make before reaching his place at the table, smiling, and waving a delicate handkerchief, which he held in his hand: "Spilt c'logne, tryin' to scent my hic—handkerchief. Makes deuced bad smell—too much c'logne; smells—alcoholic. Thom's, bear a hand, 's good f'low. No? All right, go on with your waitin'. B-ic—business b'fore pleasure, 's feller says. Play it alone, I guess."

The boy had shrunk back in dismay, and Hicks contrived to reach his place by one of those precipitate dashes with which drunken men attain a point, when the luck is with them. He looked smilingly round the circle of faces. Staniford and the captain exchanged threatening looks of intelligence, while Mr. Watterson and Dunham subordinately waited their motion. But the advantage, as in such cases, was on the side of Hicks. He knew it, with a drunkard's subtlety, and was at his ease.

"No app'tite, friends; but thought I'd come out, keep you from feeling lonesome." He laughed and hiccuped, and smiled upon them all. "Well, cap'n," he continued, "'covered from 'tigues day, sterday? You look blooming's usual. Thom's, pass the—pass the—victuals lively, my son, and fetch along coffee soon. Some the friends up late, and want their coffee. Nothing like coffee, carry off'fee's." He winked to the men, all round; and then added, to Lydia: "Sorry see you in this state—I mean, sorry see me—Can't make it that way either; up stump on both routes. What I mean is, sorry hadn't coffee first. But *you're* all right—all right! Like see anybody offer you disrespec', 'n I'm around. Tha's all."

Till he addressed her, Lydia had remained motionless, first with bewilderment, and then with open abhorrence. She could hardly have seen in South Bradfield a man who had been drinking. Even in haying, or other sharpest stress of farmwork, our farmer and his men stay themselves with nothing stronger than molasses-water, or, in extreme cases, cider with a little corn soaked in it; and the Mill Village, where she had taught school, was under the iron rule of a local vote for prohibition. She stared in stupefaction at Hicks's heated, foolish face; she started at his wild movements, and listened with dawning intelligence to his hiccup-broken speech, with its thickened sibilants and its wandering emphasis. When he turned to her, and accompanied his words with a reassuring gesture, she recoiled, and as if breaking an ugly fascination she gave a low, shuddering cry, and looked at Staniford.

"Thomas," he said, "Miss Blood was going to take her dessert on deck to-day. Dunham?"

Dunham sprang to his feet, and led her out of the cabin.

The movement met Hicks's approval. "Tha's right; 'sert on deck, 'joy landscape and pudding together,—Rhine steamer style. All right. Be up there m'self soon's I get my coffee." He winked again with drunken sharpness. "I know wha's what. Be up there m'self, 'n a minute."

"If you offer to go up," said Staniford, in a low voice, as soon as Lydia was out of the way, "I'll knock you down!"

"Captain," said Mr. Watterson, venturing, perhaps for the first time in his whole maritime history, upon a suggestion to his superior officer, "shall I clap him in irons?"

"Clap him in irons!" roared Captain Jenness. "Clap him in bed! Look here, you!" He turned to Hicks, but the latter, who had been bristling at Staniford's threat, now relaxed in a crowing laugh:—

"Tha's right, captain. Irons no go, 'cept in case mutiny; bed perfectly legal 't all times. Bed is good. But trouble is t' enforce it."

"Where's your bottle?" demanded the captain, rising from the seat in which a paralysis of fury had kept him hitherto. "I want your bottle."

"Oh, bottle's all right! Bottle's under pillow. Empty,—empty's Jonah's gourd; 'nother sea-faring party,—Jonah. S'cure the shadow ere the substance fade. Drunk all the brandy, old boy. Bottle's a canteen; 'vantage of military port to houseless stranger. Brought the brandy on board under my coat; nobody noticed,—so glad get me back. Prodigal son's return,—fatted calf under his coat."

The reprobate ended his boastful confession with another burst of hiccuping, and Staniford helplessly laughed.

"Do me proud," said Hicks. "Proud, I 'sure you. Gentleman, every time, Stanny. Know good thing when you see it—hear it, I mean."

"Look here, Hicks," said Staniford, choosing to make friends with the mammon of unrighteousness, if any good end might be gained by it. "You know you're drunk, and you're not fit to be about. Go back to bed, that's a good fellow; and come out again, when you're all right. You don't want to do anything you'll be sorry for."

"No, no! No, you don't, Stanny. Coffee'll make me all right. Coffee always does. Coffee—Heaven's lash besh gift to man. 'Scovered subse-subs'quently to grape. See? Comes after claret in course of nature. Captain doesn't understand the 'lusion. All right, captain. Little learning dangerous thing." He turned sharply on Mr. Watterson, who had remained inertly in his place. "Put me in irons, heh! *You* put me in irons, you old Triton. Put *me* in irons, will you?" His amiable mood was passing; before one could say so, it was past. He was meditating means of active offense. He gathered up the carving-knife and fork, and held them close under Mr. Watterson's nose. "Smell that!" he said, and frowned as darkly as a man of so little eyebrow could.

At this senseless defiance Staniford, in spite of himself, broke into another laugh, and even Captain Jenness grinned. Mr. Watterson sat with his head drawn as far back as possible, and with his nose wrinkled at the affront offered it. "Captain," he screamed, appealing even in this extremity to his superior, "shall I fetch him *one?*"

"No, no!" cried Staniford, springing from his chair; "don't hit him! He isn't responsible. Let's get him into his room."

"Fetch me *one*, heh?" said Hicks, rising, with dignity, and beginning to turn up his cuffs. "*One!* It'll take more than one, fetch *me*. Stan' up, 'f you're man enough." He was squaring at Mr. Watterson, when he detected signs of strategic approach in Staniford and Captain Jenness. He gave a wild laugh, and shrank into a corner. "No! No, you don't, boys," he said.

They continued their advance, one on either side, and reinforced by Mr. Watterson hemmed him in. The drunken man has the advantage of his sober brother in never seeming to be on the alert. Hicks apparently entered into the humor of the affair. "Sur-hic-surrender!" he said, with a smile in his heavy eyes. He darted under the extended arms of Captain Jenness, who was leading the centre of the advance, and before either wing could touch him he was up the gangway and on the deck.

Captain Jenness indulged one of those expressions, very rare with him, which are supposed to be forgiven to good men in moments of extreme perplexity, and Mr. Watterson profited by the precedent to unburden his heart in a paraphrase of the captain's language. Staniford's laugh had as much cursing in it as their profanity.

He mechanically followed Hicks to the deck, prepared to renew the attempt for his capture there. But Hicks had not stopped near Dunham and Lydia. He had gone forward on the other side of the ship, and was leaning quietly on the rail, and looking into the sea. Staniford paused irresolute for a moment, and then sat down beside Lydia, and they all tried to feign that nothing unpleasant had happened, or was still impending. But their talk had the wandering inconclusiveness which was inevitable, and the eyes of each from time to time furtively turned toward Hicks.

For half an hour he hardly changed his position. At the end of that time, they found him looking intently at them; and presently he began to work slowly back to the waist of the ship, but kept to his own side. He was met on the way by the second mate, when nearly opposite where they sat.

"Ain't you pretty comfortable where you are?" they heard the mate asking. "Guess I wouldn't go aft any further just yet."

"*You're* all right, Mason," Hicks answered. "Going below —down cellar, 's feller says; go to bed."

"Well, that's a pious idea," said the mate. "You couldn't do better than that. I'll lend you a hand."

"Don't care 'f I do," responded Hicks, taking the mate's proffered arm. But he really seemed to need it very little; he walked perfectly well, and he did not look across at the others again.

At the head of the gangway he encountered Captain Jenness and Mr. Watterson, who had completed the perquisition they had remained to make in his state-room. Mr. Watterson came up empty-handed; but the captain bore the canteen in which the common enemy had been so artfully conveyed on board. He walked, darkly scowling, to the rail, and flung the canteen into the sea. Hicks, who had saluted his appearance with a glare as savage as his own, yielded to his whimsical sense of the futility of this vengeance. He gave his fleeting, drunken laugh: "Good old boy, Captain Jenness. Means well—means well. But lacks—lacks—forecast. Pounds of cure, but no prevention. Not much on bite, but death on bark. Heh?" He waggled his hand offensively at the captain, and disappeared, loosely floundering down the cabin stairs, holding hard by the hand-rail, and fumbling round with his foot for the steps before he put it down.

"As soon as he's in his room, Mr. Watterson, you lock him in." The captain handed his officer a key, and walked away forward, with a hang-dog look on his kindly face, which he kept averted from his passengers.

The sound of Hicks's descent had hardly ceased when clapping and knocking noises were heard again, and the face of the troublesome little wretch reappeared. He waved Mr. Watterson aside with his left hand, and in default of specific orders the latter allowed him to mount to the deck again. Hicks stayed himself a moment, and lurched to where Staniford and Dunham sat with Lydia.

"What I wish say Miss Blood is," he began,—"what I

wish say is, peculiar circumstances make no difference with man if man's gentleman. What I say is, everybody 'spec's—What I say is, circumstances don't alter cases; lady's a lady—What I want do is beg you fellows' pardon—beg *her* pardon—if anything I said that firs' morning—"

"Go away!" cried Staniford, beginning to whiten round the nostrils. "Hold your tongue!"

Hicks fell back a pace, and looked at him with the odd effect of now seeing him for the first time. "What *you* want?" he asked. "What you mean? Slingin' criticism ever since you came on this ship! What you mean by it? Heh? What you mean?"

Staniford rose, and Lydia gave a start. He cast an angry look at her. "Do you think I'd hurt him?" he demanded.

Hicks went on: "Sorry, very sorry, 'larm a lady,—specially lady we all respec'. But this particular affair. Touch—touches my honor. You said," he continued, "'f I came on deck, you'd knock me down. Why don't you do it? Wha's the matter with you? Sling criticism ever since you been on ship, and 'fraid do it! 'Fraid, you hear? 'F-ic—'fraid, I say." Staniford slowly walked away forward, and Hicks followed him, threatening him with word and gesture. Now and then Staniford thrust him aside, and addressed him some expostulation, and Hicks laughed and submitted. Then, after a silent excursion to the other side of the ship, he would return and renew his one-sided quarrel. Staniford seemed to forbid the interference of the crew, and alternately soothed and baffled his tedious adversary, who could still be heard accusing him of slinging criticism, and challenging him to combat. He leaned with his back to the rail, and now looked quietly into Hicks's crazy face, when the latter paused in front of him, and now looked down with a worried, wearied air. At last he crossed to the other side, and began to come aft again.

"Mr. Dunham!" cried Lydia, starting up. "I know what Mr. Staniford wants to do. He wants to keep him away from me. Let me go down to the cabin. I can't walk; *please* help me!" Her eyes were full of tears, and the hand trembled that she laid on Dunham's arm, but she controlled her voice.

He softly repressed her, while he intently watched Staniford. "No, no!"

"But he can't bear it much longer," she pleaded. "And if he should—"

"Staniford would never strike him," said Dunham, calmly. "Don't be afraid. Look! He's coming back with him; he's trying to get him below; they'll shut him up there. That's the only chance. Sit down, please." She dropped into her seat, hid her eyes for an instant, and then fixed them again on the two young men.

Hicks had got between Staniford and the rail. He seized him by the arm, and, pulling him round, suddenly struck at him. It was too much for his wavering balance: his feet shot from under him, and he went backwards in a crooked whirl and tumble, over the vessel's side.

Staniford uttered a cry of disgust and rage. "Oh, you little brute!" he shouted, and with what seemed a single gesture he flung off his coat and the low shoes he wore, and leaped the railing after him.

The cry of "Man overboard!" rang round the ship, and Captain Jenness's order, "Down with your helm! Lower a boat, Mr. Mason!" came, quick as it was, after the second mate had prepared to let go; and he and two of the men were in the boat, and she was sliding from her davits, while the Aroostook was coming up to the light wind and losing headway.

When the boat touched the water, two heads had appeared above the surface terribly far away. "Hold on, for God's sake! We'll be there in a second."

"All right!" Staniford's voice called back. "Be quick." The heads rose and sank with the undulation of the water. The swift boat appeared to crawl.

By the time it reached the place where they had been seen, the heads disappeared, and the men in the boat seemed to be rowing blindly about. The mate stood upright. Suddenly he dropped and clutched at something over the boat's side. The people on the ship could see three hands on her gunwale; a figure was pulled up into the boat, and proved to be Hicks; then Staniford, seizing the gunwale with both hands, swung himself in.

A shout went up from the ship, and Staniford waved his hand. Lydia waited where she hung upon the rail, clutching it hard with her hands, till the boat was alongside. Then from white she turned fire-red, and ran below and locked herself in her room.

XVII

Dunham followed Staniford to their room, and helped him off with his wet clothes. He tried to say something ideally fit in recognition of his heroic act, and he articulated some bald commonplaces of praise, and shook Staniford's clammy hand. "Yes," said the latter, submitting; "but the difficulty about a thing of this sort is that you don't know whether you haven't been an ass. It has been pawed over so much by the romancers that you don't feel like a hero in real life, but a hero of fiction. I've a notion that Hicks and I looked rather ridiculous going over the ship's side; I know we did, coming back. No man can reveal his greatness of soul in wet clothes. Did Miss Blood laugh?"

"Staniford!" said Dunham, in an accent of reproach. "You do her great injustice. She felt what you had done in the way you would wish,—if you cared."

"What did she say?" asked Staniford, quickly.

"Nothing. But—"

"That's an easy way of expressing one's admiration of heroic behavior. I hope she'll stick to that line. I hope she won't feel it at all necessary to say anything in recognition of my prowess; it would be extremely embarrassing. I've got Hicks back again, but I couldn't stand any gratitude for it. Not that I'm ashamed of the performance. Perhaps if it had been anybody but Hicks, I should have waited for them to lower a boat. But Hicks had peculiar claims. You couldn't let a man you disliked so much welter round a great while. Where is the poor old fellow? Is he clothed and in his right mind again?"

"He seemed to be sober enough," said Dunham, "when he came on board; but I don't think he's out yet."

"We must let Thomas in to gather up this bathing-suit," observed Staniford. "What a Newportish flavor it gives the place!" He was excited, and in great gayety of spirits.

He and Dunham went out into the cabin, where they found Captain Jenness pacing to and fro. "Well, sir," he said, taking Staniford's hand, and crossing his right with his left, so as to include Dunham in his congratulations, "you ought to have been a sailor!" Then he added, as if the unqualified praise might seem fulsome, "But if you'd been a sailor, you wouldn't have tried a thing like that. You'd have had more sense. The chances were ten to one against you."

Staniford laughed. "Was it so bad as that? I shall begin to respect myself."

The captain did not answer, but his iron grip closed hard upon Staniford's hand, and he frowned in keen inspection of Hicks, who at that moment came out of his state-room, looking pale and quite sobered. Captain Jenness surveyed him from head to foot, and then from foot to head, and pausing at the level of his eyes he said, still holding Staniford by the hand: "The trouble with a man aboard ship is that he can't turn a blackguard out-of-doors just when he likes. The Aroostook puts in at Messina. You'll be treated well till we get there, and then if I find you on my vessel five minutes after she comes to anchor, I'll heave you overboard, and I'll take care that nobody jumps after you. Do you hear? And you won't find me doing any such fool kindness as I did when I took you on board, soon again."

"Oh, I say, Captain Jenness," began Staniford.

"He's all right," interrupted Hicks. "I'm a blackguard; I know it; and I don't think I was worth fishing up. But you've done it, and I mustn't go back on you, I suppose." He lifted his poor, weak, bad little face, and looked Staniford in the eyes with a pathos that belied the slang of his speech. The latter released his hand from Captain Jenness and gave it to Hicks, who wrung it, as he kept looking him in the eyes, while his lips twitched pitifully, like a child's. The captain gave a quick snort either of disgust or of sympathy, and turned abruptly about and bundled himself up out of the cabin.

"I say!" exclaimed Staniford, "a cup of coffee wouldn't be bad, would it? Let's have some coffee, Thomas, about as quick as the cook can make it," he added, as the boy came out from his stateroom with a lump of wet clothes in his hands. "You wanted some coffee a little while ago," he said to Hicks, who hung his head at the joke.

For the rest of the day Staniford was the hero of the ship. The men looked at him from a distance, and talked of him together. Mr. Watterson hung about whenever Captain Jenness drew near him, as if in the hope of overhearing some acceptable expression in which he could second his superior officer. Failing this, and being driven to despair, "Find the water pretty cold, sir?" he asked at last; and after that seemed to feel that he had discharged his duty as well as might be under the extraordinary circumstances.

The second mate, during the course of the afternoon, contrived to pass near Staniford. "Why, there wa'n't no *need* of your doing it," he said, in a bated tone. "I could ha' had him out with the boat, *soon enough.*"

Staniford treasured up these meagre expressions of the general approbation, and would not have had them different. From this time, within the narrow bounds that brought them all necessarily together in some sort, Hicks abolished himself as nearly as possible. He chose often to join the second mate at meals, which Mr. Mason, in accordance with the discipline of the ship, took apart both from the crew and his superior officers. Mason treated the voluntary outcast with a sort of sarcastic compassion, as a man whose fallen state was not without its points as a joke to the indifferent observer, and yet might appeal to the pity of one who knew such cases through the misery they inflicted. Staniford heard him telling Hicks about his brother-in-law, and dwelling upon the peculiar relief which the appearance of his name in the mortality list gave all concerned in him. Hicks listened in apathetic patience and acquiescence; but Staniford thought that he enjoyed, as much as he could enjoy anything, the second officer's frankness. For his own part, he found that having made bold to keep this man in the world he had assumed a curious responsibility towards him. It became his business to show him that he was not shunned by his fellow-creatures, to hearten and cheer him up. It was heavy work. Hicks with his joke was sometimes odious company, but he was also sometimes amusing; without it, he was of a terribly dull conversation. He accepted Staniford's friendliness too meekly for good comradery; he let it add, apparently, to his burden of gratitude, rather than lessen it. Staniford smoked with him, and told him stories; he walked up and down with him, and made a point of parading their good understanding, but his spirits seemed to sink the lower. "Deuce take him!" mused his benefactor; "he's in love with her!" But he now had the satisfaction, such as it was, of seeing that if he was in love he was quite without hope. Lydia had never relented in her abhorrence of Hicks since the day of his disgrace. There seemed no scorn in her condemnation, but neither was there any mercy. In her simple life she had kept unsophisticated the severe morality of a child, and it was this that judged him, that found him unpardonable and outlawed him. He had never ventured to speak to her since that day, and Staniford never saw her look at him except when Hicks was not looking, and then with a repulsion which was very curious. Staniford could have pitied him, and might have interceded so far as to set him nearer right in her eyes; but he felt that she avoided him, too; there were no more walks on the deck, no more readings in the cabin; the checker-board, which professed to be the History of England, In 2 Vols., remained a closed book. The good companionship of a former time, in which they had so often seemed like brothers and sister, was gone. "Hicks has smashed our Happy Family," Staniford said to Dunham, with little pleasure in his joke. "Upon my word, I think I had better have left him in the water." Lydia kept a great deal in her own room; sometimes when Staniford came down into the cabin he found her there, talking with Thomas of little things that amuse children; sometimes when he went on deck in the evening she would be there in her accustomed seat, and the second mate, with face and figure half averted, and staying himself by one hand on the shrouds, would be telling her something to which she listened with lifted chin and attentive eyes. The mate would go away when Staniford appeared, but that did not help matters, for then Lydia went too. At table she said very little; she had the effect of placing herself more and more under the protection of the captain. The golden age, when they had all laughed and jested so freely and fearlessly together, under her pretty sovereignty, was past, and they seemed far dispersed in a common exile. Staniford imagined she grew pale and thin; he asked Dunham if he did not see it, but Dunham had not observed. "I think matters have taken a very desirable shape, socially," he said. "Miss Blood will reach her friends as fancy-free as she left home."

"Yes," Staniford assented vaguely; "that's the great object."

After a while Dunham asked, "She's never said anything to you about your rescuing Hicks?"

"Rescuing? What rescuing? They'd have had him out in another minute, any way," said Staniford, fretfully. Then he brooded angrily upon the subject: "But I can tell you what: considering all the circumstances, she might very well have said something. It looks obtuse, or it looks hard. She must have known that it all came about through my trying to keep him away from her."

"Oh, yes; she knew that," said Dunham; "she spoke of it at the time. But I thought—"

"Oh, she did! Then I think that it would be very little if she recognized the mere fact that something had happened."

"Why, you said you hoped she wouldn't. You said it would be embarrassing. You're hard to please, Staniford."

"I shouldn't choose to have her speak for *my* pleasure," Staniford returned. "But it argues a dullness and coldness in her—"

"I don't believe she's dull; I don't believe she's cold," said Dunham, warmly.

"What *do* you believe she is?"

"Afraid."

"Pshaw!" said Staniford.

The eve of their arrival at Messina, he discharged one more duty by telling Hicks that he had better come on to Trieste with them. "Captain Jenness asked me to speak to you about it," he said. "He feels a little awkward, and thought I could open the matter better."

"The captain's all right," answered Hicks, with unruffled humility, "but I'd rather stop at Messina. I'm going to get home as soon as I can,—strike a bee-line."

"Look here!" said Staniford, laying his hand on his shoulder. "How are you going to manage for money?"

"Monte di Pieta," replied Hicks. "I've been there before. Used to have most of my things in the care of the state when I was studying medicine in Paris. I've got a lot of rings and trinkets that'll carry me through, with what's left of my watch."

"Are you sure?"

"Sure."

"Because you can draw on me, if you're going to be short."

"Thanks," said Hicks. "There's something I should like to ask you," he added, after a moment. "I see as well as you do that Miss Blood isn't the same as she was before. I want to know—I can't always be sure afterwards—whether I did or said anything out of the way in her presence."

"You were drunk," said Staniford, frankly, "but beyond that you were irreproachable, as regarded Miss Blood. You were even exemplary."

"Yes, I know," said Hicks, with a joyless laugh. "Sometimes it takes that turn. I don't think I could stand it if I had shown her any disrespect. She's a lady,—a perfect lady; she's the best girl I ever saw."

"Hicks," said Staniford, presently, "I haven't bored you in regard to that little foible of yours. Aren't you going to try to do something about it?"

"I'm going home to get them to shut me up somewhere," answered Hicks. "But I doubt if anything can be done. I've studied the thing; I am a doctor,—or I would be if I were not a drunkard,—and I've diagnosed the case pretty thoroughly. For three months or four months, now, I shall be all right. After that I shall go to the bad for a few weeks; and I'll have to scramble back the best way I can. Nobody can help me. That was the mistake this last time. I shouldn't have wanted anything at Gibraltar if I could have had my spree out at Boston. But I let them take me before it was over, and ship me off. I thought I'd try it. Well, it was like a burning fire every minute, all the way. I thought I should die. I tried to get something from the sailors; I tried to steal Gabriel's cooking-wine. When I got that brandy in Gibraltar I was wild. Talk about heroism! I tell you it was superhuman, keeping that canteen corked till night! I was in hopes I could get through it,—sleep it off,—and nobody be any the wiser. But it wouldn't work. O Lord, Lord, Lord!"

Hicks was as common a soul as could well be. His conception of life was vulgar, and his experience of it was probably vulgar. He had a good mind enough, with abundance of that humorous brightness which may hereafter be found the most national quality of the Americans; but his ideals were pitiful, and the language of his heart was a drolling slang. Yet his doom lifted him above his low conditions, and made him tragic; his despair gave him the dignity of a mysterious expiation, and set him apart with all those who suffer beyond human help. Without deceiving himself as to the quality of the man, Staniford felt awed by the darkness of his fate.

"Can't you try somehow to stand up against it, and fight it off? You're so young yet, it can't—"

The wretched creature burst into tears. "Oh, try,—try! You don't know what you're talking about. Don't you suppose I've had reasons for trying? If you could see how my mother looks when I come out of one of my drunks,— and my father, poor old man! It's no use; I tell you it's no use. I shall go just so long, and then I shall want it, and *will* have it, unless they shut me up for life. My God, I wish I was dead! Well!" He rose from the place where they had been sitting together, and held out his hand to Staniford. "I'm going to be off in the morning before you're out, and I'll say good-by now. I want you to keep this chair, and give it to Miss Blood, for me, when you get to Trieste."

"I will, Hicks," said Staniford, gently.

"I want her to know that I was ashamed of myself. I think she'll like to know it."

"I will say anything to her that you wish," replied Staniford.

"There's nothing else. If ever you see a man with my

complaint fall overboard again, think twice before you jump after him."

He wrung Staniford's hand, and went below, leaving him with a dull remorse that he should ever have hated Hicks, and that he could not quite like him even now.

But he did his duty by him to the last. He rose at dawn, and was on deck when Hicks went over the side into the boat which was to row him to the steamer for Naples, lying at anchor not far off. He presently returned, to Staniford's surprise, and scrambled up to the deck of the Aroostook. "The steamer sails to-night," he said, "and perhaps I couldn't raise the money by that time. I wish you'd lend me ten napoleons. I'll send 'em to you from London. There's my father's address: I'm going to telegraph to him." He handed Staniford a card, and the latter went below for the coins. "Thanks," said Hicks, when he reappeared with them. "Send 'em to you where?"

"Care Blumenthals', Venice. I'm going to be there some weeks."

In the gray morning light the lurid color of tragedy had faded out of Hicks. He was merely a baddish-looking young fellow whom Staniford had lent ten napoleons that he might not see again. Staniford watched the steamer uneasily, both from the Aroostook and from the shore, where he strolled languidly about with Dunham part of the day. When she sailed in the evening, he felt that Hicks's absence was worth twice the money.

XVIII

The young men did not come back to the ship at night, but went to a hotel, for the greater convenience of seeing the city. They had talked of offering to show Lydia about, but their talk had not ended in anything. Vexed with himself to be vexed at such a thing, Staniford at the bottom of his heart still had a soreness which the constant sight of her irritated. It was in vain that he said there was no occasion, perhaps no opportunity, for her to speak, yet he was hurt that she seemed to have seen nothing uncommon in his risking his own life for that of a man like Hicks. He had set the action low enough in his own speech; but he knew that it was not ignoble, and it puzzled him that it should be so passed over. She had not even said a word of congratulation upon his own escape. It might be that she did not know how, or did not think it was her place to speak. She was curiously estranged. He felt as if he had been away, and she had grown from a young girl into womanhood during his absence. This fantastic conceit was strongest when he met her with Captain Jenness one day. He had found friends at the hotel, as one always does in Italy, if one's world is at all wide,—some young ladies, and a lady, now married, with whom he had once violently flirted. She was willing that he should envy her husband; that amused him in his embittered mood; he let her drive him about; and they met Lydia and the captain, walking together. Staniford started up from his lounging ease, as if her limpid gaze had searched his conscience, and bowed with an air which did not escape his companion.

"Ah! Who's that?" she asked, with the boldness which she made pass for eccentricity.

"A lady of my acquaintance," said Staniford, at his laziest again.

"A lady?" said the other, with an inflection that she saw hurt. "Why the marine animal, then? She bowed very prettily; she blushed prettily, too."

"She's a very pretty girl," replied Staniford.

"Charming! But why blush?"

"I've heard that there are ladies who blush for nothing."

"Is she Italian?"

"Yes,—in voice."

"Oh, an American *prima donna*!" Staniford did not answer. "Who is she? Where is she from?"

"South Bradfield, Mass." Staniford's eyes twinkled at her pursuit, which he did not trouble himself to turn aside, but baffled by mere impenetrability.

The party at the hotel suggested that the young men should leave their ship and go on with them to Naples; Dunham was tempted, for he could have reached Dresden sooner by land; but Staniford overruled him, and at the end of four days they went back to the Aroostook. They said it was like getting home, but in fact they felt the change from the airy heights and breadths of the hotel to the small cabin and the closets in which they slept; it was not so great alleviation as Captain Jenness seemed to think that one of them could now have Hicks's stateroom. But Dunham took everything sweetly, as his habit was; and, after all, they were meeting their hardships voluntarily. Some of the ladies came with them in the boat which rowed them to the Aroostook; the name made them laugh; that lady who wished Staniford to regret her waved him her hand kerchief as the boat rowed away again. She had with difficulty been kept from coming on board by the refusal of the others to come with her. She had contrived to associate herself with him again in the minds of the others, and this, perhaps, was all that she desired. But the sense of her frivolity—her not so much vacant-mindedness as vacant-heartedness—was like a stain, and he painted in Lydia's face when they first met the reproach which was in his own breast.

Her greeting, however, was frank and cordial; it was a real welcome. Staniford wondered if it were not more frank and cordial than he quite liked, and whether she was merely relieved by Hicks's absence, or had freed herself from that certain subjection in which she had hitherto been to himself.

Yet it was charming to see her again as she had been in the happiest moments of the past, and to feel that, Hicks being out of her world, her trust of everybody in it was perfect once more. She treated that interval of coldness and diffidence as all women know how to treat a thing which they wish not to have been; and Staniford, a man on whom no pleasing art of her sex was ever lost, admired and gratefully accepted the effect of this. He fell luxuriously into the old habits again. They had still almost the time of a steamer's voyage to Europe before them; it was as if they were newly setting sail from America. The first night after they left Messina Staniford found her in her place in the waist of the ship, and sat down beside her there, and talked; the next night she did not come; the third she came, and he asked her to walk with him. The elastic touch of her hand on his arm, the rhythmic movement of her steps beside him, were things that seemed always to have been. She told him of what she had seen and done in Messina. This glimpse of Italy had vividly animated her; she had apparently found a world within herself as well as without.

With a suddenly depressing sense of loss, Staniford had a prevision of splendor in her, when she should have wholly blossomed out in that fervid air of art and beauty; he would fain have kept her still a wilding rosebud of the New England wayside. He hated the officers who should wonder at her when she first came into the Square of St. Mark with her aunt and uncle.

Her talk about Messina went on; he was thinking of her, and not of her talk; but he saw that she was not going to refer to their encounter. "You make me jealous of the objects of interest in Messina," he said. "You seem to remember seeing everything but me, there."

She stopped abruptly. "Yes," she said, after a deep breath, "I saw you there;" and she did not offer to go on again.

"Where were you going, that morning?"

"Oh, to the cathedral. Captain Jenness left me there, and I looked all through it till he came back from the consulate."

"Left you there alone!" cried Staniford.

"Yes; I told him I should not feel lonely, and I should not stir out of it till he came back. I took one of those little pine chairs and sat down, when I got tired, and looked at the people coming to worship, and the strangers with their guide-books."

"Did any of them look at you?"

"They stared a good deal. It seems to be the custom in Europe; but I told Captain Jenness I should probably have to go about by myself in Venice, as my aunt's an invalid, and I had better get used to it."

She paused, and seemed to be referring the point to Staniford.

"Yes,—oh, yes," he said.

"Captain Jenness said it was their way, over here," she resumed; "but he guessed I had as much right in a church as anybody."

"The captain's common sense is infallible," answered Staniford. He was ashamed to know that the beautiful young girl was as improperly alone in church as she would have been in a cafe, and he began to hate the European world for the fact. It seemed better to him that the Aroostook should put about and sail back to Boston with her, as she was,—better that she should be going to her aunt in South Bradfield than to her aunt in Venice. "We shall soon be at our journey's end, now," he said, after a while.

"Yes; the captain thinks in about eight days, if we have good weather."

"Shall you be sorry?"

"Oh, I like the sea very well."

"But the new life you are coming to,—doesn't that alarm you sometimes?"

"Yes, it does," she admitted, with a kind of reluctance.

"So much that you would like to turn back from it?"

"Oh, no!" she answered quickly. Of course not, Staniford thought; nothing could be worse than going back to South Bradfield. "I keep thinking about it," she added. "You say Venice is such a very strange place. Is it any use my having seen Messina?"

"Oh, all Italian cities have something in common."

"I presume," she went on, "that after I get there everything will become natural. But I don't like to look forward. It— scares me. I can't form any idea of it."

"You needn't be afraid," said Staniford. "It's only more beautiful than anything you can imagine."

"Yes—yes; I know," Lydia answered.

"And do you really dread getting there?"

"Yes, I dread it," she said.

"Why," returned Staniford lightly, "so do I; but it's for a different reason, I'm afraid. I should like such a voyage as this to go on forever. Now and then I think it will; it seems always to have gone on. Can you remember when it began?"

"A great while ago," she answered, humoring his fantasy,

W. D. Howells

"but I can remember." She paused a long while. "I don't know," she said at last, "whether I can make you understand just how I feel. But it seems to me as if I had died, and this long voyage was a kind of dream that I was going to wake up from in another world. I often used to think, when I was a little girl, that when I got to heaven it would be lonesome—I don't know whether I can express it. You say that Italy—that Venice—is so beautiful; but if I don't know any one there—" She stopped, as if she had gone too far.

"But you do know somebody there," said Staniford. "Your aunt—"

"Yes," said the girl, and looked away.

"But the people in this long dream,—you're going to let some of them appear to you there," he suggested.

"Oh, yes," she said, reflecting his lighter humor, "I shall want to see them, or I shall not know I am the same person, and I must be sure of myself, at least."

"And you wouldn't like to go back to earth—to South Bradfield again?" he asked presently.

"No," she answered. "All that seems over forever. I couldn't go back there and be what I was. I could have stayed there, but I couldn't go back."

Staniford laughed. "I see that it isn't the other world that's got hold of you! It's *this* world! I don't believe you'll be unhappy in Italy. But it's pleasant to think you've been so contented on the Aroostook that you hate to leave it. I don't believe there's a man on the ship that wouldn't feel personally flattered to know that you liked being here. Even that poor fellow who parted from us at Messina was anxious that you should think as kindly of him as you could. He knew that he had behaved in a way to shock you, and he was very sorry. He left a message with me for you. He thought you would like to know that he was ashamed of himself."

"I pitied him," said Lydia succinctly. It was the first time that she had referred to Hicks, and Staniford found it in character for her to limit herself to this sparse comment. Evidently, her compassion was a religious duty. Staniford's generosity came easy to him.

"I feel bound to say that Hicks was not a bad fellow. I disliked him immensely, and I ought to do him justice, now he's gone. He deserved all your pity. He's a doomed man; his vice is irreparable; he can't resist it." Lydia did not say anything: women do not generalize in these matters; perhaps they cannot pity the faults of those they do not love. Staniford only forgave Hicks the more. "I can't say that up to the last moment I thought him anything but a poor, common little creature; and yet I certainly did feel a greater kindness for him after—what I—after what had happened. He left something more than a message for you, Miss Blood; he left his steamer chair yonder, for you."

"For me?" demanded Lydia. Staniford felt her thrill and grow rigid upon his arm, with refusal. "I will not have it. He had no right to do so. He—he—was dreadful! I will give it to you!" she said, suddenly. "He ought to have given it to you. You did everything for him; you saved his life."

It was clear that she did not sentimentalize Hicks's case; and Staniford had some doubt as to the value she set upon what he had done, even now she had recognized it.

W. D. Howells

He said, "I think you overestimate my service to him, possibly. I dare say the boat could have picked him up in good time."

"Yes, that's what the captain and Mr. Watterson and Mr. Mason all said," assented Lydia.

Staniford was nettled. He would have preferred a devoted belief that but for him Hicks must have perished. Besides, what she said still gave no clew to her feeling in regard to himself. He was obliged to go on, but he went on as indifferently as he could. "However, it was hardly a question for me at the time whether he could have been got out without my help. If I had thought about it at all—which I didn't—I suppose I should have thought that it wouldn't do to take any chances."

"Oh, no," said Lydia, simply, "you couldn't have done anything less than you did."

In his heart Staniford had often thought that he could have done very much less than jump overboard after Hicks, and could very properly have left him to the ordinary life-saving apparatus of the ship. But if he had been putting the matter to some lady in society who was aggressively praising him for his action, he would have said just what Lydia had said for him,—that he could not have done anything less. He might have said it, however, in such a way that the lady would have pursued his retreat from her praises with still fonder applause; whereas this girl seemed to think there was nothing else to be said. He began to stand in awe of her heroic simplicity. If she drew every-day breath in that lofty air, what could she really think of him, who preferred on principle the atmosphere of the valley? "Do you know, Miss Blood," he said gravely, "that you pay me a very high compliment?"

"How?" she asked.

"You rate my maximum as my mean temperature." He felt that she listened inquiringly. "I don't think I'm habitually up to a thing of that kind," he explained.

"Oh, no," she assented, quietly; "but when he struck at you so, you had to do everything."

"Ah, you have the pitiless Puritan conscience that takes the life out of us all!" cried Staniford, with sudden bitterness. Lydia seemed startled, shocked, and her hand trembled on his arm, as if she had a mind to take it away. "I was a long time laboring up to that point. I suppose you are always there!"

"I don't understand," she said, turning her head round with the slow motion of her beauty, and looking him full in the face.

"I can't explain now. I will, by and by,—when we get to Venice," he added, with quick lightness.

"You put off everything till we get to Venice," she said, doubtfully.

"I beg your pardon. It was you who did it the last time."

"Was it?" She laughed. "So it was! I was thinking it was you."

It consoled him a little that she should have confused them in her thought, in this way. "What was it you were to tell me in Venice?" he asked.

"I can't think, now."

"Very likely something of yourself—or myself. A third person might say our conversational range was limited."

"Do you think it is very egotistical?" she asked, in the gay tone which gave him relief from the sense of oppressive elevation of mind in her.

"It is in me,—not in you."

"But I don't see the difference."

"I will explain sometime,"

"When we get to Venice?"

They both laughed. It was very nonsensical; but nonsense is sometimes enough.

When they were serious again, "Tell me," he said, "what you thought of that lady in Messina, the other day."

She did not affect not to know whom he meant. She merely said, "I only saw her a moment."

"But you thought something. If we only see people a second we form some opinion of them."

"She is very fine-appearing," said Lydia.

Staniford smiled at the countrified phrase; he had observed that when she spoke her mind she used an instinctive good language; when she would not speak it, she fell into the phraseology of the people with whom she had lived. "I see you don't wish to say, because you think she is a friend of mine. But you can speak out freely. We were not friends; we were enemies, if anything."

Staniford's meaning was clear enough to himself; but Lydia paused, as if in doubt whether he was jesting or not, before she asked, "Why were you riding with her then?"

"I was driving with her," he replied, "I suppose, because she asked me."

"*Asked* you!" cried the girl; and he perceived her moral recoil both from himself and from a woman who could be so unseemly. That lady would have found it delicious if she could have known that a girl placed like Lydia was shocked at her behavior. But he was not amused. He was touched by the simple self-respect that would not let her suffer from what was not wrong in itself, but that made her shrink from a voluntary semblance of unwomanliness. It endeared her not only to his pity, but to that sense which in every man consecrates womanhood, and waits for some woman to be better than all her sex. Again he felt the pang he had remotely known before. What would she do with these ideals of hers in that depraved Old World,—so long past trouble for its sins as to have got a sort of sweetness and innocence in them,—where her facts would be utterly irreconcilable with her ideals, and equally incomprehensible?

They walked up and down a few turns without speaking again of that lady. He knew that she grew momently more constrained toward him; that the pleasure of the time was spoiled for her; that she had lost her trust in him, and this half amused, half afflicted him. It did not surprise him when, at their third approach to the cabin gangway, she withdrew her hand from his arm and said, stiffly, "I think I will go down." But she did not go at once. She lingered, and after a certain hesitation she said, without looking at him, "I didn't express what I wanted to, about Mr. Hicks, and—what you did. It is what I thought you would do."

W. D. Howells

"Thanks," said Staniford, with sincere humility. He understood how she had had this in her mind, and how she would not withhold justice from him because he had fallen in her esteem; how rather she would be the more resolute to do him justice for that reason.

XIX

He could see that she avoided being alone with him the next day, but he took it for a sign of relenting, perhaps helpless relenting, that she was in her usual place on deck in the evening. He went to her, and, "I see that you haven't forgiven me," he said.

"Forgiven you?" she echoed.

"Yes," he said, "for letting that lady ask me to drive with her."

"I never said—" she began.

"Oh, no! But I knew it, all the same. It was not such a very wicked thing, as those things go. But I liked your not liking it. Will you let me say something to you?"

"Yes," she answered, rather breathlessly.

"You must think it's rather an odd thing to say, as I ask leave. It is; and I hardly know how to say it. I want to tell you that I've made bold to depend a great deal upon your good opinion for my peace of mind, of late, and that I can't well do without it now."

She stole the quickest of her bird-like glances at him, but

W. D. Howells

did not speak; and though she seemed, to his anxious fancy, poising for flight, she remained, and merely looked away, like the bird that will not or cannot fly.

"You don't resent my making you my outer conscience, do you, and my knowing that you're not quite pleased with me?"

She looked down and away with one of those turns of the head, so precious when one who beholds them is young, and caught at the fringe of her shawl. "I have no right," she began.

"Oh, I give you the right!" he cried, with passionate urgence. "You have the right. Judge me!" She only looked more grave, and he hurried on. "It was no great harm of her to ask me; that's common enough; but it was harm of me to go if I didn't quite respect her,—if I thought her silly, and was willing to be amused with her. One hasn't any right to do that. I saw this when I saw you." She still hung her head, and looked away. "I want you to tell me something," he pursued. "Do you remember once—the second time we talked together—that you said Dunham was in earnest, and you wouldn't answer when I asked you about myself? Do you remember?"

"Yes," said the girl.

"I didn't care, then. I care very much now. You don't think me—you think I can be in earnest when I will, don't you? And that I can regret—that I really wish—" He took the hand that played with the shawl-fringe, but she softly drew it away.

"Ah, I see!" he said. "You can't believe in me. You don't believe that I can be a good man—like Dunham!"

She answered in the same breathless murmur, "I think you are good." Her averted face drooped lower.

"I will tell you all about it, some day!" he cried, with joyful vehemence. "Will you let me?"

"Yes," she answered, with the swift expulsion of breath that sometimes comes with tears. She rose quickly and turned away. He did not try to keep her from leaving him. His heart beat tumultuously; his brain seemed in a whirl. It all meant nothing, or it meant everything.

"What is the matter with Miss Blood?" asked Dunham, who joined him at this moment. "I just spoke to her at the foot of the gangway stairs, and she wouldn't answer me."

"Oh, I don't know about Miss Blood—I don't know what's the matter," said Staniford. "Look here, Dunham; I want to talk with you—I want to tell you something—I want you to advise me—I—There's only one thing that can explain it, that can excuse it. There's only one thing that can justify all that I've done and said, and that can not only justify it, but can make it sacredly and eternally right,—right for her and right for me. Yes, it's reason for all, and for a thousand times more. It makes it fair for me to have let her see that I thought her beautiful and charming, that I delighted to be with her, that I— Dunham," cried Staniford, "I'm in love!"

Dunham started at the burst in which these ravings ended. "Staniford," he faltered, with grave regret, "I *hope* not!"

"You hope not? You—you—What do you mean? How else can I free myself from the self-reproach of having trifled with her, of—"

Dunham shook his head compassionately. "You can't do it

that way. Your only safety is to fight it to the death,—to run from it."

"But if I don't *choose* to fight it?" shouted Staniford,—"if I don't *choose* to run from it? If I—"

"For Heaven's sake, hush! The whole ship will hear you, and you oughtn't to breathe it in the desert. I saw how it was going! I dreaded it; I knew it; and I longed to speak. I'm to blame for not speaking!"

"I should like to know what would have authorized you to speak?" demanded Staniford, haughtily.

"Only my regard for you; only what urges me to speak now! You *must* fight it, Staniford, whether you choose or not. Think of yourself,—think of her! Think—you have always been my ideal of honor and truth and loyalty—think of her husband—"

"Her husband!" gasped Staniford. "Whose husband? What the deuce—*who* the deuce—are you talking about, Dunham?"

"Mrs. Rivers."

"Mrs. Rivers? That flimsy, feather-headed, empty-hearted—eyes-maker! That frivolous, ridiculous—Pah! And did you think that I was talking of *her*? Did you think I was in love with *her*?"

"Why," stammered Dunham, "I supposed—I thought—At Messina, you know—"

"Oh!" Staniford walked the deck's length away. "Well, Dunham," he said, as he came back, "you've spoilt a pretty scene with your rot about Mrs. Rivers. I was going to be romantic! But perhaps I'd better say in ordinary newspaper English that I've just found out that I'm in love with Miss Blood."

"With *her!*" cried Dunham, springing at his hand.

"Oh, come now! Don't *you* be romantic, after knocking *my* chance."

"Why, but Staniford!" said Dunham, wringing his hand with a lover's joy in another's love and his relief that it was not Mrs. Rivers. "I never should have dreamt of such a thing!"

"Why?" asked Staniford, shortly.

"Oh, the way you talked at first, you know, and—"

"I suppose even people who get married have something to take back about each other," said Staniford, rather sheep-ishly. "However," he added, with an impulse of frankness, "I don't know that I should have dreamt of it myself, and I don't blame you. But it's a fact, nevertheless."

"Why, of course. It's splendid! Certainly. It's magnificent!" There was undoubtedly a qualification, a reservation, in Dunham's tone. He might have thought it right to bring the inequalities of the affair to Staniford's mind. With all his effusive kindliness of heart and manner, he had a keen sense of social fitness, a nice feeling for convention. But a man does not easily suggest to another that the girl with whom he has just declared himself in love is his inferior. What Dunham finally did say was: "It jumps with all your ideas—all your old talk about not caring to marry a society girl—"

"Society might be very glad of such a girl!" said Staniford, stiffly.

"Yes, yes, certainly; but I mean—"

"Oh, I know what you mean. It's all right," said Staniford. "But it isn't a question of marrying yet. I can't be sure she understood me,—I've been so long understanding myself. And yet, she must, she must! She must believe it by this time, or else that I'm the most infamous scoundrel alive. When I think how I have sought her out, and followed her up, and asked her judgment, and hung upon her words, I feel that I oughtn't to lose a moment in being explicit. I don't care for myself; she can take me or leave me, as she likes; but if she doesn't understand, she mustn't be left in suspense as to my meaning." He seemed to be speaking to Dunham, but he was really thinking aloud, and Dunham waited for some sort of question before he spoke. "But it's a great satisfaction to have had it out with myself. I haven't got to pretend any more that I hang about her, and look at her, and go mooning round after her, for this no-reason and that; I've got the best reason in the world for playing the fool,—I'm in love!" He drew a long, deep breath. "It simplifies matters immensely to have reached the point of acknowledging that. Why, Dunham, those four days at Messina almost killed me! They settled it. When that woman was in full fascination it made me gasp. I choked for a breath of fresh air; for a taste of spring-water; for—Lurella!" It was a long time since Staniford had used this name, and the sound of it made him laugh. "It's droll—but I always think of her as Lurella; I wish it *was* her name! Why, it was like heaven to see her face when I got back to the ship. After we met her that day at Messina, Mrs. Rivers tried her best to get out of me who it was, and where I met her. But I flatter myself that I was equal to *that* emergency."

Dunham said nothing, at once. Then, "Staniford," he faltered, "she got it out of me."

"Did you tell her who Lu—who Miss Blood was?"

"Yes."

"And how I happened to be acquainted with her?"

"Yes."

"And that we were going on to Trieste with her?"

"She had it out of me before I knew," said Dunham. "I didn't realize what she was after; and I didn't realize how peculiar the situation might seem—"

"I see nothing peculiar in the situation," interrupted Staniford, haughtily. Then he laughed consciously. "Or, yes, I do; of course I do! You must know *her* to appreciate it, though." He mused a while before he added: "No wonder Mrs. Rivers was determined to come aboard! I wish we had let her,—confound her! She'll think I was ashamed of it. There's nothing to be ashamed of! By Heaven, I should like to hear any one—" Staniford broke off, and laughed, and then bit his lip, smiling. Suddenly he burst out again, frowning: "I won't view it in that light. I refuse to consider it from that point of view. As far as I'm concerned, it's as regular as anything else in life. It's the same to me as if she were in her own house, and I had come there to tell her that she has my future in her hand. She's such a lady by instinct that she's made it all a triumph, and I thank God that I haven't done or said anything to mar it. Even that beast of a Hicks didn't; it's no merit. I've made love to her,—I own it; of course I have, because I was in love with her; and my fault has been that I haven't made love to her openly, but have gone on fancying that I was studying her character, or some rubbish of that sort. But the fault is easily repaired." He turned about, as if he were going to look for Lydia at once, and ask her to be his wife. But he halted abruptly, and sat down. "No; that won't do," he said. "That won't do at all." He remained thinking, and Dunham, unwilling to interrupt his reverie, moved a few paces off. "Dunham, don't go. I want your advice. Perhaps I don't see it in the right light."

"How is it you see it, my dear fellow?" asked Dunham.

"I don't know whether I've a right to be explicit with her, here. It seems like taking an advantage. In a few days she will be with her friends—"

"You must wait," said Dunham, decisively. "You can't speak to her before she is in their care; it wouldn't be the thing. You're quite right about that."

"No, it wouldn't be the thing," groaned Staniford. "But how is it all to go on till then?" he demanded desperately.

"Why, just as it has before," answered Dunham, with easy confidence.

"But is that fair to her?"

"Why not? You mean to say to her at the right time all that a man can. Till that time comes I haven't the least doubt she understands you."

"Do you think so?" asked Staniford, simply. He had suddenly grown very subject and meek to Dunham.

"Yes," said the other, with the superiority of a betrothed lover; "women are very quick about those things."

"I suppose you're right," sighed Staniford, with nothing of his wonted arrogant pretension in regard to women's moods and minds, "I suppose you're right. And you would go on just as before?"

"I would, indeed. How could you change without making her unhappy—if she's interested in you?"

"That's true. I could imagine worse things than going on just as before. I suppose," he added, "that something more explicit has its charms; but a mutual understanding is very pleasant,—if it *is* a mutual understanding." He looked inquiringly at Dunham.

"Why, as to that, of course I don't know. You ought to be the best judge of that. But I don't believe your impressions would deceive you."

"Yours did, once," suggested Staniford, in suspense.

"Yes; but I was not in love with her," explained Dunham.

"Of course," said Staniford, with a breath of relief. "And you think—Well, I must wait!" he concluded, grimly. "But don't—don't mention this matter, Dunham, unless I do. Don't keep an eye on me, old fellow. Or, yes, you must! You can't help it. I want to tell you, Dunham, what makes me think she may be a not wholly uninterested spectator of my—sentiments." He made full statement of words and looks and tones. Dunham listened with the patience which one lover has with another.

XX

The few days that yet remained of their voyage were falling in the latter half of September, and Staniford tried to make the young girl see the surpassing loveliness of that season under Italian skies; the fierceness of the summer is then past, and at night, when chiefly they inspected the firmament, the heaven has begun to assume something of the intense blue it wears in winter. She said yes, it was very beautiful, but she could not see that the days were finer, or the skies bluer, than those of September at home; and he laughed at her loyalty to the American weather. "Don't *you* think so, too?" she asked, as if it pained her that he should like Italian weather better.

"Oh, yes,—yes," he said. Then he turned the talk on her, as he did whenever he could. "I like your meteorological patriotism. If I were a woman, I should stand by America in everything."

"Don't you as a man?" she pursued, still anxiously.

"Oh, certainly," he answered. "But women owe our continent a double debt of fidelity. It's the Paradise of women, it's their Promised Land, where they've been led up out of the Egyptian bondage of Europe. It's the home of their freedom. It is recognized in America that women have consciences and souls."

Lydia looked very grave. "Is it—is it so different with women in Europe?" she faltered.

"Very," he replied, and glanced at her half-laughingly, half-tenderly.

After a while, "I wish you would tell me," she said, "just what you mean. I wish you would tell me what is the difference."

"Oh, it's a long story. I will tell you—when we get to Venice." The well-worn jest served its purpose again; she laughed, and he continued: "By the way, just when will that be? The captain says that if this wind holds we shall be in Trieste by Friday afternoon. I suppose your friends will meet you there on Saturday, and that you'll go back with them to Venice at once."

"Yes," assented Lydia.

"Well, if I should come on Monday, would that be too soon?"

"Oh, no!" she answered. He wondered if she had been vaguely hoping that he might go directly on with her to Venice. They were together all day, now, and the long talks went on from early morning, when they met before breakfast on deck, until late at night, when they parted there, with blushed and laughed good-nights. Sometimes the trust she put upon his unspoken promises was terrible; it seemed to condemn his reticence as fantastic and hazardous. With her, at least, it was clear that this love was the first; her living and loving were one. He longed to testify the devotion which he felt, to leave it unmistakable and safe past accident; he thought of making his will, in which he should give her everything, and declare her supremely dear; he could only rid himself of this by drawing up the paper in writing, and then he easily tore it in pieces.

They drew nearer together, not only in their talk about each other, but in what they said of different people in their relation to themselves. But Staniford's pleasure in the metaphysics of reciprocal appreciation, his wonder at the quickness with which she divined characters he painfully analyzed, was not greater than his joy in the pretty hitch of the shoulder with which she tucked her handkerchief into the back pocket of her sack, or the picturesqueness with, which she sat facing him, and leant upon the rail, with her elbow wrapped in her shawl, and the fringe gathered in the hand which propped her cheek. He scribbled his sketch-book full of her contours and poses, which sometimes he caught unawares, and which sometimes she sat for him to draw. One day, as they sat occupied in this, "I wonder," he said, "if you have anything of my feeling, nowadays. It seems to me as if the world had gone on a pleasure excursion, without taking me along, and I was enjoying myself very much at home."

"Why, yes," she said, joyously; "do you have that feeling, too?"

"I wonder what it is makes us feel so," he ventured.

"Perhaps," she returned, "the long voyage."

"I shall hate to have the world come back, I believe," he said, reverting to the original figure. "Shall you?"

"You know I don't know much about it," she answered, in lithe evasion, for which she more than atoned with a conscious look and one of her dark blushes. Yet he chose, with a curious cruelty, to try how far she was his.

"How odd it would be," he said, "if we never should have a chance to talk up this voyage of ours when it is over!"

She started, in a way that made his heart smite him. "Why, you said you—" And then she caught herself, and struggled pitifully for the self-possession she had lost. She turned her head away; his pulse bounded.

"Did you think I wouldn't? I am living for that." He took the hand that lay in her lap; she seemed to try to free it, but she had not the strength or will; she could only keep her face turned from him.

XXI

They arrived Friday afternoon in Trieste, and Captain
Jenness telegraphed his arrival to Lydia's uncle as he went
up to the consulate with his ship's papers. The next
morning the young men sent their baggage to a hotel, but
they came back for a last dinner on the Aroostook. They
all pretended to be very gay, but everybody was perturbed
and distraught. Staniford and Dunham had paid their way
handsomely with the sailors, and they had returned with
remembrances in florid scarfs and jewelry for Thomas
and the captain and the officers. Dunham had thought
they ought to get something to give Lydia as a souvenir of
their voyage; it was part of his devotion to young ladies to
offer them little presents; but Staniford overruled him,
and said there should be nothing of the kind. They agreed
to be out of the way when her uncle came, and they said
good-by after dinner. She came on deck to watch them
ashore. Staniford would be the last to take leave. As he
looked into her eyes, he saw brave trust of him, but he
thought a sort of troubled wonder, too, as if she could not
understand his reticence, and suffered from it. There was
the same latent appeal and reproach in the pose in which
she watched their boat row away. She stood with one
hand resting on the rail, and her slim grace outlined
against the sky. He waved his hand; she answered with a
little languid wave of hers; then she turned away. He felt
as if he had forsaken her.

The afternoon was very long. Toward night-fall he eluded Dunham, and wandered back to the ship in the hope that she might still be there. But she was gone. Already everything was changed. There was bustle and discomfort; it seemed years since he had been there. Captain Jenness was ashore somewhere; it was the second mate who told Staniford of her uncle's coming.

"What sort of person was he?" he asked vaguely.

"Oh, well! *Dum* an Englishman, any way," said Mason, in a tone of easy, sociable explanation.

The scruple to which Staniford had been holding himself for the past four or five days seemed the most incredible of follies,—the most fantastic, the most cruel. He hurried back to the hotel; when he found Dunham coming out from the *table d'hote* he was wild.

"I have been the greatest fool in the world, Dunham," he said. "I have let a quixotic quibble keep me from speaking when I ought to have spoken."

Dunham looked at him in stupefaction. "Where have you been?" he inquired.

"Down to the ship. I was in hopes that she might be still there. But she's gone."

"The Aroostook *gone*?"

"Look here, Dunham," cried Staniford, angrily, "this is the second time you've done that! If you are merely thick-witted, much can be forgiven to your infirmity; but if you've a mind to joke, let me tell you you choose your time badly."

"I'm not joking. I don't know what you're talking about. I may be thick-witted, as you say; or you may be scatter-witted," said Dunham, indignantly. "What are you after, any way?"

"What was my reason for not being explicit with her; for going away from her without one honest, manly, downright word; for sneaking off without telling her that she was more than life to me, and that if she cared for me as I cared for her I would go on with her to Venice, and meet her people with her?"

"Why, I don't know," replied Dunham, vaguely. "We agreed that there would be a sort of—that she ought to be in their care before—"

"Then I can tell you," interrupted Staniford, "that we agreed upon the greatest piece of nonsense that ever was. A man can do no more than offer himself, and if he does less, after he's tried everything to show that he's in love with a woman, and to make her in love with him, he's a scamp to refrain from a bad motive, and an ass to refrain from a good one. Why in the name of Heaven *shouldn't* I have spoken, instead of leaving her to eat her heart out in wonder at my delay, and to doubt and suspect and dread—Oh!" he shouted, in supreme self-contempt.

Dunham had nothing to urge in reply. He had fallen in with what he thought Staniford's own mind in regard to the course he ought to take; since he had now changed his mind, there seemed never to have been any reason for that course.

"My dear fellow," he said, "it isn't too late yet to see her, I dare say. Let us go and find what time the trains leave for Venice."

"Do you suppose I can offer myself in the *salle d'attente*?" sneered Staniford. But he went with Dunham to the coffee-room, where they found the Osservatore Triestino and the time-table of the railroad. The last train left for Venice at ten, and it was now seven; the Austrian Lloyd steamer for Venice sailed at nine.

"Pshaw!" said Staniford, and pushed the paper away. He sat brooding over the matter before the table on which the journals were scattered, while Dunham waited for him to speak. At last he said, "I can't stand it; I must see her. I don't know whether I told her I should come on to-morrow night or not. If she should be expecting me on Monday morning, and I should be delayed—Dunham, will you drive round with me to the Austrian Lloyd's wharf? They may be going by the boat, and if they are they'll have left their hotel. We'll try the train later. I should like to find out if they are on board. I don't know that I'll try to speak with them; very likely not."

"I'll go, certainly," answered Dunham, cordially.

"I'll have some dinner first," said Staniford. "I'm hungry."

It was quite dark when they drove on to the wharf at which the boat for Venice lay. When they arrived, a plan had occurred to Staniford, through the timidity which had already succeeded the boldness of his desperation. "Dunham," he said, "I want you to go on board, and see if she's there. I don't think I could stand not finding her. Besides, if she's cheerful and happy, perhaps I'd better not see her. You can come back and report. Confound it, you know, I should be so conscious before that infernal uncle of hers. You understand!"

"Yes, yes," returned Dunham, eager to serve Staniford in a case like this. "I'll manage it."

"Well," said Staniford, beginning to doubt the wisdom of either going aboard, "do it if you think best. I don't know—"

"Don't know what?" asked Dunham, pausing in the door of the *fiacre*.

"Oh, nothing, nothing! I hope we're not making fools of ourselves."

"You're morbid, old fellow!" said Dunham, gayly. He disappeared in the darkness, and Staniford waited, with set teeth, till he came back. He seemed a long time gone. When he returned, he stood holding fast to the open fiacre-door, without speaking.

"Well!" cried Staniford, with bitter impatience.

"Well what?" Dunham asked, in a stupid voice.

"Were they there?"

"I don't know. I can't tell."

"Can't tell, man? Did you go to see?"

"I think so. I'm not sure."

A heavy sense of calamity descended upon Staniford's heart, but patience came with it. "What's the matter, Dunham?" he asked, getting out tremulously.

"I don't know. I think I've had a fall, somewhere. Help me in."

Staniford got out and helped him gently to the seat, and then mounted beside him, giving the order for their return.

"Where is your hat?" he asked, finding that Dunham was bareheaded.

"I don't know. It doesn't matter. Am I bleeding?"

"It's so dark, I can't see."

"Put your hand here." He carried Staniford's hand to the back of his head.

"There's no blood; but you've had an ugly knock there."

"Yes, that's it," said Dunham. "I remember now; I slipped and struck my head." He lapsed away in a torpor; Staniford could learn nothing more from him.

The hurt was not what Staniford in his first anxiety had feared, but the doctor whom they called at the hotel was vague and guarded as to everything but the time and care which must be given in any event. Staniford despaired; but there was only one thing to do. He sat down beside his friend to take care of him.

His mind was a turmoil of regrets, of anxieties, of apprehensions; but he had a superficial calmness that enabled him to meet the emergencies of the case. He wrote a letter to Lydia which he somehow knew to be rightly worded, telling her of the accident. In terms which conveyed to her all that he felt, he said that he should not see her at the time he had hoped, but promised to come to Venice as soon as he could quit his friend. Then, with a deep breath, he put that affair away for the time, and seemed to turn a key upon it.

He called a waiter, and charged him to have his letter posted at once. The man said he would give it to the *portier*, who was sending out some other letters. He returned, ten minutes later, with a number of letters which he said the portier had found for him at the post-office. Staniford glanced at them. It was no time to read them then, and he put them into the breast pocket of his coat.

XXII

At the hotel in Trieste, to which Lydia went with her uncle before taking the train for Venice, she found an elderly woman, who made her a courtesy, and, saying something in Italian, startled her by kissing her hand.

"It's our Veronica," her uncle explained; "she wants to know how she can serve you." He gave Veronica the wraps and parcels he had been carrying. "Your aunt thought you might need a maid."

"Oh, no!" said Lydia. "I always help myself."

"Ah, I dare say," returned her uncle. "You American ladies are so—up to snuff, as you say. But your aunt thought we'd better have her with us, in any case."

"And she sent her all the way from Venice?"

"Yes."

"Well, I never did!" said Lydia, not lightly, but with something of contemptuous severity.

Her uncle smiled, as if she had said something peculiarly acceptable to him, and asked, hesitatingly, "When you say you never did, you know, what is the full phrase?"

Lydia looked at him. "Oh! I suppose I meant I never heard of such a thing."

"Ah, thanks, thanks!" said her uncle. He was a tall, slender man of fifty-five or sixty, with a straight gray mustache, and not at all the typical Englishman, but much more English-looking than if he had been. His bearing toward Lydia blended a fatherly kindness and a colonial British gallantry, such as one sees in elderly Canadian gentlemen attentive to quite young Canadian ladies at the provincial watering-places. He had an air of adventure, and of uncommon pleasure and no small astonishment in Lydia's beauty. They were already good friends; she was at her ease with him; she treated him as if he were an old gentleman. At the station, where Veronica got into the same carriage with them, Lydia found the whole train very queer-looking, and he made her describe its difference from an American train. He said, "Oh, yes—yes, engine," when she mentioned the locomotive, and he apparently prized beyond its worth the word cow-catcher, a fixture which Lydia said was wanting to the European locomotive, and left it very stubby. He asked her if she would allow him to set it down; and he entered the word in his note-book, with several other idioms she had used. He said that he amused himself in picking up these things from his American friends. He wished to know what she called this and that and the other thing, and was equally pleased whether her nomenclature agreed or disagreed with his own. Where it differed, he recorded the fact, with her leave, in his book. He plied her with a thousand questions about America, with all parts of which he seemed to think her familiar; and she explained with difficulty how very little of it she had seen. He begged her not to let him bore her, and to excuse the curiosity of a Britisher, "As I suppose you'd call me," he added.

Lydia lifted her long-lashed lids half-way, and answered,

"No, I shouldn't call you so."

"Ah, yes," he returned, "the Americans always disown it. But I don't mind it at all, you know. I like those native expressions." Where they stopped for refreshments he observed that one of the dishes, which was flavored to the national taste, had a pretty tall smell, and seemed disappointed by Lydia's unresponsive blankness at a word which a countryman of hers—from Kentucky—had applied to the odor of the Venetian canals. He suffered in like measure from a like effect in her when he lamented the complications that had kept him the year before from going to America with Mrs. Erwin, when she revisited her old stomping-ground.

As they rolled along, the warm night which had fallen after the beautiful day breathed through the half-dropped window in a rich, soft air, as strange almost as the flying landscape itself. Mr. Erwin began to drowse, and at last he fell asleep; but Veronica kept her eyes vigilantly fixed upon Lydia, always smiling when she caught her glance, and offering service. At the stations, so orderly and yet so noisy, where the passengers were held in the same meek subjection as at Trieste, people got in and out of the carriage; and there were officers, at first in white coats, and after they passed the Italian frontier in blue, who stared at Lydia. One of the Italians, a handsome young hussar, spoke to her. She could not know what he said; but when he crossed over to her side of the carriage, she rose and took her place beside Veronica, where she remained even after he left the carriage. She was sensible of growing drowsy. Then she was aware of nothing till she woke up with her head on Veronica's shoulder, against which she had fallen, and on which she had been patiently supported for hours. "Ecco Venezia!" cried the old woman, pointing to a swarm of lights that seemed to float upon an expanse of sea. Lydia did not understand;

she thought she was again on board the Aroostook, and that the lights she saw were the lights of the shipping in Boston harbor. The illusion passed, and left her heart sore. She issued from the glare of the station upon the quay before it, bewildered by the ghostly beauty of the scene, but shivering in the chill of the dawn, and stunned by the clamor of the gondoliers. A tortuous course in the shadow of lofty walls, more deeply darkened from time to time by the arch of a bridge, and again suddenly pierced by the brilliance of a lamp that shot its red across the gloom, or plunged it into the black water, brought them to a palace gate at which they stopped, and where, after a dramatic ceremony of sliding bolts and the reluctant yielding of broad doors on a level with the water, she passed through a marble-paved court and up a stately marble staircase to her uncle's apartment. "You're at home, now, you know," he said, in a kindly way, and took her hand, very cold and lax, in his for welcome. She could not answer, but made haste to follow Veronica to her room, whither the old woman led the way with a candle. It was a gloomily spacious chamber, with sombre walls and a lofty ceiling with a faded splendor of gilded paneling. Some tall, old-fashioned mirrors and bureaus stood about, with rugs before them on the stone floor; in the middle of the room was a bed curtained with mosquito-netting. Carved chairs were pushed here and there against the wall. Lydia dropped into one of these, too strange and heavy-hearted to go to bed in that vastness and darkness, in which her candle seemed only to burn a small round hole. She longed forlornly to be back again in her pretty state-room on the Aroostook; vanishing glimpses and echoes of the faces and voices grown so familiar in the past weeks haunted her; the helpless tears ran down her cheeks.

There came a tap at her door, and her aunt's voice called, "Shall I come in?" and before she could faintly consent, her aunt pushed in, and caught her in her arms, and kissed her, and broke into a twitter of welcome and compassion. "You poor child! Did you think I was going to let you go to sleep without seeing you, after you'd come half round the world to see me?" Her aunt was dark and slight like Lydia, but not so tall; she was still a very pretty woman, and she was a very effective presence now in the long white morning-gown of camel's hair, somewhat fantastically embroidered in crimson silk, in which she drifted about before Lydia's bewildered eyes. "Let me see how you look! Are you as handsome as ever?" She held the candle she carried so as to throw its light full upon Lydia's face. "Yes!" she sighed. "How pretty you are! And at your age you'll look even better by daylight! I had begun to despair of you; I thought you couldn't be all I remembered; but you are,—you're more! I wish I had you in Rome, instead of Venice; there would be some use in it. There's a great deal of society there,—*English* society; but never mind: I'm going to take you to church with me to-morrow,—the English service; there are lots of English in Venice now, on their way south for the winter. I'm crazy to see what dresses you've brought; your aunt Maria has told me how she fitted you out. I've got two letters from her since you started, and they're all perfectly well, dear. Your black silk will do nicely, with bright ribbons, especially; I hope you haven't got it spotted or anything on the way over." She did not allow Lydia to answer, nor seem to expect it. "You've got your mother's eyes, Lydia, but your father had those straight eyebrows: you're very much like him. Poor Henry! And now I'm having you get something to eat. I'm not going to risk coffee on you, for fear it will keep you awake; though you can drink it in this climate with *comparative* impunity. Veronica is warming you a bowl of *bouillon*, and that's all you're to have till breakfast!"

"Why, aunt Josephine," said the girl, not knowing what bouillon was, and abashed by the sound of it, "I'm not the

W. D. Howells

least hungry. You oughtn't to take the trouble—"

"You'll be hungry when you begin to eat. I'm so impatient to hear about your voyage! I am going to introduce you to some very nice people, here,—English people. There are no Americans living in Venice; and the Americans in Europe are so queer! You've no idea how droll our customs seem here; and I much prefer the English. Your poor uncle can never get me to ask Americans. I tell him I'm American enough, and he'll have to get on without others. Of course, he's perfectly delighted to get at you. You've quite taken him by storm, Lydia; he's in raptures about your looks. It's what I told him before you came; but I couldn't believe it till I took a look at you. I couldn't have gone to sleep without it. Did Mr. Erwin talk much with you?"

"He was very pleasant. He talked—as long as he was awake," said Lydia.

"I suppose he was trying to pick up Americanisms from you; he's always doing it. I keep him away from Americans as much as I can: but he will get at them on the cars and at the hotels. He's always asking them such ridiculous questions, and I know some of them just talk nonsense to him."

Veronica came in with a tray, and a bowl of bouillon on it; and Mrs. Erwin pulled up a light table, and slid about, serving her, in her cabalistic dress, like an Oriental sorceress performing her incantations. She volubly watched Lydia while she ate her supper, and at the end she kissed her again. "Now you feel better," she said. "I knew it would cheer you up more than any one thing. There's nothing like something to eat when you're homesick. I found that out when I was off at school."

Lydia was hardly kissed so much at home during a year as she had been since meeting Mrs. Erwin. Her aunt Maria sparely embraced her when she went and came each week from the Mill Village; anything more than this would have come of insincerity between them; but it had been agreed that Mrs. Erwin's demonstrations of affection, of which she had been lavish during her visit to South Bradfield, might not be so false. Lydia accepted them submissively, and she said, when Veronica returned for the tray, "I hate to give you so much trouble. And sending her all the way to Trieste on my account,—I felt ashamed. There wasn' a thing for her to do."

"Why, of course not!" exclaimed her aunt. "But what did you think I was made of? Did you suppose I was going to have you come on a night-journey alone with your uncle? It would have been all over Venice; it would have been ridiculous. I sent Veronica along for a dragon."

"A dragon? I don't understand," faltered Lydia.

"Well, you will," said her aunt, putting the palms of her hands against Lydia's, and so pressing forward to kiss her. "We shall have breakfast at ten. Go to bed!"

XXIII

When Lydia came to breakfast she found her uncle alone in the room, reading Galignani's Messenger. He put down his paper, and came forward to take her hand. "You are all right this morning, I see, Miss Lydia," he said. "You were quite up a stump, last night, as your countrymen say."

At the same time hands were laid upon her shoulders from behind, and she was pulled half round, and pushed back, and held at arm's-length. It was Mrs. Erwin, who, entering after her, first scanned her face, and then, with one devouring glance, seized every detail of her dress—the black silk which had already made its effect—before she kissed her. "You *are* lovely, my dear! I shall spoil you, I know; but you're worth it! What lashes you have, child! And your aunt Maria made and fitted that dress? She's a genius!"

"Miss Lydia," said Mr. Erwin, as they sat down, "is of the fortunate age when one rises young every morning." He looked very fresh himself in his clean-shaven chin, and his striking evidence of snowy wristbands and shirt-bosom. "Later in life, you can't do that. She looks as blooming," he added, gallantly, "as a basket of chips,—as you say in America."

"Smiling," said Lydia, mechanically correcting him.

"Ah! It is? Smiling,—yes; thanks. It's very good either way; very characteristic. It would be curious to know the origin of a saying like that. I imagine it goes back to the days of the first settlers. It suggests a wood-chopping period. Is it—ah—in general use?" he inquired.

"Of course it isn't, Henshaw!" said his wife.

"You've been a great while out of the country, my dear," suggested Mr. Erwin.

"Not so long as not to know that your Americanisms are enough to make one wish we had held our tongues ever since we were discovered, or had never been discovered at all. I want to ask Lydia about her voyage. I haven't heard a word yet. Did your aunt Maria come down to Boston with you?"

"No, grandfather brought me."

"And you had good weather coming over? Mr. Erwin told me you were not seasick."

"We had one bad storm, before we reached Gibraltar; but I wasn't seasick."

"Were the other passengers?"

"One was." Lydia reddened a little, and then turned somewhat paler than at first.

"What is it, Lydia?" her aunt subtly demanded. "Who was the one that was sick?"

"Oh, a gentleman," answered Lydia.

Her aunt looked at her keenly, and for whatever reason

abruptly left the subject. "Your silk," she said, "will do very well for church, Lydia."

"Oh, I say, now!" cried her husband, "you're not going to make her go to church to-day!"

"Yes, I am! There will be more people there to-day than any other time this fall. She must go."

"But she's tired to death,—quite tuckered, you know."

"Oh, I'm rested, now," said Lydia. "I shouldn't like to miss going to church."

"Your silk," continued her aunt, "will be quite the thing for church." She looked hard at the dress, as if it were not quite the thing for breakfast. Mrs. Erwin herself wore a morning-dress of becoming delicacy, and an airy French cap; she had a light fall of powder on her face. "What kind of overthing have you got?" she asked.

"There's a sack goes with this," said the girl, suggestively.

"That's nice! What is your bonnet?"

"I haven't any bonnet. But my best hat is nice. I could—"

"*No* one goes to church in a hat! You can't do it. It's simply impossible."

"Why, my dear," said her husband, "I saw some very pretty American girls in hats at church, last Sunday."

"Yes, and everybody *knew* they were Americans by their hats!" retorted Mrs. Erwin.

"*I* knew they were Americans by their good looks," said

Mr. Erwin, "and what you call their stylishness."

"Oh, it's all well enough for you to talk. *You're* an Englishman, and you could wear a hat, if you liked. It would be set down to character. But in an American it would be set down to greenness. If you were an American, you would have to wear a bonnet."

"I'm glad, then, I'm not an American," said her husband; "I don't think I should look well in a bonnet."

"Oh, stuff, Henshaw! You know what I mean. And I'm not going to have English people thinking we're ignorant of the common decencies of life. Lydia shall not go to church in a hat; she had better *never* go. I will lend her one of my bonnets. Let me see, *which* one." She gazed at Lydia in critical abstraction. "I wear rather young bonnets," she mused aloud, "and we're both rather dark. The only difficulty is I'm so much more delicate—" She brooded upon the question in a silence, from which she burst exulting. "The very thing! I can fuss it up in no time. It won't take two minutes to get it ready. And you'll look just killing in it." She turned grave again. "Henshaw," she said, "I *wish* you would go to church this morning!"

"I would do almost anything for you, Josephine; but really, you know, you oughtn't to ask that. I was there last Sunday; I can't go every Sunday. It's bad enough in England; a man ought to have some relief on the Continent."

"Well, well. I suppose I oughtn't to ask you," sighed his wife, "especially as you're going with us to-night."

"I'll go to-night, with pleasure," said Mr. Erwin. He rose when his wife and Lydia left the table, and opened the door for them with a certain courtesy he had; it struck

W. D. Howells

even Lydia's uneducated sense as something peculiarly sweet and fine, and it did not overawe her own simplicity, but seemed of kind with it.

The bonnet, when put to proof, did not turn out to be all that it was vaunted. It looked a little odd, from the first; and Mrs. Erwin, when she was herself dressed, ended by taking it off, and putting on Lydia the hat previously condemned. "You're divine in that," she said. "And after all, you are a traveler, and I can say that some of your things were spoiled coming over,—people always get things ruined in a sea voyage,—and they'll think it was your bonnet."

"I kept my things very nicely, aunt Josephine," said Lydia conscientiously. "I don't believe anything was hurt."

"Oh, well, you can't tell till you've unpacked; and we're not responsible for what people happen to think, you know. Wait!" her aunt suddenly cried. She pulled open a drawer, and snatched two ribbons from it, which she pinned to the sides of Lydia's hat, and tied in a bow under her chin; she caught out a lace veil, and drew that over the front of the hat, and let it hang in a loose knot behind. "Now," she said, pushing her up to a mirror, that she might see, "it's a bonnet; and I needn't say *any*thing!"

They went in Mrs. Erwin's gondola to the palace in which the English service was held, and Lydia was silent, as she looked shyly, almost fearfully, round on the visionary splendors of Venice.

Mrs. Erwin did not like to be still. "What are you thinking of, Lydia?" she asked.

"Oh! I suppose I was thinking that the leaves were beginning to turn in the sugar orchard," answered Lydia faithfully. "I was thinking how still the sun would be in the pastures, there, this morning. I suppose the stillness here put me in mind of it. One of these bells has the same tone as our bell at home."

"Yes," said Mrs. Erwin. "Everybody finds a familiar bell in Venice. There are enough of them, goodness knows. I don't see why you call it still, with all this clashing and banging. I suppose this seems very odd to you, Lydia," she continued, indicating the general Venetian effect. "It's an old story to me, though. The great beauty of Venice is that you get more for your money here than you can anywhere else in the world. There isn't much society, however, and you mustn't expect to be very gay."

"I have never been gay," said Lydia.

"Well, that's no reason you shouldn't be," returned her aunt. "If you were in Florence, or Rome, or even Naples, you could have a good time. There! I'm glad your uncle didn't hear me say that!"

"What?" asked Lydia.

"Good time; that's an Americanism."

"Is it?"

"Yes. He's perfectly delighted when he catches me in one. I try to break myself of them, but I don't always know them myself. Sometimes I feel almost like never talking at all. But you can't do that, you know."

"No," assented Lydia.

"And you have to talk Americanisms if you're an American. You mustn't think your uncle isn't obliging,

Lydia. He is. I oughtn't to have asked him to go to church,—it bores him so much. I used to feel terribly about it once, when we were first married. But things have changed very much of late years, especially with all this scientific talk. In England it's quite different from what it used to be. Some of the best people in society are skeptics now, and that makes it quite another thing." Lydia looked grave, but she said nothing, and her aunt added, "I wouldn't have asked him, but I had a little headache, myself."

"Aunt Josephine," said Lydia, "I'm afraid you're doing too much for me. Why didn't you let me come alone?"

"Come alone? To church!" Mrs. Erwin addressed her in a sort of whispered shriek. "It would have been perfectly scandalous."

"To go to church alone?" demanded Lydia, astounded.

"Yes. A young girl mustn't go *any*where alone."

"Why?"

"I'll explain to you, sometime, Lydia; or rather, you'll learn for yourself. In Italy it's very different from what it is in America." Mrs. Erwin suddenly started up and bowed with great impressiveness, as a gondola swept towards them. The gondoliers wore shirts of blue silk, and long crimson sashes. On the cushions of the boat, beside a hideous little man who was sucking the top of an ivory-handled stick, reclined a beautiful woman, pale, with purplish rings round the large black eyes with which, faintly smiling, she acknowledged Mrs. Erwin's salutation, and then stared at Lydia.

"Oh, you may look, and you may look, and you may

look!" cried Mrs. Erwin, under her breath. "You've met more than your match at last! The Countess Tatocka," she explained to Lydia. "That was her palace we passed just now,—the one with the iron balconies. Did you notice the gentleman with her? She always takes to those monsters. He's a Neapolitan painter, and ever so talented,—clever, that is. He's dead in love with her, they say."

"Are they engaged?" asked Lydia.

"Engaged!" exclaimed Mrs. Erwin, with her shriek in dumb show. "Why, child, she's married!"

"To *him*?" demanded the girl, with a recoil.

"No! To her husband."

"To her husband?" gasped Lydia. "And she—"

"Why, she isn't quite well seen, even in Venice," Mrs. Erwin explained. "But she's rich, and her *conversazioni* are perfectly brilliant. She's very artistic, and she writes poetry,—Polish poetry. I *wish* she could hear you sing, Lydia! I know she'll be frantic to see you again. But I don't see how it's to be managed; her house isn't one you can take a young girl to. And *I* can't ask her: your uncle detests her."

"Do you go to her house?" Lydia inquired stiffly.

"Why, as a foreigner, *I* can go. Of course, Lydia, you can't be as particular about everything on the Continent as you are at home."

The former oratory of the Palazzo Grinzelli, which served as the English chapel, was filled with travelers of both the English-speaking nationalities, as distinguishable by their

W. D. Howells

dress as by their faces. Lydia's aunt affected the English style, but some instinctive elegance betrayed her, and every Englishwoman there knew and hated her for an American, though she was a precisian in her liturgy, instant in all the responses and genuflexions. She found opportunity in the course of the lesson to make Lydia notice every one, and she gave a telegrammic biography of each person she knew, with a criticism of the costume of all the strangers, managing so skillfully that by the time the sermon began she was able to yield the text a statuesquely close attention, and might have been carved in marble where she sat as a realistic conception of Worship.

The sermon came to an end; the ritual proceeded; the hymn, with the hemming and hawing of respectable inability, began, and Lydia lifted her voice with the rest. Few of the people were in their own church; some turned and stared at her; the bonnets and the back hair of those who did not look were intent upon her; the long red neck of one elderly Englishman, restrained by decorum from turning his head toward her, perspired with curiosity. Mrs. Erwin fidgeted, and dropped her eyes from the glances which fell to her for explanation of Lydia, and hurried away with her as soon as the services ended. In the hall on the water-floor of the palace, where they were kept waiting for their gondola a while, she seemed to shrink even from the small, surly greetings with which people whose thoughts are on higher things permit themselves to recognize fellow-beings of their acquaintance in coming out of church. But an old lady, who supported herself with a cane, pushed through the crowd to where they stood aloof, and, without speaking to Mrs. Erwin, put out her hand to Lydia; she had a strong, undaunted, plain face, in which was expressed the habit of doing what she liked. "My dear," she said, "how wonderfully you sing! Where did you get that heavenly voice? You are an American; I see that by your beauty. You are Mrs. Erwin's niece, I suppose, whom she expected. Will you come and sing to me? You must bring her, Mrs. Erwin."

She hobbled away without waiting for an answer, and Lydia and her aunt got into their gondola. "*Oh*! How glad I am!" cried Mrs. Erwin, in a joyful flutter. "She's the very tip-top of the English here; she has a whole palace, and you meet the very best people at her house. I was afraid when you were singing, Lydia, that they would think your voice was too good to be good form,—that's an expression you must get; it means everything,—it sounded almost professional. I wanted to nudge you to sing a little lower, or different, or something; but I couldn't, everybody was looking so. No matter. It's all right now. If *she* liked it, nobody else will dare to breathe. You can see that she has taken a fancy to you; she'll make a great pet of you."

"Who is she?" asked Lydia, bluntly.

"Lady Fenleigh. Such a character,—so eccentric! But really, I suppose, very hard to live with. It must have been quite a release for poor Sir Fenleigh."

"She didn't seem in mourning," said Lydia. "Has he been dead long?"

"Why, he isn't dead at all! He is what you call a grass-widower. The best soul in the world, everybody says, and very, very fond of her; but she couldn't stand it; he was *too* good, don't you understand? They've lived apart a great many years. She's lived a great deal in Asia Minor,—somewhere. She likes Venice; but of course there's no telling how long she may stay. She has another house in Florence, all ready to go and be lived in at a day's notice. I wish I had presented you! It did go through my head; but it didn't seem as if I *could* get the Blood out. It *is* a fearful name, Lydia; I always felt it so when I was a girl, and I was *so* glad to marry out of it; and it sounds so terribly American. I think you must take your mother's name, my dear. Latham is rather flattish, but it's worlds better than Blood."

"I am not ashamed of my father's name," said Lydia.

"But you'll have to change it some day, at any rate,— when you get married."

Lydia turned away. "I will be called Blood till then. If Lady Fenleigh—"

"Yes, my dear," promptly interrupted her aunt, "I know that sort of independence. I used to have whole Declarations of it. But you'll get over that, in Europe. There was a time—just after the war—when the English quite liked our sticking up for ourselves; but that's past now. They like us to be outlandish, but they don't like us to be independent. How did you like the sermon? Didn't you think we had a nicely-dressed congregation?"

"I thought the sermon was very short," answered Lydia.

"Well, that's the English way, and I like it. If you get in all the service, you *must* make the sermon short."

Lydia did not say anything for a little while. Then she asked, "Is the service the same at the evening meeting?"

"Evening meeting?" repeated Mrs. Erwin.

"Yes,—the church to-night."

"Why, child, there isn't any church to-night! What *are* you talking about?"

"Didn't uncle—didn't Mr. Erwin say he would go with us to-night?"

Mrs. Erwin seemed about to laugh, and then she looked embarrassed. "Why, Lydia," she cried at last, "he didn't mean church; he meant—opera!"

"Opera! Sunday night! Aunt Josephine, do you go to the theatre on Sabbath evening?"

There was something appalling in the girl's stern voice. Mrs. Erwin gathered herself tremulously together for defense. "Why, of course, Lydia, I don't approve of it, though I never *was* Orthodox. Your uncle likes to go; and if everybody's there that you want to see, and they will give the best operas Sunday night, what are you to do?"

Lydia said nothing, but a hard look came into her face, and she shut her lips tight.

"Now you see, Lydia," resumed her aunt, with an air of deductive reasoning from the premises, "the advantage of having a bonnet on, even if it's only a make-believe. I don't believe a soul knew it. All those Americans had hats. You were the only American girl there with a bonnet. I'm sure that it had more than half to do with Lady Fenleigh's speaking to you. It showed that you had been well brought up."

"But I never wore a bonnet to church at home," said Lydia.

"That has nothing to do with it, if they thought you did. And Lydia," she continued, "I was thinking while you were singing there that I wouldn't say anything at once about your coming over to cultivate your voice. That's got to be such an American thing, now. I'll let it out little by little,—and after Lady Fenleigh's quite taken you under her wing. Perhaps we may go to Milan with you, or to Naples,—there's a conservatory there, too; and we can pull up stakes as easily as not. Well!" said Mrs. Erwin, interrupting herself, "I'm glad Henshaw wasn't by to hear *that* speech. He'd have had it down among his Americanisms instantly. I don't know whether it *is* an Americanism; but he puts down all the outlandish sayings he gets hold of to Americans; he has no end of English slang in his book. Everything has opened *beautifully*, Lydia, and I intend you shall have the *best* time!" She looked fondly at her brother's child. "You've no idea how much you remind me of your poor father. You have his looks exactly. I always thought he would come out to Europe before he died. We used to be so proud of his looks at home! I can remember that, though I was the youngest, and he was ten years older than I. But I always did worship beauty. A perfect Greek, Mr. Rose-Black calls me: you'll see him; he's an English painter staying here; he comes a *great* deal."

"Mrs. Erwin, Mrs. Erwin!" called a lady's voice from a gondola behind them. The accent was perfectly English, but the voice entirely Italian. "Where are you running to?"

"Why, Miss Landini!" retorted Mrs. Erwin, looking back over her shoulder. "Is that you? Where in the world are *you* going?"

"Oh, I've been to pay a visit to my old English teacher. He's awfully ill with rheumatism; but awfully! He can't turn in bed."

"Why, poor man! This is my niece whom I told you I was expecting! Arrived last night! We've been to church!"

Mrs. Erwin exclaimed each of the facts.

The Italian girl stretched her hand across the gunwales of the boats, which their respective gondoliers had brought skillfully side by side, and took Lydia's hand. "I'm glad to see you, my dear. But my God, how beautiful you Americans are! But you don't look American, you know; you look Spanish! I shall come a great deal to see you, and practice my English."

"Come home with, us now, Miss Landini, and have lunch," said Mrs. Erwin.

"No, my dear, I can't. My aunt will be raising the devil if I'm not there to drink coffee with her; and I've been a great while away now. Till tomorrow!" Miss Landini's gondolier pushed his boat away, and rowed it up a narrow canal on the right.

"I suppose," Mrs. Erwin explained, "that she's really her mother,—everybody says so; but she always calls her aunt. Dear knows who her father was. But she's a very bright girl, Lydia, and you'll like her. Don't you think she speaks English wonderfully for a person who's never been out of Venice?"

"Why does she swear?" asked Lydia, stonily.

"*Swear*? Oh, I know what you mean. That's the funniest thing about Miss Landini. Your uncle says it's a shame to correct her; but I do, whenever I think of it. Why, you know, such words as God and devil don't sound at all wicked in Italian, and ladies use them quite commonly. She understands that it isn't good form to do so in English, but when she gets excited she forgets. Well, you can't say but what *she* was impressed, Lydia!"

After lunch, various people came to call upon Mrs. Erwin. Several of them were Italians who were learning English, and they seemed to think it inoffensive to say that they were glad of the opportunity to practice the language with Lydia. They talked local gossip with her aunt, and they spoke of an approaching visit to Venice from the king; it seemed to Lydia that the king's character was not good.

Mr. Rose-Black, the English artist, came. He gave himself the effect of being in Mrs. Erwin's confidence, apparently without her authority, and he bestowed a share of this intimacy upon Lydia. He had the manner of a man who had been taken up by people above him, and the impudence of a talent which had not justified the expectations formed of it. He softly reproached Mrs. Erwin for running away after service before he could speak to her, and told her how much everybody had been enchanted by her niece's singing. "At least, they said it was your niece."

"Oh, yes, Mr. Rose-Black, let me introduce you to Miss—" Lydia looked hard, even to threatening, at her aunt, and Mrs. Erwin added, "Blood."

"I beg your pardon," said Mr. Rose-Black, with his picked-up politeness, "I didn't get the name."

"Blood," said Mrs. Erwin, more distinctly.

"Aoh!" said Mr. Rose-Black, in a cast-off accent of jaded indifferentism, just touched with displeasure. "Yes," he added, dreamily, to Lydia, "it was divine, you know. You might say it needed training; but it had the *naive* sweetness we associate with your countrywomen. They're greatly admired in England now, you know, for their beauty. Oh, I assure you, it's quite the thing to admire American ladies. I want to arrange a little lunch at my studio for Mrs. Erwin and yourself; and I want you to abet me in it, Miss Blood." Lydia stared at him, but he was not troubled. "I'm going to ask to sketch you. Really, you know, there's a poise—something bird-like—a sort of repose in movement—" He sat in a corner of the sofa, with his head fallen back, and abandoned to an absent enjoyment of Lydia's pictorial capabilities. He was very red; his full beard, which started as straw color, changed to red when it got a little way from his face. He wore a suit of rough blue, the coat buttoned tightly about him, and he pulled a glove through his hand as he talked. He was scarcely roused from his reverie by the entrance of an Italian officer, with his hussar jacket hanging upon one shoulder, and his sword caught up in his left hand. He ran swiftly to Mrs. Erwin, and took her hand.

"Ah, my compliments! I come practice my English with you a little. Is it well said, a little, or do you say a small?"

"A little, cavaliere," answered Mrs. Erwin, amiably. "But you must say a good deal, in this case."

"Yes, yes,—good deal. For what?"

"Let me introduce you to my niece. Colonel Pazzelli," said Mrs. Erwin.

"Ah! Too much honor, too much honor!" murmured the cavaliere. He brought his heels together with a click, and drooped towards Lydia till his head was on a level with his hips. Recovering himself, he caught up his eye-glasses, and bent them on Lydia. "Very please, very honored, much—" He stopped, and looked confused, and Lydia turned pale and red.

"Now, won't you play that pretty *barcarole* you played the other night at Lady Fenleigh's?" entreated Mrs. Erwin.

Colonel Pazzelli wrenched himself from the fascination of Lydia's presence, and lavished upon Mrs. Erwin the hoarded English of a week. "Yes, yes; very nice, very good. With much pleasure. I thank you. Yes, I play." He was one of those natives who in all the great Italian cities haunt English-speaking societies; they try to drink tea without grimacing, and sing for the ladies of our race, who innocently pet them, finding them so very like other women in their lady-like sweetness and softness; it is said they boast among their own countrymen of their triumphs. The cavaliere unbuckled his sword, and laying it across a chair sat down at the piano. He played not one but many barcaroles, and seemed loath to leave the instrument.

"Now, Lydia," said Mrs. Erwin, fondly, "won't you sing us something?"

"Do!" called Mr. Rose-Black from the sofa, with the intonation of a spoiled first-cousin, or half-brother.

"I don't feel like singing to-day," answered Lydia, immovably. Mrs. Erwin was about to urge her further, but other people came in,—some Jewish ladies, and then a Russian, whom Lydia took at first for an American. They all came and went, but Mr. Rose-Black remained in his corner of the sofa, and never took his eyes from Lydia's face. At last he went, and then Mr. Erwin looked in.

"Is that beast gone?" he asked. "I shall be obliged to show him the door, yet, Josephine. You ought to snub him. He's worse than his pictures. Well, you've had a whole raft of folks today,—as your countrymen say."

"Yes, thank Heaven," cried Mrs. Erwin, "and they're all gone. I don't want Lydia to think that I let everybody come to see me on Sunday. Thursday is my day, Lydia, but a few privileged friends understand that they can drop in Sunday afternoon." She gave Lydia a sketch of the life and character of each of these friends. "And now I must tell you that your manner is very good, Lydia. That reserved way of yours is quite the thing for a young girl in Europe: I suppose it's a gift; I never could get it, even when I *was* a girl. But you mustn't show any *hauteur*, even when you dislike people, and you refused to sing with *rather* too much *aplomb*. I don't suppose it was noticed though,—those ladies coming in at the same time. Really, I thought Mr. Rose-Black and Colonel Pazzelli were trying to outstare each other! It was certainly amusing. I never saw such an evident case, Lydia! The poor cavaliere looked as if he had seen you somewhere before in a dream, and was struggling to make it all out."

Lydia remained impassive. Presently she said she would go to her room, and write home before dinner. When she went out Mrs. Erwin fetched a deep sigh, and threw herself upon her husband's sympathy.

"She's terribly unresponsive," she began. "I supposed she'd be in raptures with the place, at least, but you wouldn't know there was anything at all remarkable in Venice from anything she's said. We have met ever so many interesting people to-day,—the Countess Tatocka, and Lady Fenleigh, and Miss Landini, and everybody, but I don't really think she's said a word about a soul. She's too queer for anything."

"I dare say she hasn't the experience to be astonished from," suggested Mr. Erwin easily. "She's here as if she'd been dropped down from her village."

"Yes, that's true," considered his wife. "But it's hard, with Lydia's air and style and self-possession, to realize that she *is* merely a village girl."

"She may be much more impressed than she chooses to show," Mr. Erwin continued. "I remember a very curious essay by a French writer about your countrymen: he contended that they were characterized by a savage stoicism through their contact with the Indians."

"Nonsense, Henshaw! There hasn't been an Indian *near* South Bradfield for two hundred years. And besides that, am *I* stoical?"

"I'm bound to say," replied her husband, "that so far as you go, you're a complete refutation of the theory."

"I hate to see a young girl so close," fretted Mrs. Erwin. "But perhaps," she added, more cheerfully, "she'll be the easier managed, being so passive. She doesn't seem at all willful,—that's one comfort."

She went to Lydia's room just before dinner, and found the girl with her head fallen on her arms upon the table, where she had been writing. She looked up, and faced her aunt with swollen eyes.

"Why, poor thing!" cried Mrs. Erwin. "What is it, dear? What is it, Lydia?" she asked, tenderly, and she pulled Lydia's face down upon her neck.

"Oh, nothing," said Lydia. "I suppose I was a little homesick; writing home made me."

She somewhat coldly suffered Mrs. Erwin to kiss her and smooth her hair, while she began to talk with her of her grandfather and her aunt at home. "But this is going to be home to you now," said Mrs. Erwin, "and I'm not going to let you be sick for any other. I want you to treat me just like a mother, or an older sister. Perhaps I shan't be the wisest mother to you in the world, but I mean to be one of the best. Come, now, bathe your eyes, my dear, and let's go to dinner. I don't like to keep your uncle waiting." She did not go at once, but showed Lydia the appointments of the room, and lightly indicated what she had caused to be done, and what she had done with her own hands, to make the place pretty for her. "And now shall I take your letter, and have your uncle post it this evening?" She picked up the letter from the table. "Hadn't you any wax to seal it? You know they don't generally mucilage their envelopes in Europe."

Lydia blushed. "I left it open for you to read. I thought you ought to know what I wrote."

Mrs. Erwin dropped her hands in front of her, with the open letter stretched between them, and looked at her niece in rapture. "Lydia," she cried, "one would suppose you had lived all your days in Europe! Showing me your letter, this way,—why, it's quite like a Continental girl."

"I thought it was no more than right you should see what I was writing home," said Lydia, unresponsively.

"Well, no matter, even if it *was* right," replied Mrs. Erwin. "It comes to the same thing. And now, as you've been quite a European daughter, I'm going to be a real American mother." She took up the wax, and sealed Lydia's letter without looking into it. "There!" she said, triumphantly.

She was very good to Lydia all through dinner, and made her talk of the simple life at home, and the village characters whom she remembered from her last summer's visit. That amused Mr. Erwin, who several times, when, his wife was turning the talk upon Lydia's voyage over, intervened with some new question about the life of the queer little Yankee hill-town. He said she must tell Lady

Fenleigh about it,—she was fond of picking up those curios; it would make any one's social fortune who could explain such a place intelligibly in London; when they got to having typical villages of the different civilizations at the international expositions,—as no doubt they would,—somebody must really send South Bradfield over. He pleased himself vastly with this fancy, till Mrs. Erwin, who had been eying Lydia critically from time to time, as if making note of her features and complexion, said she had a white cloak, and that in Venice, where one need not dress a great deal for the opera, Lydia could wear it that night.

Lydia looked up in astonishment, but she sat passive during her aunt's discussion of her plans. When they rose from table, she said, at her stiffest and coldest, "Aunt Josephine, I want you to excuse me from going with you to-night. I don't feel like going."

"Not feel like going!" exclaimed her aunt in dismay. "Why, your uncle has taken a box!"

Lydia opposed nothing to this argument. She only said, "I would rather not go."

"Oh, but you *will*, dear," coaxed her aunt. "You would enjoy it so much."

"I thought you understood from what I said to-day," replied Lydia, "that I could not go."

"Why, no, I didn't! I knew you objected; but if I thought it was proper for you to go—"

"I should not go at home," said Lydia, in the same immovable fashion.

"Of course not. Every place has its customs, and in Venice it has *always* been the custom to go to the opera on Sunday night." This fact had no visible weight with Lydia, and after a pause her aunt added, "Didn't Paul himself say to do in Rome as the Romans do?"

"No, aunt Josephine," cried Lydia, indignantly, "he did *not*!"

Mrs. Erwin turned to her husband with a face of appeal, and he answered, "Really, my dear, I think you're mistaken. I always had the impression that the saying was—an Americanism of some sort."

"But it doesn't matter," interposed Lydia decisively. "I couldn't go, if I didn't think it was right, whoever said it."

"Oh, well," began Mrs. Erwin, "if you wouldn't mind what *Paul* said—" She suddenly checked herself, and after a little silence she resumed, kindly, "I won't try to force you, Lydia. I didn't realize what a very short time it is since you left home, and how you still have all those ideas. I wouldn't distress you about them for the world, my dear. I want you to feel at home with me, and I'll make it as like home for you as I can in everything. Henshaw, I think you must go alone, this evening. I will stay with Lydia."

"Oh, no, no! I couldn't let you; I can't let you! I shall not know what to do if I keep you at home. Oh, don't leave it that way, please! I shall feel so badly about it—"

"Why, we can both stay," suggested Mr. Erwin, kindly.

Lydia's lips trembled and her eyes glistened, and Mrs. Erwin said, "I'll go with you, Henshaw. I'll be ready in half an hour. I won't dress *much*." She added this as if not to dress a great deal at the opera Sunday night might somehow be accepted as an observance of the Sabbath.

XXIV

The next morning Veronica brought Lydia a little scrawl
from her aunt, bidding the girl come and breakfast with
her in her room at nine.

"Well, my dear," her aunt called to her from her pillow,
when she appeared, "you find me flat enough, this
morning. If there was anything wrong about going to the
opera last night, I was properly punished for it. Such
wretched stuff as *I* never heard! And instead of the new
ballet that they promised, they gave an old thing that I had
seen till I was sick of it. You didn't miss much, I can tell
you. How fresh and bright you *do* look, Lydia!" she
sighed. "Did you sleep well? Were you lonesome while
we were gone? Veronica says you were reading the whole
evening. Are you fond of reading?"

"I don't think I am, very," said Lydia. "It was a book that I
began on the ship. It's a novel." She hesitated. "I wasn't
reading it; I was just looking at it."

"What a queer child you are! I suppose you were dying to
read it, and wouldn't because it was Sunday. Well!" Mrs.
Erwin put her hand under her pillow, and pulled out a
gossamer handkerchief, with which she delicately touched
her complexion here and there, and repaired with an
instinctive rearrangement of powder the envious ravages

W. D. Howells

of a slight rash about her nose. "I respect your high principles beyond anything, Lydia, and if they can only be turned in the right direction they will never be any disadvantage to you." Veronica came in with the breakfast on a tray, and Mrs. Erwin added, "Now, pull up that little table, and bring your chair, my dear, and let us take it easy. I like to talk while I'm breakfasting. Will you pour out my chocolate? That's it, in the ugly little pot with the wooden handle; the copper one's for you, with coffee in it. I never could get that repose which seems to come perfectly natural to you. I was always inclined to be a little rowdy, my dear, and I've had to fight hard against it, without any help from *either* of my husbands; men like it; they think it's funny. When I was first married, I was very young, and so was he; it was a real love match; and my husband was very well off, and when I began to be delicate, nothing would do but he must come to Europe with me. How little I ever expected to outlive him!"

"You don't look very sick now," began Lydia.

"Ill," said her aunt. "You must say ill. Sick is an Americanism."

"It's in the Bible," said Lydia, gravely.

"Oh, there are a great many words in the *Bible* you can't use," returned her aunt. "No, I don't look ill now, and I'm worlds better. But I couldn't live a year in any other climate, I suppose. You seem to take after your mother's side. Well, as I was saying, the European ways didn't come natural to me, at all. I used to have a great deal of gayety when I was a girl, and I liked beaux and attentions; and I had very free ways. I couldn't get their stiffness here for years and years, and all through my widowhood it was one wretched failure with me. Do what I would, I was always violating the most essential rules, and the worst of it was that it only seemed to make me the more popular. I do believe it was nothing but my rowdiness that attracted Mr. Erwin; but I determined when I had got an Englishman I would make one bold strike for the proprieties, and have them, or die in the attempt. I determined that no Englishwoman I ever saw should outdo me in strict conformity to all the usages of European society. So I cut myself off from all the Americans, and went with nobody but the English."

"Do you like them better?" asked Lydia, with the blunt, child-like directness that had already more than once startled her aunt.

"*Like* them! I detest them! If Mr. Erwin were a real Englishman, I think I should go crazy; but he's been so little in his own country—all his life in India, nearly, and the rest on the Continent,—that he's quite human; and no American husband was ever more patient and indulgent; and *that*'s saying a good deal. He would be glad to have nothing but Americans around; he has an enthusiasm for them,—or for what he supposes they are. Like the English! You ought to have heard them during our war; it would have made your blood boil! And then how they came crawling round after it was all over, and trying to pet us up! Ugh!"

"If you feel so about them," said Lydia, as before, "why do you want to go with them so much?"

"My dear," cried her aunt, "*to beat them with their own weapons on their own ground*,—to show them that an American can be more European than any of them, if she chooses! And now you've come here with looks and temperament and everything just to my hand. You're more beautiful than any English girl ever dreamt of being; you're very distinguished-looking; your voice is perfectly divine; and you're colder than an iceberg. *Oh*, if I only had one winter with you in Rome, I think I should die in peace!" Mrs. Erwin paused, and drank her chocolate, which she had been letting cool in the eagerness of her discourse. "But, never mind," she continued, "we will do the best we can here. I've seen English girls going out two or three together, without protection, in Rome and Florence; but I mean that you shall be quite Italian in that respect. The Italians never go out without a chaperone of some sort, and you must never be seen without me, or your uncle, or Veronica. Now I'll tell you how you must do at parties, and so on. You must be very retiring; you're that, any way; but you must always keep close to me. It doesn't do for young people to talk much together in society; it makes scandal about a girl. If you dance, you must always hurry back to me. Dear me!" exclaimed Mrs. Erwin, "I remember how, when I was a girl, I used to hang on to the young men's arms, and promenade with them after a dance, and go out to supper with them, and flirt on the stairs,—*such* times! But that wouldn't do here, Lydia. It would ruin a girl's reputation; she could hardly walk arm in arm with a young man if she was engaged to him." Lydia blushed darkly red, and then turned paler than usual, while her aunt went on. "You might do it, perhaps, and have it set down to American eccentricity or under-breeding, but I'm not going to have that. I intend you to be just as dull and diffident in society as if you were an Italian, and *more* than if you were English. Your voice, of course, is a difficulty. If you sing, that will make you conspicuous, in spite of everything. But I don't see why that can't be turned to advantage; it's no worse than your beauty. Yes, if you're so splendid-looking and so gifted, and at the same time as stupid as the rest, it's so much clear gain. It will come easy for you to be shy with men, for I suppose you've hardly ever talked with any, living up there in that out-of-the-way village; and your manner is very good. It's reserved, and yet it isn't green.

The way," continued Mrs. Erwin, "to treat men in Europe is to behave as if they were guilty till they prove themselves innocent. All you have to do is to reverse all your American ideas. But here I am, lecturing you as if you had been just such a girl as I was, with half a dozen love affairs on her hands at once, and no end of gentlemen friends. Europe won't be hard for you, my dear, for you haven't got anything to unlearn. But *some* girls that come over!—it's perfectly ridiculous, the trouble they get into, and the time they have getting things straight. They take it for granted that men in good society are gentlemen,— what we mean by gentlemen."

Lydia had been letting her coffee stand, and had scarcely tasted the delicious French bread and the sweet Lombard butter of which her aunt ate so heartily. "Why, child," said Mrs. Erwin, at last, "where is your appetite? One would think you were the elderly invalid who had been up late. Did you find it too exciting to sit at home *looking* at a novel? What was it? If it's a new story I should like to see it. But you didn't bring a novel from South Bradfield with you?"

"No," said Lydia, with a husky reluctance. "One of the— passengers gave it to me."

"Had you many passengers? But of course not. That was what made it so delightful when I came over that way. I was newly married then, and with spirits—oh dear me!— for anything. It was one adventure, the whole way; and we got so well acquainted, it was like one family. I suppose your grandfather put you in charge of some family. I know artists sometimes come out that way, and people for their health."

"There was no family on our ship," said Lydia. "My state-room had been fixed up for the captain's wife—"

"Our captain's wife was along, too," interposed Mrs. Erwin. "She was such a joke with us. She had been out to Venice on a voyage before, and used to be always talking about the Du-*cal* Palace. And did they really turn out of their state-room for you?"

"She was not along," said Lydia.

"Not along?" repeated Mrs. Erwin, feebly. "Who—who were the other passengers?"

"There were three gentlemen," answered Lydia.

"Three gentlemen? Three men? Three—And you—and—" Mrs. Erwin fell back upon her pillow, and remained gazing at Lydia, with a sort of remote bewildered pity, as at perdition, not indeed beyond compassion, but far beyond help. Lydia's color had been coming and going, but now it settled to a clear white. Mrs. Erwin commanded herself sufficiently to resume: "And there were—there were—no other ladies?"

"No."

"And you were—"

"I was the only woman on board," replied Lydia. She rose abruptly, striking the edge of the table in her movement, and setting its china and silver jarring. "Oh, I know what you mean, aunt Josephine, but two days ago I couldn't have dreamt it! From the time the ship sailed till I reached this wicked place, there wasn't a word said nor a look looked to make me think I wasn't just as right and safe there as if I had been in my own room at home. They were never anything but kind and good to me. They never let me think that they could be my enemies, or that I must suspect them and be on the watch against them. They were Americans! I had to wait for one of your Europeans to teach me that,—for that officer who was here yesterday—"

"The cavaliere? Why, where—"

"He spoke to me in the cars, when Mr. Erwin was asleep! Had he any right to do so?"

"He would think he had, if he thought you were alone," said Mrs. Erwin, plaintively. "I don't see how we could resent it. It was simply a mistake on his part. And now you see, Lydia—"

"Oh, I see how my coming the way I have will seem to all these people!" cried Lydia, with passionate despair. "I know how it will seem to that married woman who lets a man be in love with her, and that old woman who can't live with her husband because he's too good and kind, and that girl who swears and doesn't know who her father is, and that impudent painter, and that officer who thinks he has the right to insult women if he finds them alone! I wonder the sea doesn't swallow up a place where even Americans go to the theatre on the Sabbath!"

"Lydia, Lydia! It isn't so bad as it seems to you," pleaded her aunt, thrown upon the defensive by the girl's outburst. "There are ever so many good and nice people in Venice, and I know them, too,—Italians as well as foreigners. And even amongst those you saw, Miss Landini is one of the kindest girls in the world, and she had just been to see her old teacher when we met her,—she half takes care of him; and Lady Fenleigh's a perfect mother to the poor; and I never was at the Countess Tatocka's except in the most distant way, at a ball where everybody went; and is it better to let your uncle go to the opera alone, or to go with him? You told me to go with him yourself; and they consider Sunday over, on the Continent, after morning service, any way!"

"Oh, it makes no difference!" retorted Lydia, wildly. "I am going away. I am going home. I have money enough to get to Trieste, and the ship is there, and Captain Jenness will take me back with him. Oh!" she moaned. "*He* has been in Europe, too, and I suppose he's like the rest of you; and he thought because I was alone and helpless he had the right to—Oh, I see it, I see now that he never meant anything, and—Oh, oh, oh!" She fell on her knees beside the bed, as if crushed to them by the cruel doubt that suddenly overwhelmed her, and flung out her arms on Mrs. Erwin's coverlet—it was of Venetian lace sewed upon silk, a choice bit from the palace of one of the ducal families—and buried her face in it.

Her aunt rose from her pillow, and looked in wonder and trouble at the beautiful fallen head, and the fair young figure shaken with sobs. "He—who—what are you talking about, Lydia? Whom do you mean? Did Captain Jenness—"

"No, no!" wailed the girl, "the one that gave me the book."

"The one that gave you the book? The book you were looking at last night?"

"Yes," sobbed Lydia, with her voice muffled in the coverlet.

Mrs. Erwin lay down again with significant deliberation. Her face was still full of trouble, but of bewilderment no longer. In moments of great distress the female mind is apt to lay hold of some minor anxiety for its distraction, and to find a certain relief in it. "Lydia," said her aunt in a broken voice, "I wish you wouldn't cry in the coverlet: it doesn't hurt the lace, but it stains the silk." Lydia swept her handkerchief under her face but did not lift it. Her aunt accepted the compromise. "How came he to give you the book?"

"Oh, I don't know. I can't tell. I thought it was because— because— It was almost at the very beginning. And after that he walked up and down with me every night, nearly; and he tried to be with me all he could; and he was always saying things to make me think—Oh dear, oh *dear*, oh dear! And he *tried* to make me care for him! Oh, it was cruel, cruel!"

"You mean that he made love to you?" asked her aunt.

"Yes—no—I don't know. He tried to make me care for him, and to make me think he cared for me."

"Did he say he cared for you? Did he—"

"No!"

Mrs. Erwin mused a while before she said, "Yes, it was cruel indeed, poor child, and it was cowardly, too."

"Cowardly?" Lydia lifted her face, and flashed a glance of tearful fire at her aunt. "He is the bravest man in the world! And the most generous and high-minded! He jumped into the sea after that wicked Mr. Hicks, and saved his life, when he disliked him worse than anything!"

"*Who* was Mr. Hicks?"

"He was the one that stopped at Messina. He was the one that got some brandy at Gibraltar, and behaved so dreadfully, and wanted to fight him."

"Whom?"

"This one. The one who gave me the book. And don't you see that his being so good makes it all the worse? Yes; and he pretended to be glad when I told him I thought he was good,—he got me to say it!" She had her face down again in her handkerchief. "And I suppose *you* think it was horrible, too, for me to take his arm, and talk and walk with him whenever he asked me!"

"No, not for you, Lydia," said her aunt, gently. "And don't you think now," she asked after a pause, "that he cared for you?"

"Oh, I *did* think so,—I *did* believe it; but now, *now*—"

"Now, what?"

"Now, I'm afraid that may be he was only playing with me, and putting me off; and pretending that he had something to tell me when he got to Venice, and he never meant anything by anything."

"Is he coming to—" her aunt began, but Lydia broke vehemently out again.

"If he had cared for me, why couldn't he have told me so at once, and not had me wait till he got to Venice? He *knew* I—"

"There are two ways of explaining it," said Mrs. Erwin. "He *may* have been in earnest, Lydia, and felt that he had no right to be more explicit till you were in the care of your friends. That would be the European way which you consider so bad," said Mrs. Erwin. "Under the circumstances, it was impossible for him to keep any distance, and all he could do was to postpone his declaration till there could be something like good form about it. Yes, it might have been that." She was silent, but the troubled look did not leave her face. "I am sorry for you, Lydia," she resumed, "but I don't know that I wish he was in earnest." Lydia looked up at her in dismay. "It might be far less embarrassing the other way, however painful. He may not be at all a suitable person." The tears stood in Lydia's eyes, and all her face expressed a puzzled suspense. "Where was he from?" asked Mrs. Erwin, finally; till then she had been more interested in the lover than the man.

"Boston," mechanically answered Lydia.

"What was his name?"

"Mr. Staniford," owned Lydia, with a blush.

Her aunt seemed dispirited at the sound. "Yes, I know who they are," she sighed.

"And aren't they nice? Isn't he—suitable?" asked Lydia, tremulously.

"Oh, poor child! He's only *too* suitable. I can't explain to you, Lydia; but at home he wouldn't have looked at a girl like you. What sort of looking person is he?"

"He's rather—red; and he has—light hair."

"It must be the family I'm thinking of," said Mrs. Erwin. She had lived nearly twenty years in Europe, and had seldom revisited her native city; but at the sound of a Boston name she was all Bostonian again. She rapidly sketched the history of the family to which she imagined

Staniford to belong. "I remember his sister; I used to see her at school. She must have been five or six years younger than I; and this boy—"

"Why, he's twenty-eight years old!" interrupted Lydia.

"How came he to tell you?"

"I don't know. He said that he looked thirty-four."

"Yes; *she* was always a forward thing too,—with her freckles," said Mrs. Erwin, musingly, as if lost in reminiscences, not wholly pleasing, of Miss Staniford.

"*He* has freckles," admitted Lydia.

"Yes, it's the one," said Mrs. Erwin. "He couldn't have known what your family was from anything you said?"

"We never talked about our families."

"Oh, I dare say! You talked about yourselves?"

"Yes."

"All the time?"

"Pretty nearly."

"And he didn't try to find out who or what you were?"

"He asked a great deal about South Bradfield."

"Of course, that was where he thought you had always belonged." Mrs. Erwin lay quiescent for a while, in apparent uncertainty as to how she should next attack the subject. "How did you first meet?"

Lydia began with the scene on Lucas Wharf, and little by little told the whole story up to the moment of their parting at Trieste. There were lapses and pauses in the story, which her aunt was never at a loss to fill aright. At the end she said, "If it were not for his promising to come here and see you, I should say Mr. Staniford had been flirting, and as it is he may not regard it as anything more than flirtation. Of course, there was his being jealous of Mr. Dunham and Mr. Hicks, as he certainly was; and his wanting to explain about that lady at Messina—yes, that looked peculiar; but he may not have meant anything by it. His parting so at Trieste with you, that might be either because he was embarrassed at its having got to be such a serious thing, or because he really felt badly. Lydia," she asked at last, "what made *you* think he cared for you?"

"I don't know," said the girl; her voice had sunk to a husky whisper. "I didn't believe it till he said he wanted me to be his—conscience, and tried to make me say he was good, and—"

"That's a certain kind of man's way of flirting. It may mean nothing at all. I could tell in an instant, if I saw him."

"He said he would be here this afternoon," murmured Lydia, tremulously.

"This afternoon!" cried Mrs. Erwin. "I must get up!"

At her toilette she had the exaltation and fury of a champion arming for battle.

XXV

Mr. Erwin entered about the completion of her preparations, and without turning round from her glass she said,
"I want you to think of the worst thing you can, Henshaw.
I don't see how I'm ever to lift up my head again." As if
this word had reminded her of her head, she turned it from
side to side, and got the effect in the glass, first of one
ear-ring, and then of the other. Her husband patiently
waited, and she now confronted him. "You may as well
know first as last, Henshaw, and I want you to prepare
yourself for it. Nothing can be done, and you will just
have to live through it. Lydia—has come over—on that
ship—alone,—with three young men,—and not the
shadow—not the ghost—of another woman—on board!"
Mrs. Erwin gesticulated with her hand-glass in delivering
the words, in a manner at once intensely vivid and
intensely solemn, yet somehow falling short of the due
tragic effect. Her husband stood pulling his mustache
straight down, while his wife turned again to the mirror,
and put the final touches to her personal appearance with
hands which she had the effect of having desperately
washed of all responsibility. He stood so long in this
meditative mood that she was obliged to be peremptory
with his image in the glass. "Well?" she cried.

"Why, my dear," said Mr. Erwin, at last, "they were all
Americans together, you know."

"And what difference does that make?" demanded Mrs. Erwin, whirling from his image to the man again.

"Why, of course, you know, it isn't as if they were— English." Mrs. Erwin flung down three hair-pins upon her dressing-case, and visibly despaired. "Of course you don't expect your countrymen—" His wife's appearance was here so terrible that he desisted, and resumed by saying, "Don't be vexed, my dear. I—I rather like it, you know. It strikes me as a genuine bit of American civilization."

"American civilization! Oh, Henshaw!" wailed Mrs. Erwin, "is it possible that after all I've said, and done, and lived, you still think that any one but a girl from the greenest little country place could do such a thing as that? Well, it is no use trying to enlighten English people. You like it, do you? Well, I'm not sure that the Englishman who misunderstands American things and likes them isn't a little worse than the Englishman who misunderstands them and dislikes them. You *all* misunderstand them. And would you like it, if one of the young men had been making love to Lydia?"

The amateur of our civilization hesitated and was serious, but he said at last, "Why, you know, I'm not surprised. She's so uncommonly pretty. I—I suppose they're engaged?" he suggested.

His wife held her peace for scorn. Then she said, "The gentleman is of a very good Boston family, and would no more think of engaging himself to a young girl without the knowledge of her friends than you would. Besides, he's been in Europe a great deal."

"I wish I could meet some Americans who hadn't been in Europe," said Mr. Erwin. "I should like to see what you call the simon-pure American. As for the young man's not engaging himself, it seems to me that he didn't avail himself of his national privileges. I should certainly have done it in his place, if I'd been an American."

"Well, if you'd been an American, you wouldn't," answered his wife.

"Why?"

"Because an American would have had too much delicacy."

"I don't understand that."

"I know you don't, Henshaw. And there's where you show yourself an Englishman."

"Really," said her husband, "you're beginning to crow, my dear. Come, I like that a great deal better than your cringing to the effete despotisms of the Old World, as your Fourth of July orators have it. It's almost impossible to get a bit of good honest bounce out of an American, nowadays,—to get him to spread himself, as you say."

"All that is neither here nor there, Henshaw," said his wife. "The question is how to receive Mr. Staniford— that's his name—when he comes. How are we to regard him? He's coming here to see Lydia, and she thinks he's coming to propose."

"Excuse me, but how does she regard him?"

"Oh, there's no question about that, poor child. She's *dead* in love with him, and can't understand why he didn't propose on shipboard."

"And she isn't an Englishman, either!" exulted Mr. Erwin.

"It appears that there are Americans and Americans, and that the men of your nation have more delicacy than the women like."

"Don't be silly," said his wife. "Of course, women always think what they would do in such cases, if they were men; but if men did what women think they would do if they were men, the women would be disgusted."

"Oh!"

"Yes. Her feeling in the matter is no guide."

"Do you know his family?" asked Mr. Erwin.

"I think I do. Yes, I'm sure I do."

"Are they nice people?"

"Haven't I told you they were a good Boston family?"

"Then upon my word, I don't see that we've to take any attitude at all. I don't see that we've to regard him in one way or the other. It quite remains for him to make the first move."

As if they had been talking of nothing but dress before, Mrs. Erwin asked: "Do you think I look better in this black mexicaine, or would you wear your ecru?"

"I think you look very well in this. But why—He isn't going to propose to you, I hope?"

"I must have on something decent to receive him in. What time does the train from Trieste get in?"

"At three o'clock."

W. D. Howells

"It's one, now. There's plenty of time, but there isn't any too much. I'll go and get Lydia ready. Or perhaps you'll tap on her door, Henshaw, and send her here. Of course, this is the end of her voice,—if it is the end."

"It's the end of having an extraordinarily pretty girl in the house. I don't at all like it, you know,—having her whisked away in this manner."

Mrs. Erwin refused to let her mind wander from the main point. "He'll be round as soon as he can, after he arrives. I shall expect him by four, at the latest."

"I fancy he'll stop for his dinner before he comes," said Mr. Erwin.

"Not at all," retorted his wife, haughtily. And with his going out of the room, she set her face in a resolute cheerfulness, for the task of heartening Lydia when she should appear; but it only expressed misgiving when the girl came in with her yachting-dress on. "Why, Lydia, shall you wear that?"

Lydia swept her dress with a downward glance.

"I thought I would wear it. I thought he—I should seem— more natural in it. I wore it all the time on the ship, except Sundays. He said— he liked it the best."

Mrs. Erwin shook her head. "It wouldn't do. Everything must be on a new basis now. He might like it; but it would be too romantic, wouldn't it, don't you think?" She shook her head still, but less decisively. "Better wear your silk. Don't you think you'd better wear your silk? This is very pretty, and the dark blue does become you, awfully. Still, I don't know—*I* don't know, either! A great many English wear those careless things in the house. Well, *wear* it,

Lydia! You *do* look perfectly killing in it. I'll tell you: your uncle was going to ask you to go out in his boat; he's got one he rows himself, and this is a boating costume; and you know you could time yourselves so as to get back just right, and you could come in with this on—"

Lydia turned pale. "Oughtn't I—oughtn't I—to be here?" she faltered.

Her aunt laughed gayly. "Why, he'll ask for *me*, Lydia."

"For you?" asked Lydia, doubtfully.

"Yes. And I can easily keep him till you get back. If you're here by four—"

"The train," said Lydia, "arrives at three."

"How did you know?" asked her aunt, keenly.

Lydia's eyelids fell even lower than their wont.

"I looked it out in that railroad guide in the parlor."

Her aunt kissed her. "And you've thought the whole thing out, dear, haven't you? I'm glad to see you so happy about it."

"Yes," said the girl, with a fluttering breath, "I have thought it out, and *I believe him*. I—" She tried to say something more, but could not.

Mrs. Erwin rang the bell, and sent for her husband. "He knows about it, Lydia," she said.

"He's just as much interested as we are, dear, but you needn't be worried. He's a perfect post for not showing a thing if you don't want him to. He's really quite superhuman, in that,—equal to a woman. You can talk Americanisms with him. If we sat here staring at each other till four o'clock,—he *must* go to his hotel before he comes here; and I say four at the earliest; and it's much more likely to be five or six, or perhaps evening,—I should die!"

Mr. Erwin's rowing was the wonder of all Venice. There was every reason why he should fall overboard at each stroke, as he stood to propel the boat in the gondolier fashion, except that he never yet had done so. It was sometimes his fortune to be caught on the shallows by the falling tide; but on that day he safely explored the lagoons, and returned promptly at four o'clock to the palace.

His wife was standing on the balcony, looking out for them, and she smiled radiantly down into Lydia's anxiously lifted face. But when she met the girl at the head of the staircase in the great hall, she embraced her, and said, with the same gay smile, "He hasn't come yet, dear, and of course he won't come till after dinner. If I hadn't been as silly as you are, Lydia, I never should have let you expect him sooner. He'll want to go to his hotel: and no matter how impatient he is, he'll want to dress, and be a little ceremonious about his call. You know we're strangers to him, whatever *you* are."

"Yes," said Lydia, mechanically. She was going to sit down, as she was; of her own motion she would not have stirred from the place till he came, or it was certain he would not come; but her aunt would not permit the despair into which she saw her sinking.

She laughed resolutely, and said, "I think we must give up the little sentimentality of meeting him in that dress, now.

Go and change it, Lydia. Put on your silk,—or wait: let me go with you. I want to try some little effects with your complexion. We've experimented with the simple and familiar, and now we'll see what can be done in the way of the magnificent and unexpected. I'm going to astonish the young man with a Venetian beauty; you know you look Italian, Lydia."

"Yes, he said so," answered Lydia.

"Did he? That shows he has an eye, and he'll appreciate what we are going to do."

She took Lydia to her own room, for the greater convenience of her experiments, and from that moment she did not allow her to be alone; she scarcely allowed her to be silent; she made her talk, she kept her in movement. At dinner she permitted no lapse. "Henshaw," she said, "Lydia has been telling me about a storm they had just before they reached Gibraltar. I wish you would tell her of the typhoon you were in when you first went out to India." Her husband obeyed; and then recurring to the days of his civil employment in India, he told stories of tiger-hunts, and of the Sepoy mutiny. Mrs. Erwin would not let them sit very long at table. After dinner she asked Lydia to sing, and she suffered her to sing all the American songs her uncle asked for. At eight o'clock she said with a knowing little look at Lydia, which included a sub-wink for her husband, "You may go to your cafe alone, this evening, Henshaw. Lydia and I are going to stay at home and talk South Bradfield gossip. I've hardly had a moment with her yet." But when he was gone, she took Lydia to her own room again, and showed her all her jewelry, and passed the time in making changes in the girl's toilette.

It was like the heroic endeavor of the arctic voyager who

feels the deadly chill in his own veins, and keeps himself alive by rousing his comrade from the torpor stealing over him. They saw in each other's eyes that if they yielded a moment to the doubt in their hearts they were lost.

At ten o'clock Mrs. Erwin said abruptly, "Go to bed, Lydia!" Then the girl broke down, and abandoned herself in a storm of tears. "Don't cry, dear, don't cry," pleaded her aunt. "He will be here in the morning, I know he will. He has been delayed."

"No, he's not coming," said Lydia, through her sobs.

"Something has happened," urged Mrs. Erwin.

"No," said Lydia, as before. Her tears ceased as suddenly as they had come. She lifted her head, and drying her eyes looked into her aunt's face. "Are you ashamed of me?" she asked hoarsely.

"Ashamed of you? Oh, poor child—"

"I can't pretend anything. If I had never told you about it at all, I could have kept it back till I died. But now—But you will never hear me speak of it again. It's over." She took up her candle, and stiffly suffering the compassionate embrace with which her aunt clung to her, she walked across the great hall in the vain splendor in which she had been adorned, and shut the door behind her.

XXVI

Dunham lay in a stupor for twenty-four hours, and after that he was delirious, with dim intervals of reason in which they kept him from talking, till one morning he woke and looked up at Staniford with a perfectly clear eye, and said, as if resuming the conservation, "I struck my head on a pile of chains."

"Yes," replied Staniford, with a wan smile, "and you've been out of it pretty near ever since. You mustn't talk."

"Oh, I'm all right," said Dunham. "I know about my being hurt. I shall be cautious. Have you written to Miss Hibbard? I hope you haven't!"

"Yes, I have," replied Staniford. "But I haven't sent the letter," he added, in answer to Dunham's look of distress. "I thought you were going to pull through, in spite of the doctor,—he's wanted to bleed you, and I could hardly keep his lancet out of you,—and so I wrote, mentioning the accident and announcing your complete restoration. The letter merely needs dating and sealing. I'll look it up and have it posted." He began a search in the pockets of his coat, and then went to his portfolio.

"What day is this?" asked Dunham.

W. D. Howells

"Friday," said Staniford, rummaging his portfolio.

"Have you been in Venice?"

"Look here, Dunham! If you begin in that way, I can't talk to you. It shows that you're still out of your head. How could I have been in Venice?"

"But Miss Blood; the Aroostook—"

"Miss Blood went to Venice with her uncle last Saturday. The Aroostook is here in Trieste. The captain has just gone away. He's stood watch and watch with me, while you were off on business."

"But didn't you go to Venice on Monday?"

"Well, hardly," answered Staniford.

"No, you stayed with me,—I see," said Dunham.

"Of course, I wrote to her at once," said Staniford, huskily, "and explained the matter as well as I could without making an ado about it. But now you stop, Dunham. If you excite yourself, there'll be the deuce to pay again."

"I'm not excited," said Dunham, "but I can't help thinking how disappointed—But of course you've heard from her?"

"Well, there's hardly time, yet," said Staniford, evasively.

"Why, yes, there is. Perhaps your letter miscarried."

"Don't!" cried Staniford, in a hollow under-voice, which he broke through to add, "Go to sleep, now, Dunham, or keep quiet, somehow."

Dunham was silent for a while, and Staniford continued his search, which he ended by taking the portfolio by one corner, and shaking its contents out on the table. "I don't seem to find it; but I've put it away somewhere. I'll get it." He went to another coat, that hung on the back of a chair, and fumbled in its pockets. "Hello! Here are those letters they brought me from the post-office Saturday night,— Murray's, and Stanton's, and that bore Farrington's. I forgot all about them." He ran the unopened letters over in his hand. "Ah, here's my familiar scrawl—" He stopped suddenly, and walked away to the window, where he stood with his back to Dunham.

"Staniford! What is it?"

"It's—it's my letter to *her*" said Staniford, without looking round.

"Your letter to Miss Blood—not gone?" Staniford, with his face still from him, silently nodded. "Oh!" moaned Dunham, in self-forgetful compassion. "How could it have happened?"

"I see perfectly well," said the other, quietly, but he looked round at Dunham with a face that was haggard. "I sent it out to be posted by the *portier*, and he got it mixed up with these letters for me, and brought it back."

The young men were both silent, but the tears stood in Dunham's eyes. "If it hadn't been for me, it wouldn't have happened," he said.

"No," gently retorted Staniford, "if it hadn't been for *me*, it wouldn't have happened. I made you come from Messina with me, when you wanted to go on to Naples with those people; if I'd had any sense, I should have spoken fully to her before we parted; and it was I who sent you to see if she were on the steamer, when you fell and hurt yourself. I know who's to blame, Dunham. What day did I tell you this was?"

"Friday."

"A week! And I told her to expect me Monday afternoon. A week without a word or a sign of any kind! Well, I might as well take passage in the Aroostook, and go back to Boston again."

"Why, no!" cried Dunham, "you must take the first train to Venice. Don't lose an instant. You can explain everything as soon as you see her."

Staniford shook his head. "If all her life had been different, if she were a woman of the world, it would be different; she would know how to account for some little misgivings on my part; but as it is she wouldn't know how to account for even the appearance of them. What she must have suffered all this week—I can't think of it!" He sat down and turned his face away. Presently he sprang up again. "But I'm going, Dunham. I guess you won't die now; but you may die if you like. I would go over your dead body!"

"Now you are talking sense," said Dunham.

Staniford did not listen; he had got out his railroad guide and was studying it. "No; there are only those two trains a day. The seven o'clock has gone; and the next starts at ten to-night. Great heavens! I could walk it sooner! Dunham," he asked, "do you think I'd better telegraph?"

"What would you say?"

"Say that there's been a mistake; that a letter miscarried;

that I'll be there in the morning; that—"

"Wouldn't that be taking her anxiety a little too much for granted?"

"Yes, that's true. Well, you've got your wits about you now, Dunham," cried Staniford, with illogical bitterness. "Very probably," he added, gloomily, "she doesn't care anything for me, after all."

"That's a good frame of mind to go in," said Dunham.

"Why is it?" demanded Staniford. "Did I ever presume upon any supposed interest in her?"

"You did at first," replied Dunham.

Staniford flushed angrily. But you cannot quarrel with a man lying helpless on his back; besides, what Dunham said was true.

The arrangements for Staniford's journey were quickly made,—so quickly that when he had seen the doctor, and had been down to the Aroostook and engaged Captain Jenness to come and take his place with Dunham for the next two nights, he had twelve hours on his hands before the train for Venice would leave, and he started at last with but one clear perception,—that at the soonest it must be twelve hours more before he could see her.

He had seemed intolerably slow in arriving on the train, but once arrived in Venice he wished that he had come by the steamboat, which would not be in for three hours yet. In despair he went to bed, considering that after he had tossed there till he could endure it no longer, he would still have the resource of getting up, which he would not have unless he went to bed. When he lay down, he found

W. D. Howells

himself drowsy; and while he wondered at this, he fell asleep, and dreamed a strange dream, so terrible that he woke himself by groaning in spirit, a thing which, as he reflected, he had never done before. The sun was piercing the crevice between his shutters, and a glance at his watch showed him that it was eleven o'clock.

The shadow of his dream projected itself into his waking mood, and steeped it in a gloom which he could not escape. He rose and dressed, and meagrely breakfasted. Without knowing how he came there, he stood announced in Mrs. Erwin's parlor, and waited for her to receive him.

His card was brought in to her where she lay in bed. After supporting Lydia through the first sharp shock of disappointment, she had yielded to the prolonged strain, and the girl was now taking care of her. She gave a hysterical laugh as she read the name on the card Veronica brought, and crushing it in her hand, "He's come!" she cried.

"I will not see him!" said Lydia instantly.

"No," assented her aunt. "It wouldn't be at all the thing. Besides, he's asked for me. Your uncle might see him, but he's out of the way; of course he *would* be out of the way. Now, let me see!" The excitement inspired her; she rose in bed, and called for the pretty sack in which she ordinarily breakfasted, and took a look at herself in a hand-glass that lay on the bed. Lydia did not move; she scarcely seemed to breathe; but a swift pulse in her neck beat visibly. "If it would be decent to keep him waiting so long, I could dress, and see him myself. I'm *well* enough." Mrs. Erwin again reflected. "Well," she said at last, "you must see him, Lydia."

"I—" began the girl.

"Yes, you. Some one must. It will be all right. On second thought, I believe I should send you, even if I were quite ready to go myself. This affair has been carried on so far on the American plan, and I think I shall let you finish it without my interference. Yes, as your uncle said when I told him, you're all Americans together; and you *are*. Mr. Staniford has come to see you, though he asks for me. That's perfectly proper; but I can't see him, and I want you to excuse me to him."

"What would you—what must I—" Lydia began again.

"No, Lydia," interrupted her aunt. "I won't tell you a thing. I might have advised you when you first came; but now, I—Well, I think I've lived too long in Europe to be of use in such a case, and I won't have anything to do with it. I won't tell you how to meet him, or what to say; but oh, child,"—here the woman's love of loving triumphed in her breast,—"I wish I was in your place! Go!"

Lydia slowly rose, breathless.

"Lydia!" cried her aunt. "Look at me!" Lydia turned her head. "Are you going to be hard with him?"

"I don't know what he's coming for," said Lydia dishonestly.

"But if he's coming for what you hope?"

"I don't hope for anything."

"But you did. Don't be severe. You're terrible when you're severe."

"I will be just."

"Oh, no, you mustn't, my dear. It won't do at all to be *just* with men, poor fellows. Kiss me, Lydia!" She pulled her down, and kissed her. When the girl had got as far as the door, "Lydia, Lydia!" she called after her. Lydia turned. "Do you realize what dress you've got on?" Lydia looked down at her robe; it was the blue flannel yachting-suit of the Aroostook, which she had put on for convenience in taking care of her aunt. "Isn't it too ridiculous?" Mrs. Erwin meant to praise the coincidence, not to blame the dress. Lydia smiled faintly for answer, and the next moment she stood at the parlor door.

Staniford, at her entrance, turned from looking out of the window and saw her as in his dream, with her hand behind her, pushing the door to; but the face with which she looked at him was not like the dead, sad face of his dream. It was thrillingly alive, and all passions were blent in it,—love, doubt, reproach, indignation; the tears stood in her eyes, but a fire burnt through the tears. With his first headlong impulse to console, explain, deplore, came a thought that struck him silent at sight of her. He remembered, as he had not till then remembered, in all his wild longing and fearing, that there had not yet been anything explicit between them; that there was no engagement; and that he had upon the face of things, at least, no right to offer her more than some formal expression of regret for not having been able to keep his promise to come sooner. While this stupefying thought gradually filled his whole sense to the exclusion of all else, he stood looking at her with a dumb and helpless appeal, utterly stunned and wretched. He felt the life die out of his face and leave it blank, and when at last she spoke, he knew that it was in pity of him, or contempt of him. "Mrs. Erwin is not well," she said, "and she wished me—"

But he broke in upon her: "Oh, don't talk to me of Mrs.

Erwin! It was you I wanted to see. Are *you* well? Are you alive? Do you—" He stopped as precipitately as he began; and after another hopeless pause, he went on piteously: "I don't know where to begin. I ought to have been here five days ago. I don't know what you think of me, or whether you have thought of me at all; and before I can ask I must tell you why I wanted to come then, and why I come now, and why I think I must have come back from the dead to see you. You are all the world to me, and have been ever since I saw you. It seems a ridiculously unnecessary thing to say, I have been looking and acting and living it so long; but I say it, because I choose to have you know it, whether you ever cared for me or not. I thought I was coming here to explain why I had not come sooner, but I needn't do that unless— unless—" He looked at her where she still stood aloof, and he added: "Oh, answer me something, for pity's sake! Don't send me away without a word. There have been times when you wouldn't have done that!"

"Oh, I *did* care for you!" she broke out. "You know I did—"

He was instantly across the room, beside her. "Yes, yes, I know it!" But she shrank away.

"You tried to make me believe you cared for me, by everything you could do. And I did believe you then; and yes, I believed you afterwards, when I didn't know what to believe. You were the one true thing in the world to me. But it seems that you didn't believe it yourself."

"That I didn't believe it myself? That I—I don't know what you mean."

"You took a week to think it over! I have had a week, too, and I have thought it over, too. You have come too late."

"Too late? You don't, you can't, mean—Listen to me, Lydia; I want to tell you—"

"No, there is nothing you can tell me that would change me. I know it, I understand it all."

"But you don't understand what kept me."

"I don't wish to know what made you break your word. I don't care to know. I couldn't go back and feel as I did to you. Oh, that's gone! It isn't that you did not come—that you made me wait and suffer; but you knew how it would be with me after I got here, and all the things I should find out, and how I should feel! And you stayed away! I don't know whether I can forgive you, even; oh, I'm afraid I don't; but I can never care for you again. Nothing but a case of life and death—"

"It was a case of life and death!"

Lydia stopped in her reproaches, and looked at him with wistful doubt, changing to a tender fear.

"Oh, have you been hurt? Have you been sick?" she pleaded, in a breaking voice, and made some unconscious movement toward him. He put out his hand, and would have caught one of hers, but she clasped them in each other.

"No, not I,—Dunham—"

"Oh!" said Lydia, as if this were not at all enough.

"He fell and struck his head, the night you left. I thought he would die." Staniford reported his own diagnosis, not the doctor's; but he was perhaps in the right to do this. "I had made him go down to the wharf with me; I wanted to see you again, before you started, and I thought we might find you on the boat." He could see her face relenting; her hands released each other. "He was delirious till yesterday. I couldn't leave him."

"Oh, why didn't you write to me?" She ignored Dunham as completely as if he had never lived. "You knew that I—" Her voice died away, and her breast rose.

"I did write—"

"But how,—I never got it."

"No,—it was not posted, through a cruel blunder. And then I thought —I got to thinking that you didn't care—"

"Oh," said the girl. "Could you doubt me?"

"You doubted me," said Staniford, seizing his advantage. "I brought the letter with me to prove *my* truth." She did not look at him, but she took the letter, and ran it greedily into her pocket. "It's well I did so, since you don't believe my word."

"Oh, yes,—yes, I know it," she said; "I never doubted it!" Staniford stood bemazed, though he knew enough to take the hands she yielded him; but she suddenly caught them away again, and set them against his breast. "I was very wrong to suspect you ever; I'm sorry I did; but there's something else. I don't know how to say what I want to say. But it must be said."

"Is it something disagreeable?" asked Staniford, lightly.

"It's right," answered Lydia, unsmilingly.

"Oh, well, don't say it!" he pleaded; "or don't say it

now,—not till you've forgiven me for the anxiety I've caused you; not till you've praised me for trying to do what I thought the right thing. You can't imagine how hard it was for one who hasn't the habit!"

"I do praise you for it. There's nothing to forgive *you*; but I can't let you care for me unless I know—unless"—She stopped, and then, "Mr. Staniford," she began firmly, "since I came here, I've been learning things that I didn't know before. They have changed the whole world to me, and it can never be the same again."

"I'm sorry for that; but if they haven't changed you, the world may go."

"No, not if we're to live in it," answered the girl, with the soberer wisdom women keep at such times. "It will have to be known how we met. What will people say? They will laugh."

"I don't think they will in my presence," said Staniford, with swelling nostrils. "They may use their pleasure elsewhere."

"And I shouldn't care for their laughing, either," said Lydia. "But oh, why did you come?"

"Why did I come?"

"Was it because you felt bound by anything that's happened, and you wouldn't let me bear the laugh alone? I'm not afraid for myself. I shall never blame you. You can go perfectly free."

"But I don't want to go free!"

Lydia looked at him with piercing earnestness. "Do you

think I'm proud?" she asked.

"Yes, I think you are," said Staniford, vaguely.

"It isn't for myself that I should be proud with other people. But I would rather die than bring ridicule upon one I—upon you."

"I can believe that," said Staniford, devoutly, and patiently reverencing the delay of her scruples.

"And if—and—" Her lips trembled, but she steadied her trembling voice. "If they laughed at you, and thought of me in a slighting way because—" Staniford gave a sort of roar of grief and pain to know how her heart must have been wrung before she could come to this. "You were all so good that you didn't let me think there was anything strange about it—"

"Oh, good heavens! We only did what it was our precious and sacred privilege to do! We were all of one mind about it from the first. But don't torture yourself about it, my darling. It's over now; it's past—no, it's present, and it will always be, forever, the dearest and best thing in life Lydia, do you believe that I love you?"

"Oh, I must!"

"And don't you believe that I'm telling you the truth when I say that I wouldn't, for all the world can give or take, change anything that's been?"

"Yes, I do believe you. Oh, I haven't said at all what I wanted to say! There was a great deal that I ought to say. I can't seem to recollect it."

He smiled to see her grieving at this recreance of her

W. D. Howells

memory to her conscience, "Well, you shall have a whole lifetime to recall it in."

"No, I must try to speak now. And you must tell me the truth now,—no matter what it costs either of us." She laid her hands upon his extended arms, and grasped them intensely. "There's something else. I want to ask you what *you* thought when you found me alone on that ship with all of you." If she had stopped at this point, Staniford's cause might have been lost, but she went on: "I want to know whether you were ever ashamed of me, or despised me for it; whether you ever felt that because I was helpless and friendless there, you had the right to think less of me than if you had first met me here in this house."

It was still a terrible question, but it offered a loop-hole of escape, which Staniford was swift to seize. Let those who will justify the answer with which he smiled into her solemn eyes: "I will leave you to say." A generous uncandor like this goes as far with a magnanimous and serious-hearted woman as perhaps anything else.

"Oh, I knew it, I knew it!" cried Lydia. And then, as he caught her to him at last, "Oh—oh—are you *sure* it's right?"

"I have no doubt of it," answered Staniford. Nor had he any question of the strategy through which he had triumphed in this crucial test. He may have thought that there were always explanations that had to be made afterwards, or he may have believed that he had expiated in what he had done and suffered for her any slight which he had felt; possibly, he considered that she had asked more than she had a right to do. It is certain that he said with every appearance of sincerity, "It began the moment I saw you on the wharf, there, and when I came to know my mind I kept it from you only till I could tell you here.

But now I wish I hadn't! Life is too short for such a week as this."

"No," said Lydia, "you acted for the best, and you are—good."

"I'll keep that praise till I've earned it," answered Staniford.

XXVII

In the Campo Santi Apostoli at Venice there stands, a little apart from the church of that name, a chapel which has been for many years the place of worship for the Lutheran congregation. It was in this church that Staniford and Lydia were married six weeks later, before the altar under Titian's beautiful picture of Christ breaking bread.

The wedding was private, but it was not quite a family affair. Miss Hibbard had come down with her mother from Dresden, to complete Dunham's cure, and she was there with him perfectly recovered; he was not quite content, of course, that the marriage should not take place in the English chapel, but he was largely consoled by the candles burning on the altar. The Aroostook had been delayed by repairs which were found necessary at Trieste, and Captain Jenness was able to come over and represent the ship at the wedding ceremony, and at the lunch which followed. He reserved till the moment of parting a supreme expression of good-will. When he had got a hand of Lydia's and one of Staniford's in each of his, with his wrists crossed, he said, "Now, I ain't one to tack round, and stand off and on a great deal, but what I want to say is just this: the Aroostook sails next week, and if you two are a mind to go back in her, the ship's yours, as I said to Miss Blood, here,—I mean Mis' Staniford; well, I *hain't* had much time to get used to it!—when she first come aboard there at Boston. I don't mean any pay; I want you to go back as my guests. You can use the cabin for your parlor; and I promise you I won't take any other passengers *this* time. I declare," said Captain Jenness, lowering his voice, and now referring to Hicks for the first time since the day of his escapade, "I did feel dreadful about that fellow!"

"Oh, never mind," replied Staniford. "If it hadn't been for Hicks perhaps I mightn't have been here." He exchanged glances with his wife, that showed they had talked all that matter over.

The captain grew confidential. "Mr. Mason told me he saw you lending that chap money. I hope he didn't give you the slip?"

"No; it came to me here at Blumenthals' the other day."

"Well, that's right! It all worked together for good, as you say. Now you come!"

"What do you say, my dear?" asked Staniford, on whom the poetic fitness of the captain's proposal had wrought.

Women are never blinded by romance, however much they like it in the abstract. "It's coming winter. Do you think you wouldn't be seasick?" returned the bride of an hour, with the practical wisdom of a matron.

Staniford laughed. "She's right, captain. I'm no sailor. I'll get home by the all-rail route as far as I can."

Captain Jenness threw back his head, and laughed too. "Good! That's about it." And he released their hands, so as to place one hairy paw on a shoulder of each. "You'll get along together, I guess."

"But we're just as much obliged to you as if we went, Captain Jenness. And tell all the crew that I'm homesick for the Aroostook, and thank all for being so kind to me; and I thank *you*, Captain Jenness!" Lydia looked at her husband, and then startled the captain with a kiss.

He blushed all over, but carried it off as boldly as he could. "Well, well," he said, "that's right! If you change your minds before the Aroostook sails, you let me know."

This affair made a great deal of talk in Venice, where the common stock of leisure is so great that each person may without self-reproach devote a much larger share of attention to the interests of the others than could be given elsewhere. The decorous fictions in which Mrs. Erwin draped the singular facts of the acquaintance and court-ship of Lydia and Staniford were what unfailingly asto-nished and amused him, and he abetted them without scruple. He found her worldliness as innocent as the unworldliness of Lydia, and he gave Mrs. Erwin his hearty sympathy when she ingenuously owned that the effort to throw dust in the eyes of her European acquaintance was simply killing her. He found endless refreshment in the contemplation of her attitude towards her burdensome little world, and in her reasons for enslaving herself to it. He was very good friends with both of the Erwins. When he could spare the time from Lydia, he went about with her uncle in his boat, and respected his skill in rowing it without falling overboard. He could not see why any one should be so much interested in the American character and dialect as Mr. Erwin was; but he did not object, and he reflected that after all they were not what their admirer supposed them.

The Erwins came with the Stanifords as far as Paris on

their way home, and afterwards joined them in California, where Staniford bought a ranch, and found occupation if not profit in its management. Once cut loose from her European ties, Mrs. Erwin experienced an incomparable repose and comfort in the life of San Francisco; it was, she declared, the life for which she had really been adapted, after all; and in the climate of Santa Barbara she found all that she had left in Italy. In that land of strange and surprising forms of every sort, her husband has been very happy in the realization of an America surpassing even his wildest dreams, and he has richly stored his note-book with philological curiosities. He hears around him the vigorous and imaginative locutions of the Pike language, in which, like the late Canon Kingsley, he finds a Scandinavian hugeness; and pending the publication of his Hand-Book of Americanisms, he is in confident search of the miner who uses his pronouns cockney-wise. Like other English observers, friendly and unfriendly, he does not permit the facts to interfere with his preconceptions.

Staniford's choice long remained a mystery to his acquaintances, and was but partially explained by Mrs. Dunham, when she came home. "Why, I suppose he fell in love with her," she said. "Of course, thrown together that way, as they were, for six weeks, it might have happened to anybody; but James Staniford was always the most consummate flirt that breathed; and he never could see a woman, without coming up, in that metaphysical way of his, and trying to interest her in him. He was always laughing at women, but there never was a man who cared more for them. From all that I could learn from Charles, he began by making fun of her, and all at once he became perfectly infatuated with her. I don't see why. I never could get Charles to tell me anything remarkable that she said or did. She was simply a country girl, with country ideas, and no sort of cultivation. Why, there was

W. D. Howells

nothing to her. He's done the wisest thing he could by taking her out to California. She never would have gone down, here. I suppose James Staniford knew that as well as any of us; and if he finds it worth while to bury himself with her there, we've no reason to complain. She did *sing*, wonderfully; that is, her voice was perfectly divine. But of course that's all over, now. She didn't seem to care much for it; and she really knew so little of life that I don't believe she could form the idea of an artistic career, or feel that it was any sacrifice to give it up. James Staniford was not worth any such sacrifice; but she couldn't know that either. She was good, I suppose. She was very stiff, and she hadn't a word to say for herself. I think she was cold. To be sure, she was a beauty; I really never saw anything like it,—that pale complexion some brunettes have, with her hair growing low, and such eyes and lashes!"

"Perhaps the beauty had something to do with his falling in love with her," suggested a listener. The ladies present tried to look as if this ought not to be sufficient.

"Oh, very likely," said Mrs. Dunham. She added, with an air of being the wreck of her former self, "But we all know what becomes of *beauty* after marriage."

The mind of Lydia's friends had been expressed in regard to her marriage, when the Stanifords, upon their arrival home from Europe, paid a visit to South Bradfield. It was in the depths of the winter following their union, and the hill country, stern and wild even in midsummer, wore an aspect of savage desolation. It was sheeted in heavy snow, through which here and there in the pastures, a craggy bowlder lifted its face and frowned, and along the woods the stunted pines and hemlocks blackened against a background of leafless oaks and birches. A northwest wind cut shrill across the white wastes, and from the crests of the billowed drifts drove a scud of stinging particles in their faces, while the sun, as high as that of Italy, coldly blazed from a cloudless blue sky. Ezra Perkins, perched on the seat before them, stiff and silent as if he were frozen there, drove them from Bradfield Junction to South Bradfield in the long wagon-body set on bob-sleds, with which he replaced his Concord coach in winter. At the station he had sparingly greeted Lydia, as if she were just back from Greenfield, and in the interest of personal independence had ignored a faint motion of hers to shake hands; at her grandfather's gate, he set his passengers down without a word, and drove away, leaving Staniford to get in his trunk as he might.

"Well, I declare," said Miss Maria, who had taken one end of the trunk in spite of him, and was leading the way up through the path cleanly blocked out of the snow, "that Ezra Perkins is enough to make you wish he'd *stayed* in Dakoty!"

Staniford laughed, as he had laughed at everything on the way from the station, and had probably thus wounded Ezra Perkins's susceptibilities. The village houses, separated so widely by the one long street, each with its path neatly tunneled from the roadway to the gate; the meeting-house, so much vaster than the present needs of worship, and looking blue-cold with its never-renewed single coat of white paint; the graveyard set in the midst of the village, and showing, after Ezra Perkins's disappearance, as many signs of life as any other locality, realized in the most satisfactory degree his theories of what winter must be in such a place as South Bradfield. The burning smell of the sheet-iron stove in the parlor, with its battlemented top of filigree iron work; the grimness of the horsehair-covered best furniture; the care with which the old-fashioned fire-places had been walled up, and all accessible character of the period to which the house belonged had been effaced, gave him an equal pleasure. He went about with his arm round Lydia's waist, examining these things, and yielding to the joy they caused him, when they were alone. "Oh, my darling," he said, in one of these accesses of delight, "when I think that it's my privilege to take you away from all this, I begin to feel not so very unworthy, after all."

But he was very polite, as Miss Maria owned, when Mr. and Mrs. Goodlow came in during the evening, with two or three unmarried ladies of the village, and he kept them from falling into the frozen silence which habitually expresses social enjoyment in South Bradfield when strangers are present. He talked about the prospects of Italian advancement to an equal state of intellectual and moral perfection with rural New England, while Mr. Goodlow listened, rocking himself back and forth in the hair-cloth arm-chair. Deacon Latham, passing his hand continually along the stove battlements, now and then let his fingers rest on the sheet-iron till he burnt them, and then jerked them suddenly away, to put them, back the next moment, in his absorbing interest. Miss Maria, amidst a murmur of admiration from the ladies, passed sponge-cake and coffee: she confessed afterwards that the evening had been so brilliant to her as to seem almost wicked; and the other ladies, who owned to having lain awake all night on her coffee, said that if they *had* enjoyed themselves they were properly punished for it.

When they were gone, and Lydia and Staniford had said good-night, and Miss Maria, coming in from the kitchen with a hand-lamp for her father, approached the marble-topped centre-table to blow out the large lamp of pea-green glass with red woollen wick, which had shed the full radiance of a sun-burner upon the festival, she faltered at a manifest unreadiness in the old man to go to bed, though the fire was low, and they had both resumed the drooping carriage of people in going about cold houses. He looked excited, and, so far as his unpracticed visage could intimate the emotion, joyous.

"Well, there, Maria!" he said. "You can't say but what he's a master-hand to converse, any way. I'd know as I ever see Mr. Goodlow more struck up with any one. He looked as if every word done him good; I presume it put him in mind of meetin's with brother ministers: I don't suppose but what he misses it some, here. You can't say but what he's a fine appearin' young man. I d'know as I see anything wrong in his kind of dressin' up to the nines, as you may say. As long's he's got the money, I don't see what harm it is. It's all worked for good, Lyddy's going out that way; though it did seem a mysterious providence at the time."

"Well!" began Miss Maria. She paused, as if she had been hurried too far by her feelings, and ought to give them a check before proceeding. "Well, I don't presume you'd notice it, but she's got a spot on her silk, so't a whole breadth's got to come out, and be let in again bottom side up. I guess there's a pair of 'em, for carelessness." She waited a moment before continuing: "I d'know as I like to see a husband puttin' his arm round his wife, even when he don't suppose any one's lookin'; but I d'know but what it's natural, too. But it's one comfort to see't she ain't the least mite silly about *him*. He's dreadful freckled." Miss Maria again paused thoughtfully, while her father burnt his fingers on the stove for the last time, and took them definitively away. "I don't say but what he talked well enough, as far forth as talkin' *goes*; Mr. Goodlow said at the door't he didn't know's he ever passed *many* such evenin's since he'd been in South Bradfield, and I d'know as *I* have. I presume he has his faults; we ain't any of us perfect; but he *does* seem terribly wrapped up in Lyddy. I don't say but what he'll make her a good husband, if she must *have* one. I don't suppose but what people might think, as you may say, 't she'd made out pretty well; and if Lyddy's suited, I d'know as anybody else has got any call to be over particular."

THE END

ABOUT THE AUTHOR

 **William Dean Howells** (March 1, 1837 – May 11, 1920) was an American realist author and literary critic.

Born in Martins Ferry, Ohio, originally Martinsville, to William Cooper and Mary Dean Howells, Howells was the second of eight children. His father was a newspaper editor and printer, and the father moved frequently around Ohio. Howells began to help his father with typesetting and printing work at an early age. In 1852, his father arranged to have one of Howells' poems published in the Ohio State Journal without telling him.

He wrote his first novel, The Wedding Journey, in 1872, but his literary reputation took off with the realist novel, A Modern Instance, published in 1882, which described the decay of a marriage. His 1885 novel The Rise of Silas Lapham is perhaps his best known, describing the rise and fall of an American entrepreneur in the paint business. His social views were also strongly reflected in the novels Annie Kilburn (1888) and A Hazard of New Fortunes (1890). He was particularly outraged by the trials resulting from the Haymarket Riot.

In 1904, he was one of the first seven chosen for membership in the American Academy of Arts and Letters, of which he became president.

Choose from Thousands of 1stWorldLibrary Classics By

A. M. Barnard
Ada Leverson
Adolphus William Ward
Aesop
Agatha Christie
Alexander Aaronsohn
Alexander Kielland
Alexandre Dumas
Alfred Gatty
Alfred Ollivant
Alice Duer Miller
Alice Turner Curtis
Alice Dunbar
Allen Chapman
Alleyne Ireland
Ambrose Bierce
Amelia E. Barr
Amory H. Bradford
Andrew Lang
Andrew McFarland Davis
Andy Adams
Angela Brazil
Anna Alice Chapin
Anna Sewell
Annie Besant
Annie Hamilton Donnell
Annie Payson Call
Annie Roe Carr
Annonaymous
Anton Chekhov
Archibald Lee Fletcher
Arnold Bennett
Arthur C. Benson
Arthur Conan Doyle
Arthur M. Winfield
Arthur Ransome
Arthur Schnitzler
Arthur Train
Atticus
B.H. Baden-Powell
B. M. Bower
B. C. Chatterjee
Baroness Emmuska Orczy
Baroness Orczy
Basil King
Bayard Taylor
Ben Macomber
Bertha Muzzy Bower
Bjornstjerne Bjornson

Booth Tarkington
Boyd Cable
Bram Stoker
C. Collodi
C. E. Orr
C. M. Ingleby
Carolyn Wells
Catherine Parr Traill
Charles A. Eastman
Charles Amory Beach
Charles Dickens
Charles Dudley Warner
Charles Farrar Browne
Charles Ives
Charles Kingsley
Charles Klein
Charles Hanson Towne
Charles Lathrop Pack
Charles Romyn Dake
Charles Whibley
Charles Willing Beale
Charlotte M. Braeme
Charlotte M. Yonge
Charlotte Perkins Stetson
Clair W. Hayes
Clarence Day Jr.
Clarence E. Mulford
Clemence Housman
Confucius
Coningsby Dawson
Cornelis DeWitt Wilcox
Cyril Burleigh
D. H. Lawrence
Daniel Defoe
David Garnett
Dinah Craik
Don Carlos Janes
Donald Keyhoe
Dorothy Kilner
Dougan Clark
Douglas Fairbanks
E. Nesbit
E. P. Roe
E. Phillips Oppenheim
E. S. Brooks
Earl Barnes
Edgar Rice Burroughs
Edith Van Dyne
Edith Wharton

Edward Everett Hale
Edward J. O'Biren
Edward S. Ellis
Edwin L. Arnold
Eleanor Atkins
Eleanor Hallowell Abbott
Eliot Gregory
Elizabeth Gaskell
Elizabeth McCracken
Elizabeth Von Arnim
Ellem Key
Emerson Hough
Emilie F. Carlen
Emily Bronte
Emily Dickinson
Enid Bagnold
Enilor Macartney Lane
Erasmus W. Jones
Ernie Howard Pie
Ethel May Dell
Ethel Turner
Ethel Watts Mumford
Eugene Sue
Eugenie Foa
Eugene Wood
Eustace Hale Ball
Evelyn Everett-green
Everard Cotes
F. H. Cheley
F. J. Cross
F. Marion Crawford
Fannie E. Newberry
Federick Austin Ogg
Ferdinand Ossendowski
Fergus Hume
Florence A. Kilpatrick
Fremont B. Deering
Francis Bacon
Francis Darwin
Frances Hodgson Burnett
Frances Parkinson Keyes
Frank Gee Patchin
Frank Harris
Frank Jewett Mather
Frank L. Packard
Frank V. Webster
Frederic Stewart Isham
Frederick Trevor Hill
Frederick Winslow Taylor

Friedrich Kerst	Hayden Carruth	James Branch Cabell
Friedrich Nietzsche	Helent Hunt Jackson	James DeMille
Fyodor Dostoyevsky	Helen Nicolay	James Joyce
G.A. Henty	Hendrik Conscience	James Lane Allen
G.K. Chesterton	Hendy David Thoreau	James Lane Allen
Gabrielle E. Jackson	Henri Barbusse	James Oliver Curwood
Garrett P. Serviss	Henrik Ibsen	James Oppenheim
Gaston Leroux	Henry Adams	James Otis
George A. Warren	Henry Ford	James R. Driscoll
George Ade	Henry Frost	Jane Abbott
Geroge Bernard Shaw	Henry James	Jane Austen
George Cary Eggleston	Henry Jones Ford	Jane L. Stewart
George Durston	Henry Seton Merriman	Janet Aldridge
George Ebers	Henry W Longfellow	Jens Peter Jacobsen
George Eliot	Herbert A. Giles	Jerome K. Jerome
George Gissing	Herbert Carter	Jessie Graham Flower
George MacDonald	Herbert N. Casson	John Buchan
George Meredith	Herman Hesse	John Burroughs
George Orwell	Hildegard G. Frey	John Cournos
George Sylvester Viereck	Homer	John F. Kennedy
George Tucker	Honore De Balzac	John Gay
George W. Cable	Horace B. Day	John Glasworthy
George Wharton James	Horace Walpole	John Habberton
Gertrude Atherton	Horatio Alger Jr.	John Joy Bell
Gordon Casserly	Howard Pyle	John Kendrick Bangs
Grace E. King	Howard R. Garis	John Milton
Grace Gallatin	Hugh Lofting	John Philip Sousa
Grace Greenwood	Hugh Walpole	John Taintor Foote
Grant Allen	Humphry Ward	Jonas Lauritz Idemil Lie
Guillermo A. Sherwell	Ian Maclaren	Jonathan Swift
Gulielma Zollinger	Inez Haynes Gillmore	Joseph A. Altsheler
Gustav Flaubert	Irving Bacheller	Joseph Carey
H. A. Cody	Isabel Cecilia Williams	Joseph Conrad
H. B. Irving	Isabel Hornibrook	Joseph E. Badger Jr
H.C. Bailey	Israel Abrahams	Joseph Hergesheimer
H. G. Wells	Ivan Turgenev	Joseph Jacobs
H. H. Munro	J.G.Austin	Jules Vernes
H. Irving Hancock	J. Henri Fabre	Julian Hawthrone
H. R. Naylor	J. M. Barrie	Julie A Lippmann
H. Rider Haggard	J. M. Walsh	Justin Huntly McCarthy
H. W. C. Davis	J. Macdonald Oxley	Kakuzo Okakura
Haldeman Julius	J. R. Miller	Karle Wilson Baker
Hall Caine	J. S. Fletcher	Kate Chopin
Hamilton Wright Mabie	J. S. Knowles	Kenneth Grahame
Hans Christian Andersen	J. Storer Clouston	Kenneth McGaffey
Harold Avery	J. W. Duffield	Kate Langley Bosher
Harold McGrath	Jack London	Kate Langley Bosher
Harriet Beecher Stowe	Jacob Abbott	Katherine Cecil Thurston
Harry Castlemon	James Allen	Katherine Stokes
Harry Coghill	James Andrews	L. A. Abbot
Harry Houidini	James Baldwin	L. T. Meade

L. Frank Baum
Latta Griswold
Laura Dent Crane
Laura Lee Hope
Laurence Housman
Lawrence Beasley
Leo Tolstoy
Leonid Andreyev
Lewis Carroll
Lewis Sperry Chafer
Lilian Bell
Lloyd Osbourne
Louis Hughes
Louis Joseph Vance
Louis Tracy
Louisa May Alcott
Lucy Fitch Perkins
Lucy Maud Montgomery
Luther Benson
Lydia Miller Middleton
Lyndon Orr
M. Corvus
M. H. Adams
Margaret E. Sangster
Margret Howth
Margaret Vandercook
Margaret W. Hungerford
Margret Penrose
Maria Edgeworth
Maria Thompson Daviess
Mariano Azuela
Marion Polk Angellotti
Mark Overton
Mark Twain
Mary Austin
Mary Catherine Crowley
Mary Cole
Mary Hastings Bradley
Mary Roberts Rinehart
Mary Rowlandson
M. Wollstonecraft Shelley
Maud Lindsay
Max Beerbohm
Myra Kelly
Nathaniel Hawthrone
Nicolo Machiavelli
O. F. Walton
Oscar Wilde

Owen Johnson
P.G. Wodehouse
Paul and Mabel Thorne
Paul G. Tomlinson
Paul Severing
Percy Brebner
Percy Keese Fitzhugh
Peter B. Kyne
Plato
Quincy Allen
R. Derby Holmes
R. L. Stevenson
R. S. Ball
Rabindranath Tagore
Rahul Alvares
Ralph Bonehill
Ralph Henry Barbour
Ralph Victor
Ralph Waldo Emmerson
Rene Descartes
Ray Cummings
Rex Beach
Rex E. Beach
Richard Harding Davis
Richard Jefferies
Richard Le Gallienne
Robert Barr
Robert Frost
Robert Gordon Anderson
Robert L. Drake
Robert Lansing
Robert Lynd
Robert Michael Ballantyne
Robert W. Chambers
Rosa Nouchette Carey
Rudyard Kipling
Saint Augustine
Samuel B. Allison
Samuel Hopkins Adams
Sarah Bernhardt
Sarah C. Hallowell
Selma Lagerlof
Sherwood Anderson
Sigmund Freud
Standish O'Grady
Stanley Weyman
Stella Benson
Stella M. Francis

Stephen Crane
Stewart Edward White
Stijn Streuvels
Swami Abhedananda
Swami Parmananda
T. S. Ackland
T. S. Arthur
The Princess Der Ling
Thomas A. Janvier
Thomas A Kempis
Thomas Anderton
Thomas Bailey Aldrich
Thomas Bulfinch
Thomas De Quincey
Thomas Dixon
Thomas H. Huxley
Thomas Hardy
Thomas More
Thornton W. Burgess
U. S. Grant
Upton Sinclair
Valentine Williams
Various Authors
Vaughan Kester
Victor Appleton
Victor G. Durham
Victoria Cross
Virginia Woolf
Wadsworth Camp
Walter Camp
Walter Scott
Washington Irving
Wilbur Lawton
Wilkie Collins
Willa Cather
Willard F. Baker
William Dean Howells
William le Queux
W. Makepeace Thackeray
William W. Walter
William Shakespeare
Winston Churchill
Yei Theodora Ozaki
Yogi Ramacharaka
Young E. Allison
Zane Grey